THE CURSE OF MEDUSA

(Joe Hawke #4)

Rob Jones

ISBN-13 978-1532830099
ISBN-10 1532830092

Other Books by Rob Jones

The Joe Hawke Series

The Vault of Poseidon (Joe Hawke #1)
Thunder God (Joe Hawke #2)
The Tomb of Eternity (Joe Hawke #3)
The Curse of Medusa (Joe Hawke #4)
Valhalla Gold (Joe Hawke #5)
The Aztec Prophecy (Joe Hawke #6)
The Secret of Atlantis (Joe Hawke #7)
The Lost City (Joe Hawke #8)

This novel is an action-adventure thriller and includes archaeological, military and mystery themes. I welcome constructive comments and I'm always happy to get your feedback.

Website: www.robjonesnovels.com

Facebook: https://www.facebook.com/RobJonesNovels/

Email: robjonesnovels@gmail.com

Twitter: @AuthorRobJones

<u>DEDICATION</u>

For Snowdrop

THE CURSE OF MEDUSA

<u>PROLOGUE</u>

Finnmark, Northern Norway, October 1968

Max Henriksen tightened the hood of his Parka and stamped his feet against the hard Arctic snow. It was a vain attempt to warm up, but he did it all the same.

He sighed and scanned the bleak horizon. This was one hell of a place to build a listening station, but what the National Security Agency wanted, the National Security Agency generally got.

He watched with growing impatience as Frank Laurie began to lower the hollow drill-head into the hole in the ice. It had gotten stuck somewhere a few thousand feet below the surface and the young scientist from New Jersey was now attempting to lubricate the process with some drilling fluid. He wasn't making a very good job of it.

"It's not budging, Max," he said.

Max scratched his beard. "What's the depth?"

"Seven thousand feet."

"Let me get a look in there, kid," Martinez said, moving Laurie aside and pushing his way to the drill.

1

Like Henriksen, Tony Martinez wasn't a scientist, but part of the NSA team assigned to scout the area for its suitability as a listening station. "You've got no strength in you. Let a real man do the job."

He laughed heartily as he began to rotate the drill barrel in an attempt to move the cutters into the ice again, but his laughter faded when he realized the drill wasn't going any deeper.

"This ain't right, Max," he said. "Should be nothing down there but ice and water. Am I right, Laurie?"

Laurie nodded, equally perplexed. "Nothing but ice and water."

Henriksen frowned. "Then let's see if we can drill around it."

It took them the best part of the day to work out where the drill head could penetrate at that depth and where it couldn't. They worked out whatever was blocking their way was no more than a couple of square feet.

"I for one want to know just what the hell is down there," Henriksen said.

The others agreed, and three hours later they were hoisting the mystery object up through the small tunnel made by the various attempts with the core driller.

Henriksen saw it first – a blackened object about the size of a small TV set.

"What the *hell*...?" Martinez said. "That thing look man-made to you, Max?"

Henriksen nodded grimly. It did look man-made to him.

When they got it to the surface, it was encrusted in ancient ice and hard to see, but clearly some kind of chest.

"This is freaking me out, Max," Martinez said.

"Me too," Laurie said, taking a few steps back.

Max unhooked it from the hoist and laid it in the snow. A storm was rising now and the freezing air was filling with snow once again.

Henriksen stared in wonder. "Well, I'll be damned..."

"It looks Greek," Martinez said.

"What the hell is a metal chest covered in Greek letters doing buried at this level in the Arctic ice?" Laurie said, scratching his head. "Ice at this depth is thousands of years old."

Henriksen frowned as he studied the intricate carvings on the lid of the chest. They looked older than time itself, and someone had carved them with the greatest of care. "Thule," he said in wonder, barely above a whisper.

Martinez looked over at the station commander. "Huh?"

"Thule," Henriksen repeated. "It's all I can think of."

Anxiety crept into Laurie's voice. "Yeah, I heard you the first time, Max. But what does it mean?"

Henriksen rubbed his gloved hands together. "Thule? I'll tell you when we're in the warm – come on."

They collected their ice core equipment and trudged back through the thick snow to their research station, dragging the heavy box behind them with lines from a dog sledding harness.

Inside, the electric fire whined almost as loud as the wind howling over the communications aerials on top of the building. Laurie hung his gloves up to dry while Martinez made coffee.

Henriksen simply couldn't take his eyes off the chest. Now it was warm and they were out of the wind he could get a good look at it for the first time. On closer inspection it was made mostly of wood – a heavy hardwood like walnut maybe – but the edge clamps and handles were made of something resembling iron. He could see that once there had been leather straps but they had almost completely degraded and they crumbled away in his hands when he touched them.

Laurie handed him a hot mug of coffee. "So tell me about this Thule thing."

Max looked up, startled by the interruption. "Thule was a place first written about by the ancient Greek geographer Pytheas. He described it as a location in the far north of Europe, but most scholars generally agree it was nothing more than a myth."

"Until now," Martinez said, staring at the box.

"Maybe..." Henriksen rubbed his eyes and ran his hands over the box again. He tentatively pulled on one of the drawbolts but it was locked by something – he looked closer and saw they had been nailed down.

"Someone seriously didn't want this thing opened," he muttered.

"Hey – don't mess with it, Max," Laurie said quietly. "We don't know what's in it, and... and I'm pretty sure it's not our place to find out."

Henriksen didn't agree. He was a government man, and more than that he was in the NSA. As far as he was concerned, whatever was inside this chest could represent some kind of national security threat to the United States.

"Martinez – get me a hammer and chisel."

"You got it, boss."

The tall New Yorker returned a moment later with the tools and handed them to Henriksen.

The station commander concentrated hard on the chest as he lined up the cutting edge of the chisel, rested it gently on the top of one of the hasps and tapped the handle of the chisel with the hammer's face.

He'd expected some resistance, but all that time in the ice had weakened the metal and it fell apart immediately, crumbling into black dust on the table top at the base of the chest.

"One down, one to go," Henriksen said.

Laurie looked at the other two men and took another step back from the table.

"I'm not sure about this at all..." he said, his voice drifting into the chilly air of the cabin.

"Just calm down, kid," Martinez said, "It's just a chest."

Henriksen's concentration didn't break as he raised the chisel to the second hasp and repeated the exercise, popping it open and leaving another small pile of degraded metal on the table top.

"Well... that should just about do it," he said, laying the tools beside the ancient black box.

He raised his hands to the chest and began to open the lid.

"Listen, Max..." Laurie said, his voice wobbling. "Whoever put that thing down there did it for a reason, and I bet it was a real good one, too. Maybe we should call the government or something?"

Martinez laughed and ignored the growing anxiety in the younger man's voice.

"We *are* the government, son," Henriksen said, without lifting his eyes from the chest. Then he opened the lid and stared inside. A look of confusion crossed his face.

"What the hell..?"

Martinez joined him and looked inside. "Excuse my high-school French, but what the fuck is *that*?"

"I have no idea."

Henriksen put his arms inside the chest and pulled out a strange, black box covered in more writing and secured with a leather strap. He pulled on the strap and it broke in his hands – another example of the deterioration caused by the extreme cold over such a long period of time.

"Max, *please*..."

Henriksen opened the box and a look of horror spread over his face. "Oh my *God*..."

Martinez's eyes narrowed and he covered his mouth to stop himself throwing up. "God *damn* it, Max!"

Laurie watched Henriksen slam the box shut and close the chest. Then both he and Martinez took a few steps back from the box.

"What the hell did you see, Max?"

"I...I don't... I...can't..."

Laurie saw something in Henriksen's face change as he looked at him. His eyes began to cloud over and his voice grew hoarse.

"Laurie...it was....inside the box..."

Martinez started to look the same as his boss, only now the skin on their faces looked like it was going a gray color and beginning to harden.

"What the hell is going on here, Max?" Laurie said, moving back to the door and grabbing the handle. Outside the wind had risen and was howling like a pack of hungry wolves.

Henriksen strained to speak. "Get out, Laurie! Get somewhere safe..."

Laurie watched in horror as Max Henriksen seemed almost to solidify right in front of him as he spoke. His skin went silver in complexion and turned into a strange matte texture before going completely rock-hard. A second later, the same happened to Martinez, who had tried to run away to the door but was now frozen in place with cold, dead eyes.

Laurie panicked and opened the door. He ran out into the night, and strained for some fresh air in the icy wind-chill. The storm had passed now and the moon was full and low in the sky. As he stared at it he noticed it was growing darker and getting blurry. Then he felt his chest grow heavy and it became harder to breathe.

He turned to run inside to get to the radio but found his legs were frozen to the ground. He felt it creep up his body like ice, only it was much colder and when he looked down at his hands he saw they had turned a strange silver color. Then he was rock-solid, unable to move, blink, breathe. Slowly the moon dimmed completely, and then, a second later, he was gone forever and the Arctic night wind howled around him as if he were nothing more than a piece of granite.

<u>CHAPTER ONE</u>

Present Day

The Englishman sprinted toward the edge of the cliff with all his might and leaped into the void without a second thought. Instantly he felt the air rush up and flow over him. It was a little colder at this altitude. Joe Hawke liked cold air. It brought back memories of home. Sometimes, he thought, memories are the best part of life.

He looked beneath him and saw a river far below flash in the sunlight as he plummeted toward the rocky ground. He noticed he was flying a little slower than usual and his path through the air was choppier than he normally managed. All things considered, this was not one of his best wingsuit exits but it would do, and he could always try again tomorrow. He had nothing else to do.

His suit had started flying earlier than usual, and a few seconds after leaving the cliff he was gliding through the summer air like an eagle. As he raced forward, his arms stretched out behind him, he glanced back and saw he had a tail flutter, where part of the suit in between his legs had failed to pressurize properly. The result made the fabric flap wildly as he cut through the air. He cursed – this was what was slowing him down.

No matter. The valley floor below was still thousands of feet beneath him as he sailed out further into the hot Idaho day and twisted to the right to correct the direction and speed of his descent to earth. He felt alive. He felt free.

As he ripped through the sky at nearly two hundred miles per hour, he looked down again and searched for his landing site. They'd been staying at the cabin now for a few weeks – his way of winding down and staying away from the press. It turned out that saving the world back in the Ethiopian Highlands had stirred the interest of the world's media. Sending Maxim Vetrov to his horrifying death in the catacombs inside the Tomb of Eternity had livened things up even more, despite Eden's attempts to suppress the story. At least Eden had managed to keep Hawke's name out of the papers – he'd rather be hunted across Siberia by Spetsnaz than face a press pool.

He shook it from his mind and returned to the day.

The horizon was hazy today, but the day was hot, and the ground was rushing up toward him as fast as it always did. He chose his usual landing place as his mind drifted back to Africa and the argument he'd had with the team back in Luxor. How they said they'd all been lying to him from the very beginning, that they'd mostly known each other from the start and were testing him to see if he was suitable to join their gang. He'd been angry and walked away from them – leaving even Lea Donovan behind, just hours after she had almost died. He'd been a stupid fool, and he knew it.

Now, the adrenalin pulsed through his veins as the ground zoomed toward him, but receded when he turned upwards and performed a move wingsuiters called the cobra – using forward momentum to pull up and drastically reduce speed. Then he pulled the ripcord and his parachute opened out behind him. He felt the jerk as the chute rapidly slowed his fall and he gently guided himself to the selected drop zone with the careful use of the steering lines. Moments later he jogged to a stop outside the cabin and his parachute fell gently to the dusty ground behind him.

He stepped out of the harness and unzipped the wingsuit on his way up the cabin steps, pausing to tap the little barometer she had placed on the porch. Pressure rising.

Inside he could smell cooking and heard her singing along to a song on the radio. He walked into the kitchen and opened the fridge to find a cold drink.

"Hey," she said, without turning to face him. She was busy cooking breakfast. "Good jump?"

"Yeah, not bad," Hawke said, pulling a bottle of water from the fridge and walking over to Alex Reeve. He leaned over her to smell the cooking eggs. "Looks great."

"You *know*..."

Hawke sighed. "I know what you're going to say."

"Oh yeah? So what am I going to say, Nostradamus?"

"You're going to tell me to call Lea. I could tell by your tone... Anyway, you tell me the same thing every morning, so it doesn't exactly take Nostradamus."

"Wrong. I was going to tell you to go wash up because I'm about to put *this* on the table." She lifted the pan to underline the point.

Hawke hesitated to take some bacon out of the pan. "Yeah, right. You've told me to call her about a thousand times. I'm starting to think it's all you can say – plus, I'll have my breakfast on a plate thanks, not the table."

She rolled her eyes. "How does she put up with you?"

"Did... how *did* she. She's probably moved on by now."

"That's up to you, you pig-headed fool."

"Hey! Less of the cheek, madam."

10

Alex served up three plates of bacon and eggs and walked over to the table with them. Hawke knew it had been strange for Alex to use her legs again after so long, but she seemed to have got used to it over time. She once told him that sometimes she felt like she had never been shot, and the whole thing had been nothing more than a terrible nightmare.

They sat down together and he watched the sun light up the steam rising from the plates.

She looked at him. "I know I said it before, Joe... but thanks."

Hawke put some pepper on his eggs.

"Thanks for what?"

"For saving my life in Moscow, of course. Vetrov was going to feed me alive to crocodiles."

"Don't mention it."

She paused a beat. "You *know*..."

He glanced at her, forking the food into his mouth. "What now?"

"You never actually thanked me for saving your life in Serbia."

Hawke set his knife and fork down. "Sure I did."

"No, not since we met face to face."

Hawke considered the matter and smiled. She was right. "But I thanked you over the phone the day you got me out of that hellhole."

"Yeah, I remember. I'm just saying..."

Hawke decided to play dumb. "Saying what?"

"Nothing."

He ate some of the eggs and swigged from his mug of coffee. "No, go on. What are you trying to say?"

Alex sighed and shook her head. "You can be a real pig sometimes."

"What?!"

"You know what."

11

"All right, then since we're saying thanks for saving each other's lives..." he looked her in the eye and his face grew serious. No more jokes. "Thank you, Alex."

She was silent for a moment. "Is that it?"

Hawke looked at her again, unsure if she was playing games or not. He'd known Agent Nightingale for many years, but Alex Reeve was a newcomer in his life. "What do you want me to do – tap dance it out for you in Morse Code?"

She laughed. "Sure. You should do that. I'd like to see it."

"Never going to happen." He ate another mouthful of eggs and some more bacon.

She made a show of putting down her fork and leaning back from the table to get a better look at him. "Seriously – I think you could pull off a tap dance."

"Too bad – I left my dancing shoes in London."

"They're called tap shoes."

He winked. "But aren't you glad I didn't know that?"

"So you *say...*"

"All right, game over. I said thanks. I'm sorry, okay?"

"You know, since you're in the mood to grovel, I know someone else you owe an apology to."

Hawke stopped eating and pushed back from the table. "Not this again. Leave it."

"Just saying..."

He looked at her as the sun shone through the kitchen window and danced in her hair. She was beautiful, and it got to him that she'd turned herself into a recluse after the incident in Colombia.

"She should have told me the truth," he said flatly.

"She was under orders not to tell you, Joe. You're being unreasonable."

12

He shook his head to signal his disagreement, but in his heart he knew she was right. Lea Donovan was under orders not to tell him about the mysterious ECHO team and their secret island headquarters in the Caribbean. Those orders were issued by Sir Richard Eden himself, a serious character who, in Hawke's opinion, shouldn't be crossed. Hawke respected Eden, and he loved Lea... only his pride had stopped him from accepting their invitation and joining them on Elysium.

Now, thanks to his hot temper on an even hotter day, he'd stormed out on them all back in Egypt. Now he didn't even know where Elysium, or Lea, was.

"You can shake your head, cowboy, but you know in here," she leaned forward and touched his chest with her finger, "that you're in sad and pathetic denial, not to mention totally in the wrong."

He offered a shallow nod but said nothing as he looked at the food on the third plate, untouched and slowly growing colder.

For a while they ate in silence until Alex decided finally to offer an olive branch.

"Look... I shouldn't have stuck my nose in where it doesn't belong."

"No, you were right to bring it up. I keep myself to myself most of the time, but I guess this time I need to open up and maybe I should call her or something. Thing is, I'm just no good at keeping in touch. In my life people just come and go... I haven't spoken to my family for a long time."

Alex looked up at him, and sipped her coffee. "You still haven't told me about your family in England."

"Nope."

"You definitely *have* family in England, right?"

"Yeap."

Alex rolled her eyes. "Fine, don't tell me."

Hawke ate some eggs and sipped his coffee. "Look..." he set down his knife and fork and sighed.

Alex tried again. "Just the basics would be nice – names, jobs, how you feel about them..."

"All right, well, it's complicated, but it goes like this..."

Jack Brooke appeared in the doorway with a phone to his ear. He looked worried and Alex rarely saw her father like this. Something wasn't right.

The Pentagon chief disconnected the call and stared into the middle distance.

"What is it, Dad?" said Alex.

"What's wrong, Jack?" Hawke asked.

For a few seconds Brooke didn't know how to answer. When he spoke, both Hawke and Alex wished he hadn't.

"That was Deakin at the NSA. He says they're getting chatter about an imminent attack on the United States. Serious chatter about a serious attack."

Hawke looked from Brooke to Alex and put down his knife and fork. Something told him breakfast time was over.

CHAPTER TWO

The former Special Boat Service man watched a brief flash of fear and confusion on the American Secretary of Defense's face before he banished them from his mind and brought the situation back under control. Now, a look of steely determination fixed in his eyes.

Hawke rose from the table. "What makes the chatter so convincing, Jack?"

Brooke sighed and ran a hand absent-mindedly through his silver hair. "It came through a respected German asset and correlates with other metadata we've been collecting for a while now."

Brooke straightened his tie and pulled his jacket on. The former Delta officer clearly wasn't going to waste any more time worrying. "I have to get back to Washington," he said. "The weather's clear and there's a government jet waiting for me at Friedman. I can get back in around four hours."

Alex put her fork down and stood up from the table. "I'm coming with you."

"No," Brooke said. "You're not."

"Come on, Dad! I'm ready to get back in the saddle again." Unconsciously, she glanced down at her legs when she spoke.

Brooke frowned. "I know that you can walk again, honey," he said, turning to Hawke and offering another shallow nod of gratitude. "We have Joe here to thank for that, and I'll owe him till the day I die but you're not ready to go back in the field, Alex. We don't know what the hell we're dealing with so you're just staying put.

Your mother would never forgive me if anything were to happen to you."

"Yeah," Hawke agreed. "Your Dad's right."

Alex gave him the look from hell. "Thanks a bunch, *Joe*. What I could have done with right now is a little support."

"Your Dad's right, Alex, and you know it."

Alex watched as her Dad got some things together and called Coleman into the room. Nate Coleman was the lead man in his Bureau of Diplomatic Security team. He ordered him to get the car ready and brief the other two agents about staying at the cabin to look after his daughter. She could tell by the look on her father's face that he wasn't going to change his mind. "I suppose, if you both insist on it, then there's not much I can do."

"Good girl," Brooke said. "It's safe here in the middle of nowhere, honey. We don't know what's under threat but I doubt it's the Idaho mountains."

"I guess."

"And we'll call you when we get to DC," Hawke said.

Alex smiled. "Sure... *wait* a minute!"

"What?" as Hawke spoke he jammed some toast in his mouth and slid his jacket on.

"If I can't go, then you can't go!"

"Why not?" the Englishman said matter-of-factly.

"We don't have time for this," Brooke said. "Alex, you're staying here with two of my best guys protecting you – Regan and Walsh – Joe and I are going to DC. No more discussion."

"But Dad, if –"

The unit sent to kill them arrived like lightning. They were wearing all black with balaclavas and carrying identical Heckler & Koch MP7 submachine guns fitted with suppressors.

Alex saw them first over her father's shoulder as the back of Special Agent Regan's skull blew off and he fell back into the plates of food on the table with a tremendous crash. A second later shots rang out all over the front of the cabin and then they all heard a burst of submachine gun fire and saw Agent Walsh slump to the ground on the patio – a pool of blood forming around his silent corpse.

Hawke spun around, reaching for the Beretta M9 on the breakfast bar and screaming at Jack Brooke and his daughter to dive for cover. He ducked down behind the wooden bar as more automatic fire raked the wall of Brooke's kitchen and sprayed all over the side of the living room. Shards of splintered oak panel burst all over the room as the bullets ripped through the furniture and walls. A large deer antler trophy was blasted from the wall above the fireplace and shattered on the hearth.

One of the men threw a grenade into the room and screamed at them: "Goodbye, Mr Secretary!"

Hawke saw it first and picked it up, hurling it through the open double doors of the living room where it exploded on the patio and blasted the glass from the windows and doors back into the room in a lethal shower.

Special Agent Coleman ran into the room, firing bursts from his handgun at the gunmen as he closed in on Brooke. "The car's ready, Mr Secretary. We have to get you out of here, sir!"

"Like hell you do!" Brooke shouted. "You get my girl to safety first." As he spoke he wrenched a Smith & Wesson .45 from an inside pocket and fired back at the men in the kitchen. He hit one of them, the three bullets exploding in his chest and sending him staggering back out the door where he collapsed on the porch steps.

"Look out!" Hawke tried to push Coleman to safety but it was too late. Another shooter in the garden had targeted the Special Agent and Hawke watched with horror as a small red dot laser-sight tracked up Coleman's back and stopped on the rear of his head. Coleman was dead before he hit the floor, and still the bullets came flying.

Another gunman made some headway toward the double doors before Hawke used the M9 to drop him with a lethal neck shot. His mind buzzed as he considered the various options open to them. Clearly they were under massive attack, and it was also obvious the target, just for once, wasn't him but the Secretary of Defense. He had no idea if other senior members of the US Government were also under attack, but focussed instead on defending Jack Brooke and his daughter. Everything else could be considered when they were safe.

The situation wasn't new to Hawke – he had worked in high-level security positions before, the most prominent one being when he was charged to protect a delegation of British Government ministers on a trade mission to Zambia. It went well until the last minute, and then things could have gone a lot more smoothly. At the last minute everything went badly wrong for the British delegation, but why had always been a mystery.

It was during his time in Lusaka that he had met Zhang Xiaoli, otherwise known as Lexi Zhang. Agent Dragonfly had been in the country investigating some kind of problem that concerned the State Council of the People's Republic of China, or that was how she had put it to him, at least. He had enjoyed her company. They made each other laugh, but they both felt the undercurrent of forbidden excitement, the subterfuge that was always there when dealing with an agent working for a foreign power.

That was then and this was now. Now he wasn't defending a team of middle-ranking British Civil Servants, but the man who gave all operational commands to the Pentagon – the American Secretary of Defense, one of the most powerful men on the planet – and he was under mortal threat at the hands of a team of highly trained professional assassins.

But Hawke had no time to think about the bigger picture now. Right now his priority was to lead Brooke and Alex to safety, and he had to think fast.

"Jack, can we get to the garage from here?"

Brooke nodded. "Sure, but if you're thinking about a car forget it. I don't keep my cars in the garage. I use the garage as a workshop and all the cars are parked in the outbuilding across the yard and through the trees."

"That's handy," Hawke said.

"We can get there through the garage though," Brooke said. "But it's going to be tough."

Hawke nodded. "Sounds like we have no choice, but we have to do all we can to get you out of here – both of you."

As the bullets traced over their heads, Alex held Hawke's arm. "If anyone can do it, I guess that man's you."

"I appreciate the vote of confidence," Hawke said, ducking to dodge another bullet, "but normally I have you on the other end of a headset telling me what to do."

"All right, then," Brooke said, checking his weapon. "Let's do this. We have a country to save."

CHAPTER THREE

Alan Pauling pushed his hand into the Cheetos and pulled out half a dozen of the neon-orange snacks. He stuffed them into his mouth before wiping the salty cheese on the side of his Hawaiian shirt. It was hot and humid in New Orleans – just his kind of weather – and he settled back in his seat and stretched his arms in the comforting warmth. It reminded him of home in Queensland, not that he'd ever be going back there. When all this was over, and his special skills were no longer needed, he was going to buy himself a large house on a small island somewhere very isolated.

Watching the crowds forming below in the street, Pauling hoped not for the first time that Novak had done his part of the job properly and got inside the Beast. They had all known that was the hardest part of the entire operation, and any screw ups wouldn't be known until the big moment itself. He shrugged his shoulders and ate more Cheetos. They would know soon enough.

How many of these people would survive the next few hours? Pauling had no idea. He didn't particularly care about any of them. The tiny handful of people he cared about were thousands of miles away in Australia. The Boss had told him that particular country wasn't a target, at least not yet. The Boss had his reasons for striking America, but the Boss never talked about them to anyone and Pauling knew better than to ask.

Another mouthful of Cheetos and he cracked open a Pepsi Max. Alan Pauling had a technical mind, but was not a complicated man. As far as he was concerned, all he cared about was the Golden Rule, and that was whoever has the gold, makes the rules. After this job for the Boss, he would be wealthy enough to fly away and build himself his own personal fiefdom, somewhere tropical if he could help it.

And nowhere immediately downwind of the Eastern Seaboard. After today, that would be a big mistake.

He fired up his laptop and swigged from the can of warm Pepsi. Waiting for the software to load, he peered once again through the window at the hubbub seven storeys beneath him. Enjoy it while you can, folks, he thought. Pretty soon nothing but mayhem down there.

The principle was simple enough – exploiting a simple zero-day vulnerability to change the course of history. Pauling enjoyed his work, and his study of the target vehicle's network architecture was especially interesting to him. The more sophisticated the system, the more vulnerabilities there were to attack and exploit, and that was what made this job so exciting. It didn't get much more sophisticated than this.

If the vehicle was connected to the internet, which it was, it was simply a case of acquiring the car's IP address. That was where Novak came in. With that information, Pauling was able to rewrite firmware in a chip inside the vehicle's navigation system and import his own code. With that done he would be able to control the vehicle through the exploited CAN bus. A simple hack of the night-vision camera on the front of the car would allow for a visual as he controlled the car, and after that, as far as the passengers in the target vehicle were concerned, Alan Pauling was God.

He crumpled the empty bag of Cheetos and tossed it over his shoulder before peering outside the window. He glanced at his watch. The crowd was gathering nicely, and pretty soon the car would be here.

Then it was Showtime in the Big Easy.

*

Speaker Todd Tobin loved supporting his team more than just about anything else in this world, and today was no exception. The Paul Brown Stadium in Cincinnati, Ohio was humming with excitement as his team, the Cincinnati Bengals, were preparing to kick the pants off the Seattle Seahawks. Days like this were a rare treat for Speaker Tobin, who spent most of his time in Washington glad-handing and smooth-talking people he barely knew and cared for even less.

Today was a break – hotdogs, fried onions, French's mustard, sunshine and last but not least, a great game ahead of him. He could barely contain his excitement.

Laura looked at him and rolled her eyes.

He smiled. "What?"

His wife said nothing and passed him a paper towel.

"Mustard?"

She nodded.

He knew what she was thinking – why can't he eat something less messy, at least in public? He knew she loved him all the same, and he loved her too – not least because she always seemed to have a paper towel handy when he needed one.

He leaned forward, close to her, and whispered so the security detail in the seats directly behind them couldn't hear what he was going to say. Five short words later he saw the smile spread on his wife's face. It worked every time...

"Woah!" he said, pointing at the field. "He's going to make him pay for that – they're down 24 – 7!"

Laura rolled her eyes again and smiled. Looking like she cared about football was part of the job. For her husband it was easy because he loved it, but on her part it was all fake, and that made it hard work. Sometimes she felt like her smile was about to fall off.

Tobin moaned as the Seahawks moved deep into Bengals territory thanks to a classic piece of misdirection play. "That is *not* a fair catch... come on!"

"That's what I was going to say," his wife said with a smirk.

He ignored her, watching with interest as the scrimmage played out and the quarterback spiked the ball after the snap.

"What does that mean?" Laura almost sounded interested.

Tobin turned to his wife and smiled at her lack of knowledge. "Technically it's an incomplete pass, so it means the clock is stopped and the down is exhausted." He turned back to the game so fast he missed the second eye-roll.

"Gee, *thanks* for that, honey," she said. "It's so much clearer now. It all makes sense."

Then she stopped talking and stared at her husband, her brow furrowed in bewilderment.

A small red light was meandering its way from her husband's sleeve to his chest. It continued on its path up his neck and over his face where it stopped on his forehead, just beneath the peak of his trusty old Bengals baseball cap.

"Honey, what the hell is..."

She never finished her sentence. Half a second later her husband was propelled violently backwards over the back of his seat and into the lap of the Secret Service agent behind, a bullet hole drilled into the center of his head.

23

Only then did she hear the familiar sound of the rifle shot, a second behind the bullet.

Laura Tobin screamed as a Secret Service agent pushed her hard to the ground, covering her with his body and calling in the attack over his earpiece. The other agents responded in seconds, drawing their weapons and scanning the stadium. Whoever it was, the delay between hitting Speaker Tobin and the sound of the shot meant they were a good distance away.

The crowd roared with approval, mistaking the terror attack for some kind of publicity stunt, but seconds later total anarchy came to the stadium as reality dawned on thousands of football fans and a rush for the exits ensued.

America really was under attack.

CHAPTER FOUR

President Charles Grant waved cheerily at the crowds lining the route of the motorcade as it swept along the boulevard and pulled up outside the university. Today he was going to deliver a speech at the Xavier University of Louisiana to pledge more federal funds to the city in the on-going plan to rebuild after Hurricane Katrina.

He glanced at his watch and saw the motorcade was already running six minutes late. Outside he saw those who thought his administration wasn't doing enough to help. They were lining up outside the university entrance with their placards and chanting slogans. It was all part of his job, he thought.

Grant stepped out of the car and waved once again as his Secret Service detail ushered him up along the entrance walkway. As he went, thousands of camera shutters clicked in his face from the press pack, and then he was inside. The president of the university greeted him and shook his hand. Moments later they were moving toward the main hall – the Secret Service were anxious to get the President's schedule back on time.

Grant got to the podium and did what he did best – charm people. He threw out a couple of well-timed jokes to relax the audience and flashed them his world-famous smile before launching into his speech. It wasn't his grandest speech – that was next month in Florida when he planned to deliver what was already being called the greatest speech of his career. Florida was the third worst state in the country for gun murders, and Grant wanted to bring it under control. He knew he had opposition – in both the House and the Senate not to mention the NRA. Even the Constitution was against him, but a spate of recent shootings had pushed many people over to his side of the argument.

But today's speech was important for the people of New Orleans, and that's what mattered to him right now.

As the room settled down, he leaned closer to the microphone and began to read off the autocue. Like most presidents, all his speeches were written for him by professional speech-writers and projected on a screen which he then read. His previous career as an actor helped him not only to deliver the jokes on time but to read the speeches and make it look like he was dreaming the stuff up as he went along. Today was no exception, and he weaved his way into the speech with his usual exceptional ease and professional acumen.

At the end of the speech, he was whisked from the room in a hail of applause and walked back out along the path toward the Beast. Earlier in the day, Scott Anderson, his Chief-of-Staff had joked that the enormous seven-ton Presidential limo was probably one of the safest places in Louisiana. Grant had smiled, but not laughed. He had been lucky so far, but previous presidents had not only been attacked while in office – four had been assassinated, and the President's safety was no laughing matter.

He moved steadily toward the limo, once again recalling Anderson's words about its safety, and reassured by their veracity however they had been delivered. The Beast was actually one of twelve identical limos in constant rotation. The ones not in use were secured in the basement garage of the Secret Service HQ back in DC.

Grant made one final wave as Dirk Partridge, his senior USSS agent swung open the rear door of the

Caddy. The senior secret service agent fired a string of words into his radio palm mic and glanced at his watch. Grant was scheduled to tour the rest of the city as well as make a special visit to the levee system before flying back to the capital before dusk. Time was short.

And that's when it happened.

From an unknown location, someone fired a series of gunshots into the air and total panic ensued. The people lining the President's route from Xavier to the limo screamed and scattered, raising their hands over their heads to protect themselves, more from instinct than judgement.

Agent Partridge reacted in a half-second. In a textbook manoeuvre of professionalism and bravery, and without a second thought about his own personal safety, the secret service man leaped forward and grabbed the President, moving around him like a human shield and forcing him into the back of the Beast.

Grant was in the back of the car before he had time to take a breath.

Partridge followed, throwing himself in after the President and slamming the heavy door shut behind them. He barked a series of orders into the palm mic and the driver of the Presidential limo floored the accelerator, sending the massive armored vehicle lurching forward.

In a cloud of burnout smoke from the spinning tires, the limo raced away from the university and hit Drexel Drive a few seconds later.

"Sir, are you hit?"

Grant took a second to focus on his surroundings. "No, I don't think so... What the hell just happened?"

"Someone tried to take a shot at you, Mr President. We have to get you back to Air Force One immediately."

Grant agreed. They'd had chatter about a serious attack, but latest intel had suggested it was going to be overseas and not in the United States. This changed things in a big way, and he had to get back to the White House. That was the best place to control things.

But then things got much more out of control.

He watched with horror as the driver slumped over in the front seat of the Presidential limo.

He and Partridge shared a glance. "What the hell..?"

Grant looked closer the through the glass partition and saw a gas emanating from somewhere in the footwell.

"He's been knocked out!" Partridge said. "We're going to crash!"

The President shook his head. "He's out cold all right but I don't think we're going to crash – look!"

Partridge watched with undisguised terror as the massive seven-ton Cadillac screeched along Drexel with no one at the wheel. Instead, just over the shoulders of the knocked-out driver, he saw the steering wheel jerking eerily to the left and right as someone controlled the vehicle remotely.

"What the hell *is* this?" President Grant muttered.

"It's the Boston Brakes! Someone's hacked the car, sir!" Dirk Partridge pulled at the door release but with no luck. "The locks are disabled!"

"We might not be able to get them open, but we can make sure whoever's behind this can't get them open either. This button locks them from the inside, so that's something in our favour..." Grant didn't look like he had reassured himself much.

Partridge slapped on the windows in panic. "We've got to get out of here, Mr President!"

Grant heard the growl of the General Motors V8 as it speeded up to power out of a corner. Normally a comforting sound, it now terrified him. "This car is completely sealed in the event of a biochemical attack, Partridge! What keeps me safe in here is now what's keeping me prisoner – these doors are as heavy as those on a 757 jet plane, and the only window that opens is the driver's, and then only by three inches. If you can think of a way out of here with the door locks disabled then I'm ready to hear it."

Behind them three Cadillac Escalades rushed into view.

"Don't worry, sir – the Secret Service is right behind us!" Partridge said.

He'd barely finished his sentence when they heard the sound of hydraulics.

"Oh no..."

The Beast fired smoke and tear-gas grenades out the rear fender. Installed as a protection device to assist the President in case of enemy pursuit, they were now being used against him.

Grant looked back and saw the Escalades skidding through the grenades' smoke, out of control. Two of them had a collision and smashed into a bank on the side of the street, while the third maintained its pursuit.

A police helicopter appeared overhead and began to follow them, hovering just above the remaining Escalade.

They raced into an underpass where a slow-moving Pepsi truck was trundling along in the slow lane. The two captive men watched in horror as the rear of the truck lowered to the ground and an identical presidential limousine reversed out the back and skidded forward out of view along the underpass. Moments later, their own limo was controlled into the rear of the truck and the back closed up.

In total darkness, they heard the Escalade race past the truck in pursuit of the dummy limo and knew it was over. Whoever was doing this had just kidnapped the President of the United States.

CHAPTER FIVE

In the Idaho Mountains, Hawke, Alex and the Pentagon Chief dropped to all fours and crawled through the cabin on their way to the garage. Bullets flew all around them, busting the wooden panels into splinters and covering the rug in thousands of shards of glass from the exploded windows. When Alex began to slow down, Hawke pulled her along at his side. Ahead of them, Jack Brooke smashed open the internal door to the garage and tumbled down the steps.

Hawke got to his feet and helped Alex into the garage where her father was already rummaging around.

"Joe – buy me a couple of minutes."

Hawke took cover behind a workbench and fired defensive shots from the Beretta when anyone tried to enter the garage. "They're running around to the front, Jack!"

Behind him, Brooke snatched up a couple of empty bottles of Coors and some old rag which he tore into strips. Then he flicked open the cap of a small portable gas can and inserted some clear plastic tubing. "Bastards won't be expecting this," he mumbled. He sucked on the tube and drew the gas through into the bottles.

He hurled the hastily constructed Molotov cocktail into the cabin and seconds later the door was ablaze and impassable. "Now we focus on getting out of here."

Brooke hit the electronic door mechanism and the roller doors began to wind open. Instantly they were met with more gun fire, many of the bullets blowing neat

31

circular holes through the aluminum door while others were lower and ricocheted off the smooth concrete floor of the garage.

They dived for cover behind the workbench while Hawke scanned the area outside the garage to see where the enemy was. He located three men with machine pistols who were using Brooke's old Winnebago across the yard for cover.

Hawke immediately opened fire with the M9 and hit one of the men in the chest, killing him instantly. The other two retreated further back in the shadow of the RV to a low wall running along the edge of the main driveway.

"Looks like the coast is clear," Brooke said. "But for how long, I don't know..."

"Get over to the outbuilding," Hawke said. "I'll slow the bastards down here as much as I can."

Before she could object, Brooke took his daughter's arm and pulled her away toward the line of spruce trees across the yard which divided the main property from the outbuilding where he stored his cars.

Hawke covered them as they ran, pinning down the gunmen behind the wall. Then he made a break for it, firing as he went. Two simple parkour rolls later he was sprinting through the row of spruces and heading for the outbuilding.

He heard a burst of machine pistol fire from behind him and turned to see the men closing in on him. One of the men – one with heavily gelled-hair combed back in a slick – was laughing as he fired.

"We have to get out of here, Jack!" the Englishman yelled.

"So move your ass!" Alex screamed back.

The men fired at Hawke and puffs of gravel dust flew up all around his feet. He was only just out-running the lethal rounds.

"The thought had crossed my mind, Nightingale..."

*

Angelika Schwartz watched with her usual carefully measured excitement as the battered, shot-up Cadillac DTS containing the world's most powerful man reversed out the back of the Pepsi truck. When it hit the ground, she smiled as it crawled like a wounded bear across the loading bay of their temporary home – an abandoned paint factory in New Orleans's Bywater district.

She was chewing gum and wore torn denim jeans and a leather jacket. Shifting her weight from one foot to the other she now stood with a Mossberg 500 pump-action shotgun casually resting on her shoulder. She ran a hand through her spikey pink hair and glanced at the platinum Rolex on her wrist, smiling – bang on time. The Boss would be impressed.

She waited with growing impatience while somewhere across town the rude Australian techie used the tiny night vision camera in the car's front fender to control the vehicle. He brought Cadillac One to a gentle remote-controlled stop less than three yards from her biker riding boots. The engine shut down, and a dozen men armed with submachine guns encircled the presidential limo.

She walked forward and pulled the shotgun from her shoulder. Smiling, she tapped the muzzle of the gun gently on the reinforced glass of the Caddy's rear window.

Inside, the President was in animated dialogue with his Secret Service agent.

Angelika frowned. "Out you come, Mr President. Now." Her German accent was thick, but understandable.

The politician inside looked through the bullet-proof window at her and hesitated, thinking through his options one last time. He looked nervous, but she could see a glimmer of hope in his eyes. That would be gone soon enough.

"Three seconds or we do it the hard way."

She raised her fingers to her mouth and wolf-whistled. A second later a man in black overalls stepped out of the shadows. He was holding a bundle of Composition C-4 blocks in his hands, better known to the world simply as C-4, a type of malleable plastic explosive. He began to mold the explosive in specific locations around the driver's door of the limo and then inserted several blasting caps into it before turning and giving Angelika an emotionless nod. He stepped far away from the vehicle.

Angelika pulled a detonator from her jacket and waved it at the President. "Vielen dank, Jakob... Now I will count to ten, and on ten I hit the detonator. There will be consequences for making me get you out the hard way. One..."

Inside, more heated debate, and then finally, President Grant's shoulders visibly slumped as he turned and opened the rear door. He stepped cautiously out into the warehouse.

"You did the right thing, Mr Grant."

"You can't possibly hope to get away with this," Grant said. "My people will be all over this place in minutes."

He'd barely finished speaking when Angelika smacked him across his face with the back of her gloved hand. "Silence!"

Partridge leaped forward but his attempt to defend the President was met by a savage blow in the center of his back with the butt of one of the men's guns. He fell forwards and hit the hard concrete floor, crying out in pain.

"No more silliness, Mr President, please," Angelika said coolly. "Besides, if you're referring to the tracking devices in your limousine, they are are currently residing in the chassis of the identical limo you saw in the underpass a few moments ago. That should keep your people busy for a while."

President Grant looked crestfallen for a few seconds, and rubbed the blood from the corner of his cut, bleeding lip. Then he raised his chin and straightened his shirt before replying. "Then I wouldn't want to be in the shoes of the man driving that limo."

The woman from Berlin smirked. "Sadly, once again you have misplaced your hope. Like your own vehicle, the decoy car is remote-controlled by a man in the center of New Orleans. He has orders to drive it as far from the underpass as he can until the Secret Service or police catch it or until it runs out of fuel, whichever comes first... by which time, you shall be tucked away somewhere nice and safe."

Angelika barked some orders at Jakob who padded over to the President and grabbed him roughly by his collar.

"Best not resist, Mr Grant. Jakob Müller here was a former *rhönradprofi* – a wheel gymnast and a serious bodybuilder. He's a good East German. He tells me he has the strength of five men, and few here have dared him to prove it."

On Angelika's orders, Jakob dragged Grant away from the relative safety of the limo and shoved him into the side of an old GMC van idling just inside the entrance to the factory. A moment later, Partridge was hauled off the floor and thrown in the back beside him.

*

Now, President Grant sat in the back of the windowless van in silence. Either side of him was an armed man, and opposite was the German woman and the man she had called Jakob.

After half an hour of driving mostly on the straight he felt the van lurch to the right and descend what could only be an off-ramp. Judging by the turns at the start of the journey he guessed he was somewhere to the north of New Orleans, but couldn't be sure. Instead of speculating, he focussed on what would be by now the largest manhunt in history as his team scrambled to rescue him.

A couple more turns and the van came to a juddering stop. A few seconds later Jakob grinned at him and the side door swung open. "Get out."

Grant climbed out of the van and blinked in the sunlight. He was standing in the middle of a vast industrial landscape, littered with countless buildings and chimneys all covered in pipes and air-conditioning ducts. It looked like they were in some kind of processing plant, but by the looks of things it was clearly abandoned. Grant began to grow pessimistic.

Just beyond the parking area where they had pulled up in the GMC was a cleared area with a sparkling white Sikorsky S-76. Grant knew the model because he recognized it as the same as the one Donald Trump owned – and he'd had a flight around Manhattan in that one a few weeks ago so he would know better than most. If it weren't obvious enough already, these people were well-funded.

Jakob stepped from the van and stood beside him. "Over there." He nodded at what had clearly been the main entrance to the complex, but was now partly overgrown with weeds.

Grant bristled, unaccustomed to being talked to like this, but kept silent. It wasn't every day the President of the United States got kidnapped – in fact this was the first time in history – so whoever was behind it was playing the highest stakes of all. It wouldn't be wise to anger them before finding out what they wanted, and he knew from his many Secret Service briefings that he had to play for time.

Jakob shoved him hard between the shoulder blades and with his hands tied behind his back he struggled to stay on his feet, but just managed it. He gave the man a snarl of contempt and moved slowly toward the enormous factory complex.

CHAPTER SIX

Hawke fired at the men. In response, they dived for cover in the spruce trees, giving Jack Brooke enough time to unlock the door to the outbuilding. Seconds later they were inside what looked like a small aircraft hangar with a polished concrete floor and corrugated metal walls. Parked in neat lines were several rows of luxury vehicles, shining dully in the diffused lighting of the opaque skylights above.

"Nice collection!" Hawke said, spying the cars. "Can we take the Corvette?"

Alex gave him a look. "Great idea, Einstein... only you might wanna count the seats."

"Eh?"

"There's three of us but the Corvette is a two-seater."

"Oh, I didn't realize you wanted to come."

Alex rolled her eyes and slapped his shoulder. "We can take the Jeep to the airport if we can just get out it out of here without getting shot to pieces!"

"How far away is the airport?" Hawke said.

"A little under twelve miles," Brooke said. "We go down Valley Road and then we hit 75. That takes us straight to Hailey and the airport."

"And we definitely can't take the Corvette?"

Alex gave him another of her looks. "Get in the Jeep, Limey."

"Sure thing, Septic."

Brooke and his daughter both turned to Hawke at the same time. "Huh?"

"Septic tank."

THE CURSE OF MEDUSA

"And...?"

"Septic tank, Yank."

"Oh..." Alex said, confused.

They were startled back to reality by the sound of gunfire and the sight of half a dozen bullet holes being punched into the steel walls of the outbuilding. The light now shone through the holes in beams.

"We have to get out of here... right *now*." Brooke ran his hand along the little board where he kept all his keys until he found the right ones for the Jeep. "Take these," he said, tossing them at Hawke. Then he pocketed the other keys and grabbed a shotgun from under the bench. "Assholes aren't chasing me in my own damned cars!"

Hawke climbed into the driving seat of the Jeep Grand Cherokee and fired up the 5.9 V8. A deep growling noise emanated from under the hood. He revved it and the entire vehicle rocked from side to side. A broad smile spread over Joe Hawke's face.

Brooke climbed in the back and dumped the shotgun on the seat.

"Get us out of here, Joe!"

Hawke stamped on the throttle and the two-and-a-half ton vehicle jumped forward and raced toward the double doors. The Englishman instinctively covered his face as the Jeep smashed through the doors in a cloud of dust and bent metal and then he skidded it around to the right in the direction of the property gates. It sprayed an impressive arc of dust and dead pine cones up into the hot air as it went.

Behind them, a hail of bullets erupted from the two men who were still using the spruces for cover. Hawke watched in the rear-view mirror as the men sprinted into the outbuilding.

Brooke shook his head. "Those assholes better not hotwire any of my babies."

"I think that's the plan, Jack," Hawke said, and increased the speed of the Jeep. "Only eleven miles to the airport now so let's hope they're not very good at hotwiring."

Alex sighed. "You might want to try something a little stronger than hope, Joe. Check the rear-view."

He checked the mirror and saw Brooke's beloved Corvette skidding out onto the highway behind them. It didn't take long for the gunmen to catch up with the much slower Jeep, and the three lanes of ID-75 meant Hawke had a much harder fight on his hands to keep the Corvette trapped behind them.

Brooke turned in his seat and stared forlornly through the rear window. "Oh *crap*, they're going to wreck my baby."

"I'm your baby, Dad."

Without turning he raised his hand and patted his daughter's shoulder. "I know you are, honey, and I love you."

"Yeah, that's not my shoulder, Dad."

Brooke turned to see his hand was on Hawke's shoulder and pulled it back fast.

"My apologies, Joe."

"That's okay, *Dad*," Hawke said. "And I want you to know I love you too."

Alex smiled, but Brooke simply returned his gaze to the Corvette, which was now accelerating and swinging to the right in a bid to overtake on the shoulder. Hawke responded by gripping the wheel and heaving the Jeep into the path of the flame-red sports car, but it was a feint. A second later the Corvette braked and skidded to the left, swinging out into the oncoming lane and rapidly accelerating alongside the Jeep.

The gunman in the passenger seat aimed a Remington 1100 tactical shotgun at them, leaning through the open window.

Hawke saw what was happening and hit the brakes.

The Corvette shot in front of them for a few seconds but the driver responded in a flash. He hit the brakes and raced behind the Jeep, swerving into the right-hand lane as he went. Before Hawke could respond they floored the accelerator and swung out into the path of an oncoming SUV narrowly avoiding a head-on collision as they overtook them once again. They were now in front of the Jeep.

Remington twisted around in his seat and leaned out the Corvette's window. He pulled the long shotgun out of the car and lifted it toward the center of the Jeep's windshield.

Hawke looked ahead and saw a massive Kenworth Road Train bearing down on them in the left-hand lane. He thought about skidding around it to the left but that would leave him in the fast-lane of the oncoming traffic, and the looming presence of the Kenworth meant he had no way to tell if there was anyone in that lane or not. He knew he could be a daredevil at times, but a head-on smash at nearly two hundred miles per hour was too much even for him to contemplate. Luckily Cairo Sloane wasn't here to talk him into it, he thought.

The gunman raised the weapon to his eye and prepared to fire.

Hawke had only one play.

He pulled the wheel to the right and sent the Jeep hurtling off the road.

The gunman fired, and a puff of white smoke was followed by the sound of lead shot peppering the back left of the Jeep. Hawke struggled to control the vehicle as it skidded down an embankment and smashed through a low wooden fence which marked the boundary between the highway and a sunburnt wheatfield.

Brooke pointed at the crop stretching out in front of them. "Holy crap, Joe!"

Alex screamed and instinctively raised her hands to protect her face.

The engine over-revved wildly as the Jeep bounced over the rough-ground at highway speed and plowed through the long, dry grass like a combine harvester. Clouds of dried wheat heads and stems burst into the air and left a corn-yellow trail of dust in their wake stretching all the way back to the road.

Hawke winced. "This is definitely not how I was planning on spending today..."

*

From his base in New Orleans, Alan Pauling tapped the keyboard of his laptop and increased the power on the Northrop Grumman MQ-8 Fire Scout. He watched through the camera as the unmanned autonomous helicopter drone lifted away from the back of the flatbed truck and into the air. The Rolls-Royce M250 turboshaft engine roared to life as Pauling directed the Fire Scout higher and turned it one-eight degrees to face its target.

Driving the Presidential limo by remote control had been enough of a challenge, especially when being chased by the Secret Service Escalades, but flying an armed, stolen, military drone into the heart of the American capital was in another league completely.

Through the camera he saw the familiar skyline of Washington DC appear on the horizon and smiled as he accelerated the chopper toward downtown. The drone was loaded with a startling variety of weapons, including Viper Strike GPS-assisted laser-guided glide bombs and Hellfire missiles.

That should just about do it, Pauling thought as the capital got larger on his monitor.

And then some.

CHAPTER SEVEN

Brooke pointed his shotgun through the window and got a shot off at the Corvette but it missed. The sports car was too far away now, up on the highway to their left, and accelerating out of sight.

"You think they gave up?" Alex asked.

"Maybe," Hawke said.

Brooke sighed and shook his head as he reloaded the shotgun. "I doubt it."

Hawke decelerated the Jeep as a line of Washington hawthorns rapidly approached them. The automatic box changed down to second and then first as he applied the brakes and drove down into a thicket where a narrow stream was running from west to east.

"Take her right through it, Joe," Brooke said. "It's not deep – I come through here with the horses all the time."

Hawke crossed the stream and pulled the Jeep up the opposite bank. He took an appreciative look around the shady glen.

"Nice place for a picnic."

"Damn it all," Alex said and looked at him sarcastically. "I packed the psychotic gunmen but forgot the salad dressing..."

Hawke glanced at her and smirked. "You know what I mean."

"I hate to break up what could be the beginning of a beautiful friendship," Brooke said. "But we have to get back on the road – look."

They were now in an enclosed field, bordered on all sides by the edge of a larch forest. "We ain't driving through there, believe me," Brooke said. "It's either back to the wheatfield or up to the highway."

Hawke agreed. They were penned in down here. What might have been an escape route had made them fish in a barrel, so he swung the wheel to the left and plowed through what remained of the second field. Ahead of them was the highway, but the Corvette was still nowhere in sight.

They smashed the Jeep through the wooden fence and climbed up the embankment in a wild spray of gravel chips as the tires slipped to keep traction. Checking the way was clear, Hawke pulled the battered Jeep back onto ID-75 and headed south to Hailey.

Back on the highway now, they checked the GPS and saw they were only three miles from Hailey and the airport. In the first few seconds of peace since the attacks had begun, Brooke reached for his phone and cursed when he realized it wasn't on him.

"Damn it! Must have left it back at the cabin..."

"Use mine," Alex said, reaching for her own cellphone.

As she handed him the phone, the Corvette appeared in the mirrors once again.

"Where the hell did that come from?" Alex asked.

"They were waiting behind that billboard," said Hawke. "How far from the airport are we now?"

"Less than two miles," Brooke said, twisting in the rear seat to take a better look at his pursuers. "If only we knew what the hell was going on! Maybe we should stop and fight the bastards."

"Are you crazy, Dad?"

"Alex is right, Jack. You're too valuable."

The Corvette accelerated and pulled up beside them on the passenger's side.

"I need to make a call to my guys at the airport – Hawke get us away from these crazies!"

Hawke nodded. "Sorry in advance, guys."

Alex looked at him, confused. "What for?"

Hawke spun the wheel to the right and smashed into the Corvette sending the much lighter vehicle careering off the road. It plowed into the shoulder, kicking up arcs of grit and gravel chips as the driver struggled to maintain control.

"Good work!" Brooke said, beaming as the Corvette almost lost control and spun around in a circle on the highway.

Hawke frowned. "But not good enough." He watched the sports car regain control and power out of the skid. After a tremendous squeal of tires the Corvette emerged from a thick, black cloud of burnout smoke and resumed the pursuit.

"They're determined little bastards," Hawke said.

He stamped on the Cherokee's throttle and the heavy vehicle lurched ever-forward along the highway. He pulled down the sun visor to protect his eyes from the bright summer light outside as they raced toward the airport. Behind in the mirror the same hot, white sunlight gleamed on the hood of the Corvette. He flicked his eyes away just in time to see the exit sign for the airport.

Brooke cocked his shotgun. "I don't want these assholes following us all the way to the airport."

Hawke nodded his head. "Agreed. Assholes with guns and aviation fuel don't mix."

"Slow down a bit, will you? I can't get a decent shot off at this speed."

"Be careful, Dad!"

"Don't worry about me, Alex. It's like I always say – if you can't shake 'em off, you gotta pick 'em off."

"Wasn't that your campaign slogan?" Hawke said.

Brooke didn't reply. His look said it all.

After a few seconds, both men laughed, but Alex was less amused. "I mean it, Dad."

And she did. She hadn't spoken to her father for so long she could barely remember when they had fallen apart. She and Hawke had shared the cabin for weeks now, but her father, one of the busiest men on the planet, had only joined them for the last few days. It was the most time she had spent with him in years.

They had argued at first, but having Joe Hawke and his no-nonsense attitude to life had helped bring them together. She had even started to wonder if they could go back to the way things used to be – before the Great Jack Brooke had walked out on his wife and kids. Before the straight-talking Idahoan had destroyed her family for a woman half his age, pathetically citing pressures of the job. In her heart, she was unsure if she could ever forgive him for that, but she knew one thing – she couldn't lose him now.

"Relax, darling," Brooke said, and flashed that crooked smile at her. "No asshole with that much product in his hair is going to take me out of the game."

Alex watched her father turn in his seat to face the rear as Hawke decelerated the Jeep, keeping one eye on the mirror at all times. Ahead, ID-75 bore off to the right and they began to drive into the northern reaches of Hailey. It looked like a great town – all white picket fences and horse paddocks. Hawke hoped it would still look like this by the time they flew out of it, but he couldn't be sure.

"You have to take them out before we get into the main town," Hawke said. "We can't risk killing any innocent people."

47

"Don't worry about that," Brooke said, squinting into the sights of his shotgun. "It won't take long now they're right behind us... but it breaks my heart to do this to poor old Sally."

Hawke looked at Alex and mouthed the word *"Sally?"*

"The car," she whispered back, a look of apology on her face.

Brooke fired a shot and missed, but then a second and third shot followed immediately afterwards. They both hit the Corvette, the first on the windshield and the second on the driver's front tire.

The sports car responded as Brooke expected, skidding violently to the left and leaving the road in a hurry. The passenger tried to get a shot off through his open window, but then he saw a high white fence rapidly approaching as the Chevrolet raced uncontrollably toward a field of horses.

Hawke watched in the mirror with a good degree of satisfaction as both men instinctively raised their hands to protect their faces. The Corvette smashed through the fence and plowed into the field, its front spoiler ramming into a low rise in the earth and sending the car flying up into the air and spinning over onto its roof. It crashed back to earth with a heavy crunching sound as it landed upside down in the field and spun around two or three times before coming to a stop in a cloud of burst radiator steam.

Brooke cheered loudly as he pulled himself back into the Jeep and placed the shotgun down at his side. "To the airport, Joe," was all he said.

Hawke and Alex shared a look but said nothing.

The former Special Forces man cruised the battered, hay-covered Cherokee down Main Street and followed the road as it curved around toward the airport. It was a small victory, but something told Hawke there was more trouble to come.

CHAPTER EIGHT

Klaus Kiefel sipped at the tequila as he watched his men push America's Commander-in-Chief across the expansive car park toward the deserted processing plant. It was rough stuff, but it was all the now-dead security guards had thought to bring on their shift. Perhaps he should send the one remaining guard to buy something more appropriate for his sophisticated palate, but he had a feeling she would come in much more useful than that as the evening progressed. For now, she could stay tied to the side of distillation unit.

He'd heard there were nice tequilas, but this was a *mixtos* - the cheap *plata* kind where you used lime to hide the taste. The thing about deserted processing plants, the German considered, was that there was rarely a decent selection of citrus fruits available when you needed one. He grimaced as the foul, musky liquor burned its way inside him, and casually tossed the glass over his shoulder. It struck the hood of an old abandoned Ford truck and shattered over the cracked, weed-strewn asphalt.

Kiefel and several other men armed with suppressed Heckler & Koch submachine guns had taken less than five minutes to take out the security guards of the plant. It was a professional paramilitary operation – comms lines cut, no witnesses left standing. Easily achieved by the men, all ex-members of former Iron Curtain countries' Special Forces – but it was just the beginning of a night of terror.

Now, he watched his master-plan come to fruition before his very eyes. Flanked by his liebling Angelika and the ever-loyal Jakob, Grant drew nearer to the plant. Kiefel studied his body language and thought he already looked vaguely dejected, but he also saw anger in his eyes.

With no words spoken, Kiefel opened the door and they moved inside, leaving the hot sun to climb higher in the Louisiana sky.

They walked for some time along cool corridors and sections all lined with industrial piping and conveyer belts. Eventually they arrived at a large room at the center of the abandoned plant.

The German glanced briefly at the set-up in the room – cameras, lights, MacBook Pro. All was going to plan. His dark eyes crawled momentarily over the sole remaining security guard – a young woman with a chipped, laminated name badge reading Sanchez. She was gagged and bound against a large distillation unit. She had seen her last sunrise, Kiefel considered without emotion, and then his attention turned to his new guest.

He straightened his black roll-neck and dusted himself down. "Guten Tag, Mr President," he said calmly.

"Just who the hell are you, and…"

Before he finished his sentence, Kiefel nodded and Jakob knocked the President to the floor of the room. He struggled to get up off his knees but Jakob's hand gripped his shoulder and held him down. Partridge tried to come to the President's aid but Angelika smashed him in the back of his head with her pump-action shotgun and he collapsed to the floor unconscious.

Kiefel sighed and nonchalantly adjusted his hair in the reflection of the distillation unit's shiny metal panel. "Not a very good way to introduce yourself, Mr Grant."

He turned his sharp eyes to the President and stared at him hard. "I suppose I *do* have the advantage, however, so let me introduce myself. I am Oberstleutnant Klaus Kiefel of the National People's Army of the German Democratic Republic."

Grant looked up at him, confused. "The German Democratic Republic? That country hasn't existed for over a quarter of a century."

"A regrettable historical oversight, Mr President."

"I don't understand..." Grant glanced at the lights and camera. "What is it you want?"

Kiefel nodded in sympathetic understanding of the President's confusion.

"Want... desire... need. What would you do, I wonder, if I told you that I want you to relinquish to me the gold codes?"

The look of horror on Grant's lean face was quickly replaced by a smile and then a shallow laugh. The President shook his head. "You must be out of your mind if you think you can get your hands on the gold codes simply by kidnapping me. The United States is more important than one man, Kiefel, even if that person happens to be the President."

Kiefel maintained his composure and stepped closer to Grant. "So you would not relinquish the gold codes, Mr President? How long do you think the world – the American people... your wife and children – will be able to watch you suffer in this plant?" Kiefel glanced around the old, broken down building.

"Mr Kiefel, as you well know, the gold codes are the launch codes for the entire United States nuclear arsenal. They allow me to authorize a full-scale nuclear attack against anywhere in the world, without the approval of Congress."

"I know all this, Charlie. Why are you telling me?"

Grant bristled once more at the use of his first name. Only his wife called him Charlie. "I just thought if maybe you heard it out loud you'd realize how insane it was. You can do whatever you like to me, but believe me – you will never get those codes. As we speak, they are already being changed and the power the use them will be handed over to the Vice President, under the terms of the twenty-fifth amendment to our Constitution."

"What do you mean?" Kiefel said, playing dumb.

"It means," Grant continued proudly, "that I strongly suspect you are no longer talking to the President because that office will now be in the hands of Mike Thorn, my Vice President. If the twenty-fifth has been invoked, you are currently standing in a processing plant talking to plain old Mr Charles Grant, a regular citizen with less political power than the mayor of Sandy Springs, Georgia."

Kiefel laughed for a moment, but his face snapped back to deadly serious a second later. "Mr Grant, I am perfectly aware of the twenty-fifth amendment, and we both know you are of great symbolic value to the United States whether or not that amendment has been invoked." He paused and a mischievous smirk crossed his face. "But I am not interested in your gold codes, or your little nuclear football."

Grant looked confused. "Then what game are you playing, Kiefel?"

"This is no game, I assure you... it is all very real. Soon, Angelika here will help me broadcast our first horror movie to the world. Oh – and if your hopes are resting with Vice President Mike Thorn they are sadly misplaced. Mr Thorn met with an unfortunate accident this morning outside his official residence. He is dead."

"You're lying!"

"No, I am not." Kiefel gestured casually to the camera and then to the guard, still struggling in the corner.

"And let that woman go at once!" Grant shouted.

"I think not."

"Whatever you do, I will never negotiate with terrorists!"

Klaus Kiefel nodded his head and smirked as he cast a casual glance at his watch. He had expected this.

"You will find out what I want soon enough, Mr Grant, but in the meantime – perhaps some entertainment while we wait?"

Kiefel snapped his fingers and Angelika spun a laptop around so Grant could see the monitor. A moment later a blurry image of Washington DC appeared on the screen. Everyone recognised the famous dome of the Jefferson Memorial.

"What the hell is this?" barked Grant.

"Alles zu seiner Zeit, Herr Grant."

"Huh?"

Before Kiefel could translate, they both watched – Kiefel in delight and Grant in abject horror – as a missile tore away from the camera shot on the screen and raced toward the memorial. A second later it struck its target and exploded into the right-hand side of the dome.

Grant lifted a trembling hand to his mouth as a fireball whited-out the screen for a second, then the image returned to reveal an enormous plume of black smoke rising into the air over the city. When the smoke cleared he registered with a mix of terror and revulsion that a quarter of the building's magnificent historical dome was now missing.

"You son of a bitch!" he spat. "That memorial is over two hundred years old! I swear to God you'll pay for this."

Kiefel sighed. "Hmm – this must have been the Viper, don't you think, meine Liebling?"

Angelika nodded. "Ja."

"We must try one of the Hellfires – they are much more powerful, are they not, Herr Grant?"

The rage coursing through Grant had rendered him speechless.

"A marvel of American engineering, the Hellfire missile. Yes – Angelika, instruct Pauling to use a Hellfire next – and make sure the target is equally as impressive."

Grant shook his head. "They'll blast that thing out of the sky in minutes after this!"

"Of course they will," Kiefel replied calmly. "We have factored it into our strategy. That is why we are acting so fast – ah... here we are – let us see what treat Mr Pauling has for us now."

They watched the monitor once again as the drone flew toward its next target.

The Washington Monument.

"Listen," Grant said, panic rising in his previously steady voice. "You can't do this... you have to stop!"

Kiefel raised his finger to his lips. "Please... hush, Mr Grant. You are interrupting the broadcast. It is educational."

Before another word could be said, a second missile ripped away from the drone, leaving a horribly twisted gray smoke trail in its wake. The next second it struck the monument and the screen once again whited-out. When the image flickered back on the monitor another wild cloud of black smoke and fire was at the center of the screen.

Grant reacted with horror when the smoke cleared to reveal that the entire top third of the Washington

Monument was now missing, turned into an enormous pile of rubble scattered around the monument's base.

"You must stop this attack, Kiefel!" Grant paused for a second, staring wide-eyed at the screen. "All right... all right, damn it all! I'll talk with you about what you want."

Kiefel grinned. "Of course you will, but first let us see what a Hellfire can do to the Lincoln Memorial."

Grant shook his head in disbelief as the drone swung left and flew toward the Reflecting Pool west of the now burning and destroyed Washington Monument. He knew that all hell must have broken loose in the capital by now, and that the twenty-fifth would have been invoked, putting Mike Thorn in the Oval Office – but... if Kiefel was telling the truth then that meant the line of succession would pass to the Speaker, Todd Tobin.

He had chosen Mike not only for his ability to secure votes all over the Deep South, but because he knew he would be a safe pair of hands if anything like this nightmare ever happened. Mike was a Navy vet with twenty years' command experience, including nearly a decade commanding an aircraft carrier battle group.

Mike Thorn could handle a cheap, two-bit merchant of terror like Klaus Kiefel. He was less sure about Tobin – he was a solid, decent man with a deep love of his country, but Grant wasn't sure about his ability to command a nation in a time of grave crisis.

But before he could consider the matter further, Kiefel cleared his throat and spoke again.

"Say goodbye to Mr Lincoln, Charlie."

President Grant could scarcely bring himself to watch the nightmare that was about unfold on the small screen right before his eyes.

CHAPTER NINE

Lea Donovan leaned forward in the plush leather couch and stared hard at the giant 3D Plasma TV. She was sitting in the tropical headquarters of ECHO on Elysium, an island nestling in the warm, turquoise waters of the Caribbean. It was most people's idea of paradise, but what she was seeing unfold on the TV looked more like some kind of hell on earth.

Right now, she was watching coverage of Washington DC as filmed by a news chopper hovering on the outskirts of the city. The news reader was explaining that a serious terrorist attack was underway in the United States. The President had been kidnapped, the Vice President and Speaker had both been assassinated and a no-fly zone was in force across the city. It was, announced the newsreader with grim anguish, a day of terrible national tragedy.

"That explains why the news chopper's flying so far out," Ryan said. He collapsed in the chair beside her and pulled open a bag of popcorn.

Lea glared at him. "Haven't you got *any* respect at all?"

"What?" As he spoke, some popcorn tumbled out of his mouth and landed in his lap.

"It's not a bloody Hollywood movie, Ry. This is real people we're talking about."

His face grew serious. "Yeah thanks, I got that. I'm just hungry, that's all. Want some?" He held out the bag to her and she waved it away with a scowl on her face.

"You can be so childish and insensitive sometimes."

"I'd do anything to stop the scumbags behind this," he protested. "I'm just hungry, so leave me alone."

She made no reply, but turned away to see Scarlet out on the ocean, ripping past the window-wall on a red-sailed windsurfer. Protected in the lee side of the kite, she performed a flawless back loop before blasting further out to sea. She never seemed to be still for more than a few seconds, Lea thought. Even now, as the tropical sun was pitching down at its strongest, Scarlet Sloane was still searching for adventure.

Her thoughts were interrupted by the sound of Ryan belching loudly. "Gross," he said weakly. "I think a little bit of sick just came up."

"For fuck's sake, Ryan, get a grip."

She heard a noise behind her and turned. Behind the couches in the center of the room was an impressive circular staircase of tempered glass and Brazilian cherry which lead to the mezzanine and offices on the upper level. Sir Richard Eden came bounding down it, three steps at a time, holding a slip of note paper.

Lea looked at his face. "So I guess you've heard about Washington?"

Eden shook his head. "No, what?" As he spoke he looked up at the TV set with horror.

"Terror attacks," Lea said. "Massive, apparently."

Eden's face dropped. "My God, that's terrible. " He shook his head slowly and clenched his jaw. "We need to keep an eye on developments there."

Ryan twisted in his seat. "So, we're not packing for America then, boss?"

Eden looked at him, confused. "No. Why would be going to America?"

"Um – that," Ryan said flatly, pointing at the TV set again.

"Of course not. We respond to matters concerning covert history and related anomalies."

"So Poseidon, Thunder Gods and Osiris yes, but massive terror attacks no?"

Eden nodded. "Yes, and you have popcorn grease all around your mouth."

As Ryan wiped the grease with his sleeve, Lea looked up at Eden.

"So if you're not talking about the attacks in Washington, why did you come racing down here looking like you've seen a ghost?"

Eden looked at her, to Ryan, and then back to Lea. "You'd better come with me – alone."

She followed him back to his private office. They took a seat and Eden started to speak.

When he had finished, Lea stared at her boss for a full minute in shocked silence. Then she wiped her eyes and sat up straight in her chair.

"My dad, you say?"

Eden nodded. "I know how hard this is for you, Lea. I knew Harry before you were born, and I was devastated when he died."

Lea heard the words, but none of them seemed to make any sense. Her head was spinning so much from the revelation Eden had just delivered to her – but this time not in his usual calm and measured style. This time, he had sounded slightly ruffled and uncertain of things.

"Can we trust the source?" she asked quietly.

"Without a doubt. Sean McNamara was an old mutual friend of mine and your father's, and this information comes from his sister."

Her mind wandered. It felt like everything was falling apart. They had worked so hard to locate the elixir of eternal life, only for it to be snatched away when the Tomb of Eternity mysteriously crumbled away right under their feet. Then, to make matters worse, Joe Bloody Hawke had stormed off in a sulk because she had kept ECHO and Elysium a secret from him. She wanted to tell Hawke that he was being stupid, that she *had* to keep it from him – that was the way it worked. She wanted to kiss him... she wanted to throttle him. She didn't even know where in the world he was, and now *this*.

She turned to face Eden. He was watching her, a look of understanding on his kind face.

"How many jets are available?" she asked.

"I thought you might ask that. The answer is two of the three. Sasha, Alfie and Ben are in Acapulco looking into the Wade affair."

"Oh sure, I forgot about that... so I could use one then?"

He nodded. "For Harry Donovan's girl, anything."

*

Thanks to the tufts of wheat sticking out of the Jeep's radiator grille, Hawke, Alex and Jack Brooke drew a certain amount of unwanted attention as they sped along Main Street and pulled into Friedman Memorial Airport.

Thanks to the Secretary's phone call back on the highway, his jet was fuelled and ready to go, and a small contingent of men in the Bureau of Diplomatic Security who had stayed with the aircraft met them at the gate and ushered them outside to the apron.

"We have to get back to DC in a hurry," Brooke said to Lopez, the lead BDS man. "Those sons-of-bitches killed three of my men back at the cabin and they almost killed me, my daughter and Joe Hawke here. Whoever the hell they are we need the President to respond and..."

Lopez and the other men shared a glance. He turned to the Pentagon chief. "You mean you haven't heard, sir?"

Brooke stopped dead on the asphalt and the entire entourage screeched to a halt around him. He stared at Lopez. "Heard what?"

"The President's been kidnapped, sir."

Brooke looked incredulous. "Kidnapped? That can't be possible!"

"Sorry, sir, but it's more than possible – it just happened."

Anger flashed across Brooke's face. "Well, how the hell *did* it happen?"

Lopez shrugged his shoulders. "We don't have the details, sir. It's total chaos everywhere right now. From what we can gather he was snatched when he was down in Louisiana."

"This is unbelievable."

"I know, sir."

They started walking again, faster now, and reached the plane where they stood at the bottom of the airstair. A few hundred yards to their right a group of men were refuelling an Embraer jet and readying it for takeoff.

"We gotta get back to DC right now. I'm going to need to talk to Mike Thorn. Has he been sworn in yet?"

Another glance. "Sir, the Vice President was killed this morning."

Brooke's face changed from anger to an incipient fear. "*Killed?*"

Lopez nodded. "He was shot by a sniper when he was leaving his house."

Brooke looked at his daughter and ran a trembling hand over his stubble.

"And they also got Speaker Tobin – when he was at a football game with his wife. I would have told you earlier but I presumed you knew."

"We were under attack, Lopez! We had no time to read the news." Brooke's eyes widened like saucers as he shook his head in disbelief and horror. "We're talking about the total decapitation of the US Government!"

The normally hardened BDS men began to look nervous.

"Doesn't that mean you're the President or something?" Hawke asked.

Brooke shook his head. "No, I'm fifth in the presidential line of succession."

"So who's number four?"

Brooke put his hands on his hips and stared up at the sky for a few seconds. "After the Speaker, the presidential line of succession goes to the President pro tempore of the Senate."

"And who's that?" Hawke asked.

Brooke sighed and returned his gaze from the heavens. "Teddy Kimble."

Hawke looked from Brooke to Alex and then back to Brooke. "You sound unhappy about something."

"It's nothing, it's just that…"

With his words still hanging in the air, Brooke stopped talking and looked over Hawke's shoulder, his jaw dropping in horror.

Hawke spun around to see a rocket-propelled grenade racing toward them.

"Run!" the Englishman shouted.

The group scattered in all directions as the grenade struck the port engine of the C-32 and ignited the kerosene contained in the wing. A series of enormous explosions tore through the aircraft and sent a white-hot fireball into the air over the airport.

The shockwave lifted Hawke and the others from their feet and blasted them away from the plane like rag dolls. Hawke smashed into the side of a small utility shed and fell to the asphalt with a smack. He shook his head, blinked and looked up to see the Secretary's official aircraft had turned into nothing more than a blown-out airframe of twisted blackened metal. Flames poured from every part of it. It looked like the burned carcass of some hideous, dead monster.

Hawke now watched in horror as the pilots tried to escape on rope ladders hanging out of their windows, only to be mown down by the submachine gun fire of the men who had fired the grenade.

By now, the BDS men were on their feet and helping Brooke back onto his.

Hawke ran a few yards to Alex and helped her up.

"What the hell was that?" she asked.

"Up there," Hawke said, pointing to the roof line of an industrial unit a few hundred yards beyond the airport's western perimeter fence. "I saw a puff of smoke rising into the air when we turned and saw the grenade. I'm guessing it's our friends who borrowed your Dad's Corvette, plus a few of *their* friends."

"Well whoever the hell they are," Brooke said, joining them, "they're not going to give up after one shot so get after them, Lopez!"

Lopez and the others fanned out and returned fire, temporarily pinning the enemy gunmen down. As the fighting continued, passengers, pilots and cabin crews streamed from their planes and ran for the cover of one of the hangars.

The familiar wail of sirens rose up in the hot Idaho air from behind the departure building. "Fire trucks and police..." Brooke said. He looked at the burning jet and shook his head in anger.

63

Lopez ran back over. "We took a couple of them out, but there has to be more. We need to get you out of here, Mr Secretary."

"Concurred," Hawke said. "And that's how we're going to do it."

He pointed to the United Express Embraer jet a few hundred yards behind them that he had seen the men refuelling.

"Our pilots are dead, Joe!" Brooke shouted.

"I can fly that thing no problem," he said. "It's the only plane here with the range and we know it's fuelled."

Brooke gave Hawke a double-take. "You can fly it?"

"Almost one hundred percent certain."

"Are you kidding me?" Alex said. "*Almost* one hundred percent?"

"It's me or them!" Hawke said. He pointed as another one of Lopez's men was shot through the chest and collapsed on the hot asphalt.

"Let's get out of here!" Brooke said, and the four of them ran up the airstair and into the Embraer. From the top of the airstair, Brooke called out for Lopez to get on board, but he stayed behind to pin some approaching gunmen down behind a maintenance shed.

"Get in here, Lopez!" Brooke screamed.

"Yes, sir!"

He sprinted up the airstair, but as Special Agent Lopez began to close the heavy door behind him, one of the shooters fired a bullet through his neck. The round ricocheted off the far cabin wall, causing no damage, but Lopez was gone. He clutched at his neck in horror as he fell from the Embraer and landed with a sickening wet smack on the asphalt below.

Horror flooded through Jack Brooke, but he wasted no time in securing the door and joining Hawke and his daughter in the cockpit. It was time to take the fight to the enemy.

CHAPTER TEN

The Secret Service agents bundled Senator Edward D. Kimble into the black Cadillac SUV that was idling outside his office on Capitol Hill and made the short journey to the White House. As they headed west, Kimble looked along the National Mall in horror at the devastated Washington Monument directly ahead of them.

They made a sharp right turn and skidded onto Pennsylvania Avenue. With the curfew now in force across the city for all non-approved journeys, the journey took a few short minutes and they arrived at the east entrance of the White House in double-quick time. The Cadillac swept through the gates and accelerated along the drive around the South Lawn. Seconds later Kimble was being rushed into the south entrance of the Executive Residence.

They were met by Scott Anderson, Charles Grant's Chief-of-Staff. "Welcome to the White House, sir," he said hurriedly to Kimble. He was out of breath as they paced through the residence toward the West Wing. The nervous faces of junior staffers peered up at him as he raced past them. "This won't take long, sir."

As they moved along the plush corridor, Kimble said nothing.

And then they reached the Oval Office.

Teddy Kimble was speechless for the first time in his life. He had been in the impressive room many times before, but all those times it was someone else's office, and that someone else was the President of the United

States. Charles Grant had always been in here, standing behind the desk, and the rest of the room orbited around his powerful gravitas. Now, Grant was gone, and the room was his.

Or soon would be.

But what had seemed like a good idea at the time was now starting to feel very wrong.

Anderson stepped forward. "Sir, this is Mark Paton, a lawyer and also of course a federal judge. He'll be swearing you in."

Kimble nodded grimly. "Where's the Chief Justice?"

Paton pulled a copy of the Bible from his suitcase. "Chief Justice Owens is on a fishing holiday in Montana, sir, but there's no legal stipulation that he has to administer the oath."

Grant's Chief-of-Staff turned to Kimble. "Senator, with the exception of Jack Brooke who's missing and presumed dead, the cabinet has convened by secure video-phone and approved the use of the Twenty-Fifth Amendment. Congressman Mitchell, USSS Agent King and the Secretary of Labor are here to act as witnesses. Are you ready to take the oath, Senator?"

Kimble glanced around the room at the men, and then above their heads at the portraits of George Washington and Abraham Lincoln. History started to weigh heavy on his shoulders. "I am, Mr Anderson."

Mark Paton stepped forward with a copy of the Bible in his hand and spoke. His words were solemn and quiet in the hushed, grim atmosphere of the Oval Office.

"Then please raise your right hand and repeat after me...I, Edward Dupont Kimble do solemnly swear..."

Kimble cleared his throat. "I, Edward Dupont Kimble do solemnly swear..."

"That I will faithfully execute the Office of President of the United States..."

Kimble repeated the words slowly, a slight wobble in his voice. "That I will faithfully execute the Office of President of the United States…"

"And will to the best of my ability…"

He paused for half a second to ask himself if this was really happening. "And will to the best of my ability."

Paton's voice didn't waver. "Preserve, protect and defend the Constitution of the United States."

"Preserve, protect and defend the Constitution of the United States."

"So help me God."

Kimble swallowed hard. "So help me God."

Paton lowered the Bible and shook Kimble's hand. "Congratulations, Mr President."

*

Hawke strapped himself in the pilot's seat and moved his hand up to the overhead panel. He clicked the two battery switches and a computerized voice began to squawk.

"What the hell does that mean?" asked Alex as she sat down beside him and strapped herself in.

"It means we're on battery power," Hawke replied. "But battery power's not going to get us to Washington." He switched on the fuel tank pumps and started up the auxiliary power unit. Suddenly they heard a whining sound as the APU powered up and began to run the electrical systems.

He activated the avionics, emergency lights and APU bleed. "Yeah…" he said to himself. "I'm pretty sure that's right – now engine start up."

"Well make it quick!" Brooke said, poking his head through the cabin door. "A sniper killed Lopez and look over there!"

Hawke glanced through the cockpit window and saw an intense fire-fight taking place on the perimeter fence between local police and airport security on one side, and the men who had fired the grenade on the other.

Brooke clenched his jaw. "If they get through that fence we're the next target!"

"So no pressure, then," Hawke said, and checked the powerplant section on the overhead panel to ensure the ignition switches were on auto. He flicked open the safety covers and moved the control switch for Engine One to the start position.

Alex raised an eyebrow. "You seem to know your way around."

"That's what all the girls say," Hawke said.

"And so modest, too."

He ignored her and watched the instrument panels spring to life as the aircraft began pumping fuel to the engine.

"Oil temperature and oil pressure rising," he muttered, and did the same procedure for engine two. "Now we're cooking with gas!"

"And so are those maniacs!" Brooke said, pointing at the fence. The men had overwhelmed the local police force and broken through the perimeter. They were just under half a mile from their jet.

"They're heading this way, Joe!" Alex said. "They want to kill my Dad!"

She felt Brooke squeeze her shoulder in reassurance, but she knew he would be scared too.

Hawke ignored everything and focussed, flicking off the APU bleeds now the engines were up and running and powering the aircraft. He checked the hydraulic electrical pumps were set to auto and glanced over the panels one last time, rubbing his hands together.

"Don't you have to tell this thing where it's going?" Alex said.

"Probably, but we're just going to fly east and hope for the best."

Before she could answer, Hawke pushed forward the throttles and the engines roared to life. The plane began to taxi toward the runway. "This is your captain speaking," Hawke said. "I recommend a strong drink followed by strapping yourselves into your seats, in that order, and as fast as possible."

He taxied the Embraer to Runway 13 as the gunmen climbed into an airport fire truck and raced toward them. Seconds later they were almost alongside them and began firing at the aircraft.

"Now *that* is just not cricket!" the Englishman muttered.

Hawke pushed the throttles forward and the powerful aircraft quickly gained speed. The runway grumbled angrily beneath them and the fire truck now fell far behind as they raced toward V1 speed.

Hawke pulled back on the yoke and the jet's nose rotated. They lifted into the air high above Hailey and he retracted the gear. They were already flying at nearly two hundred knots as they passed the mountain line and shot up into the blue sky, tearing through a handful of cumulus clouds on their way up.

Hawke spoke quietly into the headset. "Ladies and gentleman, no one is more surprised than your captain that we are actually safely airborne, but pleased be advised to stay in your seats with your seatbelts on until we have reached cruising altitude and I'm absolutely sure I can keep this thing in the air. Thanks."

Alex smiled. "You've done this before, right?"

Hawke smiled. "Yes and no. I'm properly trained to fly light aircraft but I'm a rotorhead really. The good news is I did take private lessons in these for a few weeks until the money ran out, so I know what everything is and what it all does." He paused and narrowed his eyes with confusion. "Except that one," he said, leaning toward a bright red button which read ESSENTIAL POWER. "I wish I knew what that one did."

Alex rolled her eyes and sighed. "Very drole, Mr Hawke."

Hawke said nothing, and set the autopilot to fly at a course of sixty-one degrees with a vertical speed of fifteen hundred feet per minute. When they hit their cruising altitude of thirty-five thousand feet, he began to relax for the first time, glancing over the controls with a mix of awe, respect and pride.

"Should be in Washington DC in around four hours," he said, tapping the top of the instrument panel as if the aircraft were a faithful dog.

"Do we even have enough fuel?" Alex asked.

"Shit – I never checked that."

Alex looked panicked. "You're kidding, right?"

"What do you think? We have enough fuel, but the flight to DC is at the far end of this little baby's range, so we won't have much to spare if we're pushed out of Washington airspace because of the attacks."

"We'll deal with that right now." They both turned to see Jack Brooke standing in the cabin doorway once again. "I want you to radio whoever the hell you have to and tell them what happened back there, and that I'm coming back to the Pentagon to straighten this shit out."

"On it," Alex said.

Brooke leaned over the pilot's seat. "And Hawke?"

"Yeah?"

"Back there, at the house when we were getting attacked."

"Yeah?"

Brooke paused a beat. He looked like he was trying to remember something important. "Did you call my daughter a septic tank?"

"Er, well..."

"Get outta here, Dad!"

Without saying another word, Brooke turned and walked back to the passenger cabin.

"That's my Dad, by the way," Alex said, and offered half a smile. "Did I ever tell you that?"

"Come to think of it," Hawke said, fixing his eyes on her. "I really don't think you did."

"I guess now you know why," she said.

Hawke guessed it was supposed to be a joke comment, but her words were tinged with sadness, and she turned away from him to look out the window as they raced over Caribou Mountain and crossed into Wyoming.

"I need to stretch my legs," she said. "Sometimes they kind of hurt."

Hawke looked at her, concerned. "Are you okay?"

She nodded and smiled. "Sure."

She unstrapped herself and walked into the main cabin. As she went, she pulled her phone from her pocket and made a quick call to an old friend.

CHAPTER ELEVEN

Hawke stared out of the cockpit window across the American continent as the jet raced toward the nation's capital. Of all things that could have crossed his mind, it was that this was the first time he'd been involved with anything like this without Lea Donovan, and it felt wrong.

He wondered again if he'd made a mistake back in Egypt when Sir Richard Eden and the others told him about the ECHO team and had invited him to join. He wanted to say yes – he had no job, for one thing, and these people had become his closest friends. But his pride had been wounded by their deceit, and he'd said he wanted nothing to do with them. He'd felt like a fool. The argument with Lea had ended in what he supposed anyone else would call a break-up, but maybe that wasn't the right word.

He hadn't heard from any of them since that day back in the desert when he'd turned his backs on them and walked away, and not for the first time he wondered what Lea and the rest of them were doing now on their private island – what had they called it – *Elysium*?

"You're thinking about her, right?"

He looked up and saw Alex had rejoined him in the cockpit. He watched her sit down in the First Officer's seat. Things had gotten so hectic in Africa he'd barely stopped to look at her, let alone talk to her face to face.

That, at least, had been corrected in the past few weeks they'd spent together in her father's hunting cabin in the mountains. It was a peaceful time, and in many ways he had wished it would never end. Watching Alex learn to walk again had been an amazing experience, for one thing, and it had helped him avoid thinking about the ECHO problem for another.

"I need to get some back-up," Hawke said ignoring Alex's question about Lea.

"My Dad has some back-up," Alex said. "It's called the US Army."

Hawke grinned, pleased to hear some levity in the chaos. "No, I mean someone I really know."

"I thought you weren't on talking terms with ECHO since you flounced off like a spoiled little girl?"

Hawke ignored the barb and sent the text. "This person's in the Everglades on a job and can be in DC fast."

"Who are we talking about?"

Before Hawke could reply, Alex's father, known to the rest of the world as the US Secretary of Defense, came and sat down in the jumpseat behind them. He rubbed his face and sighed. "Now we're out of that shitstorm, just who the hell were those guys, Joe?"

"Germans."

"I'm sorry?"

"Germans, Jack. The grenade they threw at us in your cabin was a DM51, a classic fragmentation grenade originally equipped to the West German Army back in the Cold War."

"But anyone could have got hold of them."

"Sure, but they were all carrying German submachine guns and their accents sounded German to me. I think we're dealing with Germans, Mr Secretary."

"Germans?" Brooke looked confused. "That doesn't make any sense at all! The Germans are our allies. What the hell would they launch an attack on the United States for?"

"The German *Government* is your ally, sure, but these crackerjacks could be anyone. Think Hans Grüber from Die Hard and you're roughly in the right ballpark, I reckon."

"Huh?"

"Nothing, just thinking out loud. Any details about the President and Vice President?"

Brooke nodded his head grimly. "What Lopez said is true, I'm sorry to report. Vice President Thorn is dead – he was killed at Observatory Circle this morning by a similar crew of thugs that tried to kill us today back at the cabin. So is Todd Tobin, murdered by an assassin at a football game right in front of his wife."

"And the President?"

"He was at a university in New Orleans when they kidnapped him. Our guys say that the driver of the limo may have been compromised." Another heavy sigh. "I just don't know – the whole day has descended into total chaos. All the information we have is just in crazy fragments and no one really knows what's going on. How long till we get there?"

Hawke glanced at his watch. "Just over an hour now."

*

An hour later, Joe Hawke watched the carnage unfolding in the streets of Washington as he turned the Embraer to line up with Andrews Air Force Base, just twelve miles southeast of the US capital. Smoke poured from several sites and the curfew's deserted streets lent an eerie quality to the whole scene.

"Jesus H. Christ," Brooke said, looking down from the cockpit window. "What the hell are we looking at?"

"The worst terrorist outrage on American soil, Jack," Hawke said.

Brooke nodded and rubbed the stubble on his jaw. A look of deep anger flashed in his eyes. "I want the response to this to be totally disproportionate."

"That's the President's choice, Dad," Alex said. "Not yours."

"And right now that's Teddy Kimble," he said. "And that doesn't fill me with confidence."

Hawke hoped he was wrong – he knew America needed a strong leader now more than ever. He turned to look once again at the terrible sight of smoke pouring out of the top of the Jefferson Memorial.

"My God!" Brooke said. "Even the Monument's been blown to pieces – look!"

Hawke's eyes flicked over the river to the Washington Monument, now no more than a smouldering stub sticking out of the earth. The ring of American flags that encircled its base was broken down and on fire. Here and there he saw a few terrified people running for their lives or piling their belongings into the backs of the cars.

"Looks like some are breaking the curfew."

"This could get really ugly."

Brooke banged his fist against the cabin wall. "Whatever son of a bitch is responsible for this will die for it, I swear!"

"They're trying to flee the city," Hawke said.

"Bad idea," Brooke said bluntly. "There'll be roadblocks on every exit route by now just in case the assholes behind this are still inside the Beltway."

Hawke reduced speed, extended the flaps and deployed the gear. They would be on the ground in minutes.

Moments later, their SUVs sped north through the suburbs of Camp Springs and Oxon Hill before crossing the Anacostia River on the 11th Street Bridge. At the north end of the bridge they slowed for a road-block manned by a mix of Metropolitan Police Department officers and heavily armed US Marines, but when the men saw who was inside the SUV they waved them through with salutes.

As they drove toward the Pentagon, Brooke clicked shut his phone and leaned toward the driver. "That was Scott Anderson. He says the President wants us at the White House."

The driver nodded and swung the wheel to the right.

Things were about to get serious.

CHAPTER TWELVE

Lea watched through the small porthole of the Gulfstream as the plane banked to the right and began its descent. In the glimpses she got through the cloud cover, the coast of Ireland looked beautiful, but seeing it again made her sad. It would always be home... only she'd wished the next time she came here it would be to introduce Joe Hawke to her family.

Her family.

After her father's death on the Cliffs of Moher things had gotten a little rocky in the Donovan household. Her mother had started drinking and her brothers had signed up to the Garda. Liam, the oldest, was killed in a bank robbery in Dublin, while Finn ended up in the Special Detective Unit, the Irish equivalent of the British Special Branch or the FBI. The decade between their ages turned out to be an unbridgeable gap and they rarely talked. Even now she didn't even know his address.

Now, below her she watched as the plane crossed over into Irish airspace for the first time as sunset slowly approached. Below her was County Clare, and there, with the wild waves of the North Atlantic smashing against them in their timeless assault, were the very same Cliffs of Moher. Her father's life had ended in that violent swell below her – the gunmetal gray of the sea spume and the ragged, savage Moher cliffs at Hag's Head. At four hundred feet high, she knew it had taken her father several seconds before he'd hit the rocks below.

She looked away, disgust and sorrow gnawing at her mind in equal measure. *Someone will pay for that*, she thought. There was nowhere in the world anyone could hide from her if she found the person who had killed her beloved Dad.

The pilot announced that they would be landing in around twenty-five minutes, and now they were low enough to make out individual houses and roads. Dry stone walls criss-crossed the moss-colored sheep fields beneath the executive jet, and she strained her eyes as she stared at the northern horizon to catch a glimpse of Connemara, the ancestral home of her family.

As her eyes settled on the clouds above Galway Bay, or *Loch Lurgan* as her old Nanna used to say, her mind drifted to that damned Englishman once again. The arrogant, cocky, selfish, unreasonable, pig-headed, son-of-a-bitch, *gobshite* who had turned his back on her in the Egyptian desert. She sighed. The only thing she hated more than that man was how much she loved him, and damn him for it, she thought.

With Joe Hawke on her mind, the rest of Ireland slipped past her unnoticed – the smooth, verdant rises of Tipperary, Offaly, Laois and Kildare. Then, as the pilot announced final approach and the plane turned to line up with Dublin Airport, her mind snapped back into business mode. She had only the vaguest recollections of Sean McNamara from her childhood. He was one of her father's many friends who had come and gone through the years. Why anyone would want to kill him she couldn't begin to imagine, but she knew in her heart it was linked to her father's murder.

And she was going to get to the bottom of it even if it killed her.

*

President Kimble had asked for some time alone in the Oval Office to consider what had just happened a few moments ago. It seemed like an age ago that the German had approached him with the files and made his business proposal to him. Kiefel had said that his compliance would facilitate a mutually beneficial arrangement, but any other man would have saved the time and called it what was it was – rank blackmail.

But was it so bad? The terms of the 'arrangement' were simple enough. Kiefel would use his considerable logistics and muscle to position him in the Oval Office in order that he perform one simple task, and after that he would be free of him forever – free, and the most powerful man in the world. It seemed like a reasonable proposal, and accepting the terms meant those files would go up in flames, and no one would ever need to know about his career-ending extra-curricular business activities.

He ran his hands along the edge of the desk. So this was the seat of power, he thought, looking around the room. As President pro tempore of the senate he had been in here before, naturally, but again it struck him how very different it looked from behind the Resolute Desk. He instantly felt the power at his disposal, but, and unexpectedly so, he was aware of a crushing responsibility bearing down on his shoulders like sacks of lead. All of the world would know everything about him, and every decision he took would go into the history books forever.

This, after all, was the exact same office in which Franklin Roosevelt had signed the declaration of war against Nazi Germany. This was the office where Harry Truman had given the order to drop the atomic bombs on Japan. This was the office where John Kennedy Jr.

had played under the desk while his father navigated through the Bay of Pigs.

The very same desk he was sitting behind right now.

A noise startled him from his daydream.

He looked down to see his cell phone vibrating on the President's desk – on *his* desk. He stared at it for a few seconds, reluctant to answer it because he knew who was calling.

Then he snatched it up and took the call.

"Yes?"

"Congratulations!" The voice was ice cold and almost mocking in its tone.

Kimble was silent. He started to feel sick.

"Teddy – are you there?"

"Yes…" the voice was barely a whisper.

"Well speak up then Teddy! Or should I say, speak up Mr President?"

Another pause. "Listen, Klaus… I'm not sure this is going to work out."

"Listen to me, Teddy, and listen very carefully. You can't back out now, you little shit. I made you President of the United States. You belong to me and don't you forget it."

"No… I'm sorry."

"Better. I had to kill good men to put you in the Oval Office, Teddy. Better men than you. I still have many unspeakable things to do just to keep you there, *President* Kimble. Don't you think that has a certain ring to it?"

"Yes… yes, I suppose it does." He sounded a little more relaxed now.

"Good. Now you remember why I gave you the job, right Teddy?"

"Of course."

"I want it released *immediately*."

"Sure, but…"

"No buts, Teddy."

"I'm just saying that these things probably take time. They're not going to release something like that just because I tell them to. If what you say is true we're talking about a doomsday weapon that makes nukes look like a Sunday School picnic."

"Tut tut, Teddy – I am surprised at you questioning my integrity like this. Of *course* what I say is true! And yes, we're speaking of something very dangerous indeed – but you're still talking like a common senator, the President pro tempore of the United States Senate, but you're not that man anymore, Teddy."

"No, I guess not…"

"Good guess. This morning I kidnapped Charles Grant and had the Vice President and Speaker of the House assassinated. For this reason, Teddy, and courtesy of the current order of the American presidential line of succession, you are now the President of the United States and the most powerful man on the planet, after me, naturally."

"I understand." As he spoke, he watched a young woman on the housekeeping staff gently place a tray of coffee and cookies on the table in the center of the room. Her name badge read Veronica Fisher. She glanced at him and smiled as she left the room and closed the door behind her.

Kiefel continued. "Good. And that is why when you order Archive 7 to release the item in question, they will do as they are commanded."

"Yes."

"Don't forget the catalog number, Teddy."

Kimble noticed his hand was trembling. "How could I forget?"

"Repeat after me, Mr President: X422387-0."

"Listen…"

"Say it!" Kiefel barked.

Kimble swallowed hard. "X422387-0."

"There's a good president…"

The line went dead.

Teddy Kimble was starting to wish he could turn back time.

*

Frank Watkins took the call at his desk. He was still in shock at the news of what was unfolding all around in him in his home city, and he lowered the volume on the TV set in the corner of his office as he picked up the receiver.

"What is it, Mandy?"

"It's a call from the President, sir."

Watkins looked confused for a few seconds. "The president of what," he said annoyed. "The Ford Motor Company?"

"The President of the United States, sir."

"*What?*"

"His office is on the line, sir, and they say it's urgent that the President speak with you right now."

Watkins widened his eyes and scratched his head. On CNN they were showing pictures of the Jefferson Memorial. It was on fire and looked like it had been bombed. The same thing had happened to the Washington Monument. Now, Watkins was struggling with the issue of evacuating essential staff from the museum when *this* happens. What the hell would the President of the United States want to talk to the Director of the National Museum of Natural History for?

"Sure…, I mean, of course – put him through at once, Mandy – and then go home and be with your family."

83

"Yes, sir... *thanks.*"

He listened as there was a change of ring-tones and then another woman's voice came on the line.

He cleared his throat. "Hello?"

"Dr Watkins, this is the Executive Secretary to the President speaking."

"Hello."

"I'm going to put you through to the President now."

"Thank you, and..."

The line clicked before he could finish his sentence.

"Frank, is that you?"

"This is Frank Watkins, sir, yes."

"This is President Kimble, Frank. I'm calling you from the Oval Office."

President Kimble? It had to be Teddy Kimble from the Senate. Things were moving fast, he thought. He wondered if they knew what had happened to President Grant – was he still alive or had the terrorists already done the unthinkable?

"I won't say congratulations, Mr President. I know this is a terrible time for you to be charged with all this responsibility. This is a truly dreadful crisis."

Kimble ignored the sentiment. "Frank, listen – I have to ask you something."

"Anything, Mr President."

"This is sensitive, Frank, but we need to talk about Archive 7."

Watkins narrowed his eyes. "Archive 7, sir?"

"Level 7 in the archives under the National Mall, Frank."

"I know what you're referring to, sir, it's just that..."

"Good, I need something released from the archive, Frank, and I need it done in a hurry."

Watkins's brow furrowed when he heard the new President's tone. He sounded desperate and anxious, not qualities he wanted to hear in the voice of his Commander-in-Chief, and it made him suspicious. While the existence of Archive 7 was a long-running rumor on popular conspiracy theory websites, it had never been formally confirmed. More than that, the authorities had initiated a long-running disinformation campaign via agents posing as posters on the internet to rubbish any claims of its existence.

Watkins appreciated that he was one of a small handful of men who knew the top secret storage facility existed, and the others consisted of the Federal Government's shiniest Top Brass – the President, naturally, being at the center of the inner circle.

But what he couldn't understand was why Kimble was ordering the release of something from the archive within what could only be minutes of the Twenty-Fifth Amendment being invoked. It all seemed terribly odd to Frank Watkins. He sighed quietly and put his doubts aside. In the final assessment, he was talking to the President of the United States, and one generally did not say 'no' to the Commander-in-Chief.

"What do you need, sir?"

Kimble replied without hesitation. "The item in question is X422387-0."

Watkins made a note of the serial number. There were countless thousands of items stored in Archive 7. It was impossible to know what they all were by serial number without looking them up. All he knew was if it was in Archive 7 then it meant trouble.

He tapped the number into his computer and was surprised to see he did not have the required clearance to see what it was. It simply said TOP SECRET/CODE WORD.

"This can only be released on Executive Order, sir."

"And I signed that order a few moments ago. EO 15325, Frank – it formally orders the release of Item X422387-0."

Another pause from Watkins as he contemplated the situation. There were very few things down in the archive that he was denied knowledge of, but this was obviously one of them. Again, he set his suspicions aside and gave Kimble the benefit of the doubt – whatever he was ordering out of the archive was obviously critical to the defense of the nation at this terrible time.

Reluctantly, Frank Watkins spoke into the telephone. "Yes, sir… the item in question will be released as requested."

"Excellent. My men will be over immediately."

Kimble ended the call and for a few moments Watkins simply stared into the buzzing receiver. He did not feel good about this at all.

CHAPTER THIRTEEN

After several heavy layers of White House security, Joe Hawke and Alex followed the Secretary of Defense into a West Wing elevator where they were met by two US Marines. Moments later they were at the underground level.

"This way, sir."

As they made their way along a short corridor, Hawke checked a message on his phone and smiled. His back-up was in the city.

They soon reached the entrance to the White House Situation Room and after taking salutes from the junior Marines, a senior officer showed them inside.

Hawke glanced around at the American President's emergency command bunker and took in the calm but tense atmosphere. The country's most experienced and senior military officers and CIA officials were struggling to get to grips with the attack.

He turned to Alex and tried not to look like he was in awe. "Have you ever been in here before?"

She shook her head. "Are you kidding?"

Teddy Kimble shuffled across the plush blue carpet and shook Brooke's hand. "I'm glad you're here, Mr Secretary."

Brooke gave a cursory nod in acknowledgement. "So where are we, Mr President?"

For a moment, Kimble almost looked over his shoulder to see who Brooke was talking to, but then he realized once again he was now the Commander-in-Chief. He reminded Hawke of a frightened rabbit.

"We're up to our necks in shit, Jack," Kimble said, and ran a trembling hand through a fine head of dyed hair. "They killed Mike Thorn and Todd Tobin and snatched the President right off the street down in Louisiana."

Several of the senior military men gave each other worried glances at Kimble's reference to the President. An army general cleared his throat and stepped forward. "Sir, the Twenty-Fifth Amendment was invoked an hour ago and you were sworn in on the Bible. You have to stop referring to Charles Grant as the President. You are the President, sir. You need to understand that. "

Kimble stared wide-eyed at the general and acknowledged him politely. He looked tired and on edge. "Of course, General McAlister... of course." He rubbed his eyes and took a deep breath before turning to pace nervously up and down the room for a few moments while he processed the nightmare. He wondered what a man like McAlister would do if he found out he was in league with the terrorists. Probably shoot him on the spot, he thought.

Over the next few moments information flooded into the Situation Room via a bank of secure phone lines and internet connections.

General McAlister took control of the situation with ease, his gravitas commanding a deep respect among the other men and women in the room, including Teddy Kimble.

"I want updates, ladies and gentlemen," he said, his deep voice exuding a calm determination.

"The coasts are secure, sir," said a naval officer.

A USAF man stepped up. "And we have a no-fly zone over all of Washington. Should we extend it to the entire country?"

McAlister looked to Kimble.

The President seemed to be wavering.

It was clear that the Joint Chiefs wanted to respond hard and fast, and Jack Brooke was in agreement. Kimble, on the other hand, seemed strangely reluctant to move forward.

"I'm not sure," he said quietly. "We can't be seen to over-react. The world is watching, and after certain foreign policy...*errors*," he paused and stared at McAlister, "we can't just wade into this guns blazing. We need more intelligence if we're to make an intelligent response. Remember, only DC has come under attack as of right now."

"With respect, Mr President," McAlister said loudly, "I strongly disagree. This is the most savage attack on the United States since nine-eleven. You're right – the world *is* watching, and what it needs to see is some serious leadership and a brutal smack-down of these maniacs. We need to enforce a national no-fly zone immediately."

Kimble saw he was facing growing opposition and backed down. "All right... all right. The attacks on DC were by drones so let's clear the skies except for our guys, of course."

McAlister looked at the senior USAF man in the room. "Do it!"

Kimble walked to the door. "All right, keep me updated, gentlemen."

They all snapped to attention as Scott Anderson opened the door and the two men exited.

Brooke looked to Hawke. "We need to get to the Pentagon. That's my home-ground." As he spoke his phone rang. "I have to take this." He walked to a quiet corner and spoke in hushed tones.

Alex moved closer to Hawke.

"This is as insane as it gets," she said, shaking her head.

Hawke wasn't so sure. "As insane as Poseidon, Lei Gong and Osiris all being real?"

"Okay, I'll give you *that*."

A few tense moments later, Brooke walked back over to Hawke and Alex. "That was Frank Watkins over at the Smithsonian. He's an old buddy of mine from way back and he just told me he got a very interesting phone call a few minutes ago from President Kimble."

Alex looked at the older man. In here, he no longer seemed to be her father, but another man altogether – a man she barely recognized. "A call about what?"

"He's issued an Executive Order which orders the release of something stored in Archive 7." Brooke glared at them both. "Neither one of you two has ever heard of Archive 7, got it?"

"Got it," Hawke said.

"Is that normal?" Alex asked.

Brooke shook his head. "I don't think so, especially at a time like this. The items stored in Archive 7 all relate to... how shall I put this...?"

"Stuff like Poseidon?" Hawke asked flatly.

Brooke realized the futility of beating around the bush with a man of Hawke's experience. "Exactly like Poseidon," he continued. "And a whole lot of other stuff you'd never believe as well. Why he's ordered the priority release of some kind of archaeological artefact at a time like this worries me a great deal."

Hawke stepped forward and lowered his voice. "You want me to check it out?"

"You read my mind."

Brooke turned to Hank Deakin, the head of the President's personal protection detail who was about to return to the Oval Office. "Hank, we're heading back to the Pentagon, please inform the President that's where he can contact me."

"Yes, sir, Mr Secretary."

As they headed to the door a man in a gray suit slipped into the room. He approached Deakin.

"Sir – we have a problem."

Deakin looked at Brooke and Hawke with a look of grave concern on his face.

"What is it, Doyle?" Deakin asked.

"Agent Novak, sir. He's not here."

"Is he on shift?"

"Yes, sir. As a matter of fact he's supposed to be in this room right now."

"Has he called in?"

"No, sir."

Deakin turned once again to Brooke, Hawke and Alex. All of them were thinking the same thing.

Brooke spoke first. "We need someone to get over to his place right now!"

Deakin nodded and turned to his man. "Doyle – I want you to get over to Kevin Novak's place right away, and take your best man."

"No... wait," Hawke said. He turned to Brooke. "We need to stay inside of this, Jack. We should send one of our guys with Agent Doyle."

"Who do you suggest?"

"An old friend of mine just arrived in DC and is waiting outside the White House. He can be trusted one hundred per cent."

Brooke looked confused. "How did he get to the White House in the middle of this curfew?"

"Yeah, curfews don't stop a man like Vincent Reno."

"Ah," Alex said. "So that's the mystery back-up you texted from the jet."

"Exactly."

Brooke nodded. "All right, so here's what we're going to do. Doyle and this Reno guy – get over to Novak's place and see where that leads. Meanwhile I want Hawke and one of my agents to get over to the Smithsonian and check out just what the hell Frank Watkins is talking about."

Suddenly they were on the go again. Not for the first time, Hawke found himself being grateful that Lea and the others were nowhere near this mess. The thought of her safe and sound on Elysium was of some comfort, at least.

*

The six men all had Secret Service ID and were armed with SIG Sauer P229s. They arrived at the Smithsonian a few moments after President Kimble's telephone call to Director Watkins, and moments later were ushered through the main gates and shown to the elevator.

As the elevator descended to Archive 7, no one spoke until the little light above the door indicated they had arrived. Then one of the men said: "Let's make this quick."

They moved to the security team, where Captain Aaron Reznik looked at the paperwork. He couldn't believe what he was seeing. In nearly twenty years in the US Army he'd never seen anything like this before.

"I'm going to need to show this to the Colonel. Wait here."

Reznik ordered the guards to keep the men outside the archive while he made a phone call.

"Sir, I think you need to see this."

"What is it, Reznik?"

"It's an Executive Order, sir, signed by the President of the United States."

Colonel Prescott was unmoved. "That's fine, Reznik. I'm on my way."

Reznik hung up the phone and told the men to wait. Two minutes later the heavy, metal door swung open and the tall, slim figure of Colonel Douglas Prescott appeared in the half-light. "Follow me," was all he said.

Reznik and the group of men obeyed in diligent silence as they followed the senior army man through the doorway and down a long corridor. Their footsteps echoed loudly off the brushed aluminum walls and ceiling as they walked to the end where a second door awaited them.

Prescott punched in a long keycode and the second door swung open to reveal a large warehouse, several storeys underground, built into the bedrock beneath the city itself. If any of the men were impressed by it, they didn't show it.

"Where is the object?" one of them asked.

"Over there," Prescott said quietly, his breath showing in the cold damp air of the storage facility. The whole place was full of boxes stacked up to create what looked almost like a maze. He pointed to the far wall, which contained hundreds of what looked like very large safety deposit boxes. "Follow me."

They walked across the warehouse to the far wall in silence. Something made Reznik glance over his shoulder but nothing was there except the USSS Agents. As he moved along behind the Colonel he read the codes and descriptions on the locked doors of the boxes... X193745-4: ARK OF THE COVENANT... X375837-1: POSEIDON'S TRIDENT... X422387-0: ULTRA-CLASSIFIED.

Reznik shivered. "This whole place creeps me out."

Prescott shot him a look. "That's enough, Captain!"

The Colonel tapped in another long keycode and the large door clicked open. He swung it fully open and walked inside.

The men swarmed inside the small room. "We'll take it from here, Colonel."

They moved ahead of Prescott and Reznik and formed a huddle.

"What are you men doing there?" Prescott said nervously. He reached for his gun as the men opened the heavy safe door at the end of the room and extracted something from within it.

The agents turned to reveal they were now wearing gas masks and fitting long black NBC gloves on their hands. The man who had spoken back in the elevator was now holding the most dreadful thing Reznik had ever seen, but the young American officer had no time to react. A second after his eyes settled on the horror before him, he felt himself stiffening. His breathing became more labored and now he was unable to move his legs, or even call out for help.

His desperate eyes moved just enough to see Colonel Prescott going through the same terrible ordeal – clutching at his throat but unable to move or even scream out in terror.

A wave of ice-cold panic rushed over Reznik as he realized the Colonel was turning to stone, and was now nothing more than a statue. It had happened right before his eyes, but the realization that the same thing was happening to him, mercifully, came too late, and his world came to an end before he knew that he too had turned to stone.

CHAPTER FOURTEEN

Lea checked into the Radisson Blu Royal Hotel on Dublin's Golden Lane. She had friends in the city, but they weren't part of this side of her life, and her remaining family was distant and scattered along the west coast.

She flicked the TV to a news channel and watched the terrible news flooding out of America. It looked like the attacks were restricted to Washington DC, which was a small mercy, but they still had no idea where the President was – or even if he was dead or alive. She knew Jack Brooke would be up to his neck in it and she hoped Alex Reeve was safe. For now, at least, there was nothing else she could do.

She glanced at her phone – no messages. She considered calling Hawke. Where was he in the world? She had no idea. She picked up the phone and began to dial his number, but then thought better of it. He hadn't called her, after all. She put the phone down and watched people trundling up and down the street beneath their umbrellas.

The light was beginning to fade now, and the night approached. It was all very familiar. Every time she returned to Ireland it was like she'd never been away, but at the same time she felt like she was a little more different every time she came back. She glanced at her watch and saw it was almost time to meet Devlin.

When Eden had told her about McNamara's murder, she knew she'd need help when she got back to Ireland.

Daniel Devlin was her old commanding officer from the Army Ranger Wing. He was a good man but a better soldier, and these days he spent his time propping up the bar in Flynn's on Harry Street.

She hadn't seen him for more years than she could remember, and she wondered what she was about to walk into. She'd heard stories about his fall from grace, but taken them with a good pinch of salt. Now she was about to see him face to face her concerns grew stronger, but she had nowhere else to run. He was the only person she could trust to help her, and she just hoped that he was going to be up to it.

She made the short walk to the pub in less than ten minutes and as expected, the former commandant was halfway through a Guinness and regaling the half-empty room with his old army exploits. She wondered if he could stand, let alone help her track down McNamara's killers… but then she stopped herself. Men like Devlin were hardened Special Operations military men and she had watched him do whatever it took on missions from Somalia to Kosovo. She was certain he could handle anything thrown at him tonight.

She approached him from behind, looking up at the muted TV set bringing the punters yet more news of the chaos unfolding in Washington DC.

"So how many's that you've sunk, Danny?"

Devlin turned and his face lit up. "So you really did make it back home, Mrs Bale?"

"Sure I did… someone had to drag you out of here, you know. You drink too much – you know that, don't you, Danny?"

Devlin shrugged his shoulders. "I drink to hide from myself, Lea."

"Does it work?"

"No. I'm too good at finding things."

"Same old tosspot, I see – and it's not Mrs Bale anymore... we divorced."

"Am I sorry to hear it?"

"No."

Devlin laughed and clapped his hand on her shoulder. He ordered two more pints of Guinness up at the bar while Lea secured a table in the corner. She watched him at the bar, recalling the night they had spent together all those years ago in this very city.

He walked over to her, a drink in each hand and smiled warmly at her as he sat down.

"So what have you been up to, Lea – saving the world, if I made my best guess?"

She looked at him for a second and took a sip of the stout. "Something like that, Danny."

He chuckled and shook his head from side to side. "I bet you are, too. Tell me though, why are you bothering *me* tonight? By the looks of that tan I'd say you're not spending too much time in Galway..."

"I need your help," she said, ignoring the fishing expedition to find out where she lived. "No other reason for me to get in touch with such an ugly bastard, is there now?"

He laughed, and glanced at her, his face growing more serious. "Nothing too nasty, I hope?"

She sat for a long time and said nothing. She knew the silence wouldn't bother Devlin, and she was right. He sipped his drink and occasionally scratched at the silver stubble on his chin. Then she spoke.

"It's about Dad."

"Your father?"

She nodded. "You remember what I told you about him, right?"

He nodded. "He died when you were a girl... I remember. Very sad."

Another pause. "You know, they told me I was crazy when I said I thought someone murdered him."

"I remember, Lea."

"But now it looks like I might be able to prove it."

He gave her a sideways glance, eyes narrowing. "How's that then?"

"Danny, listen – recently a close friend of mine in British intelligence…"

"Now that's an aposiopesis if ever I heard one, young Donovan."

She rolled her eyes. "I was *going* to say that he's a very good friend of mine, and he knew Dad. Anyway, he got some information recently about one of his and Dad's mutual friends – a Sean McNamara."

"What sort of information?"

"He was killed, Danny. Someone broke into his cottage in Cork and garrotted him to death with the silk cord of his own dressing gown."

Devlin winced and put his pint glass down. "Now, I asked you right at the start if it was anything too nasty. You could have given some kind of warning – that's put me right off me Arthur's."

"This is serious, Danny."

"It bloody sounds like it!"

Lea rubbed her eyes. "That it is, Danny – that it is…"

"So what's this got to do with you and me?"

"Whoever killed him was looking for something. That was obvious because the whole place was trashed, but they didn't find it."

He gave her a look. "And how do you know that?"

"Because just before he was killed, he sent Rich – my intel friend – an email."

"While he was being garrotted?"

"Sure. Turns out he'd set up an automatic emergency send function on his mobile phone. You can send a prewritten message out to any number of contacts just by holding down the volume button on your phone."

"And how many contacts did this message go to?"

"Just one – Rich."

"And it said..?"

"It said if he was reading this message, then they had come for him at last, that they were the same people who had killed my father, and that what they were looking for they would find on the side of the sun."

"On the side of the sun? I don't understand."

"That's because you don't speak Irish."

Devlin rolled his eyes and laughed. "Don't start that again."

"On the side of the sun is Taobh na Gréine in Irish, Danny."

"Still not with you."

"I can tell you never went on a self-catering holiday as a kid…"

"I grew up in South Africa, Lea, you know that. Just tell me what the hell you're talking about."

"My parents' holiday cottage was called Taobh na Gréine, Danny – a lot of those places are called that. McNamara's emergency message was telling Rich that the men who killed him and my father are searching for something, and that whatever they were looking for, Dad must have hidden in his cottage."

Devlin smiled. "You see, now – *now* – I'm right up there with you. All I need to know is why you're telling *me* about this? Surely you can hire a car and drive to the cottage without recruiting an old soak like Danny Devlin?"

Another pause. "There's something else."

"I bloody knew it! Am I going to need another drink?"

"McNamara and Dad were both doctors, Danny. Not your average GPs but research specialists. The message hinted that what the killers were searching for might have something to do with their later research work. That's all."

"That's all?! It's more than enough to be going on with! Garrotted doctors in cosy cottages? Until now I used to think it was a weird day if it stopped raining, but now I see I was wrong."

"Danny, will you help me?"

"Lea, you know that…"

Without warning, bullets drilled through the windows at the front of Flynn's and blasted shattered glass into the room with the force of a hurricane. The handful of drinkers dived for the floor and crawled over the broken glass on their way behind the bar. More bullets shredded through the woodwork and peppered the bottles of whiskey, vodka and gin neatly lined up behind the bar. A mix of glass shards and alcoholic mist rained down on those sheltering beneath.

Lea and Devlin leaped from their table and slammed themselves against the far wall. She peered around the corner through the wrecked entrance of the pub and saw three men in ski masks standing behind a black Peugeot 508 estate car. Each of them was carrying what looked like a MAT-49 – a blowback operated submachine gun used by the French Army.

The gunmen swaggered across the narrow pedestrian area toward the ruined pub.

"Like father like daughter, hein?" one of them shouted, and laughed. It sounded to Lea a lot like a French accent.

"Out you come, little piggies," said another, also French.

Devlin looked at Lea. "Don't know about you, Donovan, but I think that's one invitation I'm going to turn down."

The men sprayed more lead into the small pub, tearing up the word-work around the old bar into a thousand splinters. "Time to die, little piggies."

Lea didn't think so. "Is there a back way outta here, Danny?"

Devlin nodded. "Just through there." He nodded at the back of the bar. "That door leads to a side entrance, but I don't like our chances. It's a narrow alley and we'll get cut to shreds before we've got ten yards if they see us go down there."

"Then let's hope they don't see us go down there because I think it's our only chance!"

Devlin dusted himself down. "If you're up for it then count me in. I've never been beaten by a woman yet and I'm not going to start now."

They made a dash for it, taking advantage of the night's darkness and the shadows to reach the end of the narrow lane with their lives intact. Behind them, they heard the gunmen demolishing the small pub with their submachine guns and laughing wildly.

"Don't take this the wrong way," Devlin said, "but I really hope those guys are after you and not me."

Lea gave him a look. "Oh, they're after me all right."

He looked at her, worried. "Listen, it's not going to take them long to work out we're not in there, so let's get moving."

Lea took a breath. "But to where, Danny?"

Devlin winced as another burst of gunfire echoed down the lane. "Sounds to me like we're going to need some back-up."

CHAPTER FIFTEEN

As they pulled into the Smithsonian car park, Hawke checked his phone to see if Brooke had called, but there were no messages from anyone – and that included Lea Donovan. He didn't like the way he felt about that, and considered calling her, but then put the phone back. She hadn't called him, had she? He shook the matter from his mind – it wasn't like he had nothing else to think about.

Hawke and Special Agent Kim Taylor made their way to the main entrance of the enormous museum and saw it was deserted. No surprises there – that was part of the curfew – but what shocked them both were the dead security guards scattered behind the front desk. They instantly drew their weapons and proceeded with guns raised, spooked by what they had just seen.

They took the elevator to Watkins's office and cautiously made their way inside but when they got there they found the same thing – someone had shot Frank Watkins several times with a nine mil weapon of some description and propped him up on his chair.

"These guys are always a step ahead of us," Hawke muttered.

"Look at this," Kim said, peering at Watkins's computer.

Hawke looked at her. Back at the Pentagon, Brooke had introduced her as his best man, which had induced an eye-roll from Kim Taylor. She was tall and slim, with brown hair tied back in a bun and wore a black suit. It didn't look to Hawke like she smiled very often.

"What is it?" the Englishman asked.

"Looks like a list of classified objects stored here at the archive."

Hawke ran his eyes over the data, but the series of code numbers meant nothing to him. "But what are they referring to exactly?"

"It looks like these are catalog numbers for various items. I'm not sure what exactly – but if you look here, you can see he's written this one down on a pad, in the middle of this pretty elaborate doodle."

Hawke looked at the agent, confused. "And that's relevant why?"

Kim rolled her eyes. "This doodle took a long time – check it out. It's not the sort of thing a man with a busy mind does for amusement – *you* maybe, but not the guy who runs the Smithsonian. This was done while he was on the phone, and considering it's all around a catalog number it's safe to assume at this point that this catalog number here must be what Kimble ordered him to release from the archive."

Hawke nodded. "This just goes deeper and deeper. We have to find out what the hell was released, and that means we're going to Archive 7."

*

In the vast, deserted museum, it didn't take long to reach the storage levels and take the elevator to Archive 7. Moments after exiting the elevator they followed the same corridor used by Prescott and Reznik until they reached the heart of the secret facility.

Hawke went first, but came to a sudden stop when he stepped through the second steel doorway.

"What's the matter?" Kim asked, scarcely believing anything could be more shocking than what they had already seen upstairs.

"They're all frozen solid – like stone," Hawke said, his heart filling with horror.

"That can't be right," Kim said, but one look tempered her natural cynicism. "Oh my God…"

"My thoughts exactly."

They drew closer to the far wall of the warehouse.

"This door here," Hawke said. "Check it out."

Kim moved past the frozen man and stood beside Hawke. "What am I looking at?"

Hawke gave an ironic smile as his eyes ran over the military lettering: X375837-1: POSEIDON'S TRIDENT…. "So this is where Eddie Kosinski and his department hide all their little treasures."

"Who's Eddie Kosinski?" she asked.

"Never mind. It just helps me to know where this is. Come on – whatever was in here is long gone now and we have a President to report to."

They sprinted back through the labyrinthine corridors of the subterranean archive and got back to their car as fast as they could.

"We need to report to Jack," Hawke said.

"Nuh-uh," Kim said firmly. "I'm reporting this to the President."

"But I report to Jack."

"And I report to President Kimble. If people are getting turned to stone, he needs to know first. You call Jack after the President's been briefed."

Hawke gave way on the point and climbed into the Chevy Suburban as Kim hit speed-dial. It rang gently on speaker and Hawke still couldn't believe they were calling the direct number of the President of the United States.

Beside him, Special Agent Kim Taylor checked the mirrors and reloaded her SIG as she waited for a response.

Kimble's voice spoke in the phone, distant and isolated. "Is that you, Agent Taylor?"

"Yes, sir," Kim said. "I'm with Joe Hawke and we're on speaker."

"Good evening, Mr Hawke."

"Good evening, Mr President," Hawke said, resisting the inclination to call him Teddy.

"Agent Deakin briefed me on your mission. What did you get?"

"Frank Watkins is dead, sir."

A pause. "You mean the Secretary of the Smithsonian?"

"Yes."

"What the hell are you doing at the Smithsonian? Deakin told me we were chasing a lead about the missing agent, Novak?"

"Yes, sir, we are," Kim said. "But we got a lead about something odd happening at the Smithsonian, so we have another team going to Novak's house while Hawke and I went to check out the museum."

Kimble paused a beat. They heard a long sigh.

"You're sure Frank Watkins is dead?"

"Pretty sure. He was shot through the head. Looks like a professional job."

"Part of the terror campaign then?"

"We think so, sir," Kim said. "But there's something else."

A longer silence. Over the speaker phone Hawke could hear the sound of the Oval Office clock ticking. It sounded pretty lonely in there. "And that's what?"

"We found something a little strange, sir," Kim said.

"What are you talking about?"

"Some of the guards in Archive 7, Mr President..." Hawke said.

Kimble's voice rose. "Well, what about them, damn it?"

Kim Taylor replied. "They were turned to stone, sir."

"Turned to... *what* did you just say?"

Hawke sighed. "She said they were turned to stone, Mr President. When we were in Archive 7 chasing down our lead we found some of the guards there were just blocks of...it looked a lot like stone."

"Did you consider that you were looking at an actual statue?"

"No sir," Kim said. "It wasn't anything like that. It was like stone, but not exactly stone. I can't explain it but it's got to have something to do with today's terror attacks."

What he said next shocked them both. "I don't want you to pursue this."

"I'm sorry?" Hawke was astonished.

"You heard me, Hawke. Whatever the hell is going on at the Smithsonian and your goddam statues, we have bigger problems right now, starting with tracking down whoever the hell is firing missiles at my capital city!"

Kim spoke next. "Sir, I really think..."

Kimble shut Kim Taylor down fast and hard. "You take your orders from me, Agent Taylor, and I am ordering you to get back to the White House right now."

"Yes sir."

Kimble cut the call and they pulled out into the deserted street, Hawke at the wheel. He gave her a look.

"He *is* my Commander-in-Chief, Hawke."

"So you're just going to do as he tells you?"

She shrugged her shoulders. "Pretty much, and even better than that, as a foreign adviser to the Defense Secretary, or whatever the hell you are, you're under my command, so buckle up because we're headed back to the White House."

"No, I don't think so," Hawke said. "We should go back to the Pentagon and talk with Brooke."

"I already told you, I can't disobey the President."

Hawke rolled his eyes. "Live dangerously for once, Kim. Everyone else is doing it."

She gave him a look as he accelerated the Suburban.

"All right, but as soon as you've checked in with Brooke we go to the White House. God knows what I'll tell the President about why it took so long."

Hawke glanced down the deserted street, totally silent thanks to the curfew.

"Just tell him you hit traffic."

Kim ignored him and holstered her weapon. It was going to be a long night.

CHAPTER SIXTEEN

The tropical sunset was approaching, and now the cicadas' call filled a humid, peaceful evening on the isle of Elysium. "Looks like a bloody mess to me," Scarlet said, stubbing her cigarette out in the ashtray and immediately lighting a second. As she did so, she kept one eye on the TV.

Sir Richard Eden raised an eyebrow. "Perhaps we should extend the smoking ban to the outside areas as well?"

"If you do then you can say goodbye to me, Dickie."

Ryan suppressed a laugh and took a sip from his drink. Maria Kurikova got up from her chair and kissed him on the cheek.

"I need to make a call to Moscow," she said. "And then I want to go to bed."

He watched her slink away into the compound and take her cell phone from her pocket.

"Bloody hell – is that Joe?" Scarlet leaned in closer to the TV and studied the chaos carefully for a few seconds. She was watching a news video from around an hour and a half ago featuring the US Secretary of Defense being driven with some urgency into the White House.

"I told you Alex called me and said she needed my help," Ryan said. "But she never mentioned anything about Joe being with her."

"Well he bloody well is!" Scarlet said.

"Are you sure?" Eden said. "What did you see?"

"Joe Sodding Hawke in the front seat of an SUV with Jack Brooke and his daughter right behind him."

Eden sighed and looked over his glasses at the plasma screen on the wall of the outside area. He turned up the volume to drown out the sound of the cicadas and watched with interest as the video clip of Hawke and Brooke replayed. Beneath the image of the black SUV speeding into the White House the news ticker was running with the headline: AMERICA UNDER ATTACK.

Eden was silent for a long time before speaking. "I'm not going to say this is an easy decision but the truth is this simply isn't an ECHO mission. I can't sanction the use of our resources for this. This is an internal American situation and the Americans will handle it extremely well as they always do."

Scarlet sighed. "Fine, then don't make it a formal ECHO mission, but give me one of the jets and let me go up and make sure he's okay."

Eden stared at Scarlet with his business face. "I said no."

And that was that.

*

Vincent Reno and Agent Doyle burned out of the White House in a Black Raven Secret Service-issue Cadillac Escalade and skidded onto Pennsylvania Avenue. Doyle was at the wheel, and he knew the city inside out. Vincent passed the time by loading his PAMAS, whistling the Marseilleise as he pushed the nine mil bullets into the magazine.

Vincent had been happy to fly up from the Everglades when Hawke had called him a few hours ago. The truth was, his mission to put an end to a coke smuggler's operation in Florida was coming to an end and he was getting bored. He was about to fly out of the country to France when the attacks had grounded all civil aircraft, leaving him stranded in Miami. Hooking up with Hawke and smashing the bastards behind the attacks was just fine with him.

Doyle had been less enthusiastic to work with him, but they were the orders of the Secretary of Defense so he had no choice but to go along. Now, it had taken less than fifteen minutes to get to Palisades, the neighborhood where Kevin Novak lived on his own in a modest house near the canal. Doyle spun the wheel and took the corner so fast the Cadillac nearly tipped onto two wheels.

"That son of a bitch better have a damned good explanation for his disappearance," Doyle said as they approached the property.

"I'll take the back," Vincent said quietly. As he spoke he checked the magazine in his PAMAS G1 and slid it back into the grip, locking it in place with a gentle nudge.

"We need him to talk," Doyle said, glancing at the gun in Vincent's large hand. "If he's alive, then he stays that way, got it?"

Vincent shrugged his shoulders. "It's your country."

They didn't even stop to close the Escalade's doors when they got to the house. They drew their weapons and split up, Doyle going to the front door while Vincent climbed over a side gate and jogged up the deck steps at the back. A few seconds later Doyle rang the bell and moved his hand smoothly to the SIG under his jacket.

*

Vincent barely had time to react when the back door burst open and Kevin Novak came scuttling out. He looked up at the enormous French merc – the last person he had expected to find outside on his deck. He tried to draw his gun but he ran out of time.

"Putain!" Vincent screamed, and drove his fist into the startled man's face.

Novak staggered back into the kitchen and crashed into a chair.

Vincent moved into the kitchen to finish the job, and saw the silhouette of another, bigger man in the hall. His features were obscured by an electric light behind him, but he looked pretty out of shape and was carrying what looked like some car keys.

Vincent raised his weapon and aimed at the man in the shadows. "Stay where you are and put your hands up."

"Sod that!" came the reply, and he slipped into a doorway behind him and out of sight.

Below Vincent, Novak was struggling to his feet, one hand on his broken nose and another raised palm out to indicate he'd already had enough. Vincent didn't believe him, and punched him once again, this time knocking him out.

Then he began to sweep the house for the silhouette, wherever he was.

He paced down the hall and turned at the door he had seen the man flee toward. Now he was just a few yards from the front door and he saw Doyle standing on the stoop. He unlocked the catch with his free hand. "You want an embossed invitation to joint the party, or what, American?"

Doyle said nothing, but cocked his gun and joined the Frenchman in the hunt.

"Bastard went in there," Vincent said, pointing to the door. He opened it and saw steps descending to the basement.

"Shit!"

They heard a car engine roar to life and then a brand new bright red Dodge Viper smashed through the garage door in a burst of splinters and wood dust and skidded out into the street.

Doyle sprinted back out of the house to catch the licence number but it was too late. The 8 liter V-10 had spirited the Viper away in a cloud of burned rubber and tire squeals.

"Damn it!" Doyle screamed, and kicked over a trashcan at the side of the house.

"Don't sweat it, mon ami," Vincent said, tipping his head to the house to indicate Novak. "We might have lost the engine driver, but we still have the oily rag, n'est-ce pas?"

CHAPTER SEVENTEEN

Charles Grant tried hard to fight down his fear when Klaus Kiefel took possession of some kind of mystery delivery. Seeing half of the capital city destroyed had excited the German in an almost unnatural way, but this latest arrival seemed to delight him more than ever.

Whatever it was, it took two armed men to carry it into the room and place it in front of the boss. Sprayed on the side in black paint was a serial number: X422387-0, and Grant knew one thing – items catalogued in Archive 7 with an initial 'X' code were always related to the vital national interest of the United States.

Kiefel stared at the steel box with undisguised glee for a few moments before ordering his men to open the outer container. They obeyed and used a pair of hardened alloy bolt cutters to snap off the six padlocks with which they had secured the lid to the heavy container back in DC. Clearly they weren't taking any risks with the contents.

Kiefel beamed. "Brought to us courtesy of an experimental UAV borrowed from the German Luftwaffe a few days ago. It travels at nearly seven thousand miles per hour, Mr Grant – too fast for even *your* fighter jets to shoot down."

"How did it get past our radar?"

"It has the latest stealth technology and flies very, very high… you'll have to do better than that!"

Jakob swung open the lid and recoiled in horror, while Angelika gave an appreciative nod.

Kiefel peered inside for the first time, his eyes wide with an almost childish anticipation.

"Remove the inner container!" he said, taking a step back.

As the men carried out his instructions, Kiefel turned and pulled a gas mask from the bench behind him. His men, including Angelika and Jakob, secured their own masks from their belts, and Kiefel tossed two casually at the former President and Partridge.

"I strongly recommend you wear it," the German said coolly, and pulled his own mask on over his goatee beard.

Grant picked the mask up from the floor and brushed the dirt from it. "What about her?" he asked, nodding at the female security guard tied to the distillation unit.

"She won't be needing one, Mr Grant... You!" he snapped, pointing his finger at one of the men. "Put the box on the bench and open it."

The man, a young shaven-headed recruit in a black boiler suit moved cautiously forward and put his hands inside the steel container. For a few moments he struggled to get a good grip on the inner box, causing Kiefel to roll his eyes and sigh, but then he lifted it from the steel container and placed it carefully on the bench.

Grant stared at it through his gas mask, and then looked over at the guard with growing concern.

Kiefel did not share his disquiet. Instead, he put on a pair of military surplus NBC gloves and opened the inner box. Grant couldn't see through the German's mask, but he got the feeling he was smiling as he leaned over the small black box and started to undo a series of worn leather straps. Then, he gently pulled back the lid and peered inside.

He gasped and took a step back, shaking his head in disbelief.

"What the hell is going on?" Grant said.

Partridge looked at the President, fear and confusion on his face.

Jakob stepped forward and smashed his rifle butt in between Grant's shoulder blades and sent him crashing to his knees where he cried out in pain.

Partridge stepped forward to defend the President but Angelika cocked her pistol and pointed it at the senior USSS man. "Back in your box, puppy."

Kiefel laughed. "Jakob is simply teaching you good manners, Mr Grant. You must learn to be patient. You are not in charge any more... I am."

Kiefel pulled something from the box and held it in his shaking hands.

Grant stared up at it from the tiled floor. At first he thought it was some kind of rotting fruit – a blackened cantaloupe melon came to mind, but then Kiefel turned and proudly showed it to Angelika and the other men.

Grant was aghast to see it was a severed head – a badly decomposed one – with black and blue skin all covered in blotches and stretched tight over the skull like dried-out Chamois leather. He was mortified with disgust and thought things could get no worse when he noticed that the black mass at the top of the skull which he had presumed was hair was in fact dozens of dead, desiccated black snakes – tiny and twisted around in knots. He felt like throwing up, but he was also strangely fixated by the terrible object in Kiefel's hands.

"What the hell is that?" he asked, his words muffled by the gas mask.

"This, Mr Grant, is the head of Medusa."

Grant moved back involuntarily along the dirty floor. "What are you talking about, Kiefel? There is no such thing as Medusa! Are you insane?"

"I take offense to that remark, Mr Grant. I am calculating, scheming, and manipulative, and I also have some *bad* qualities... I am not, however, insane."

"You're wrong, Kiefel! How can you believe that thing is what you say it is, if you're not totally crazy? Medusa was a myth, damn it!"

"I see American education does not extend to the Classics! We know from our reading of Ovid that Medusa was a real, mortal being – her head of snakes... *these snakes*... was given to her by Athena as punishment for desecrating her temple when she slept with Poseidon!"

"Fairy tales..." Grant said, but he was no longer sure of it.

"Sadly, we can never know the truth, but that is Ovid's account." Kiefel held the head up to his face and stared at it almost lovingly through the mask. "Others claim Poseidon was besotted with her, but when she rejected him he grew enraged and used his divine power to turn her hair into snakes."

"You did all this killing just to get this *thing* released from Archive 7?"

Kiefel beamed. "There's no need to congratulate me, Mr Grant – it's implied."

"For God's sake, Kiefel – you need help!"

Kiefel was unmoved. "She was still incredibly beautiful, but the snakes terrified anyone who looked at her and turned them into stone... this was mighty Poseidon's revenge on the woman who had rejected him."

"Please, just stop this!" Grant watched the madman's eyes through the gas mask, distorted by the warped plastic lenses.

The German ran a hand down the skull's cheekbone. "Some say that when Perseus was sent to kill her, he took a glass shield so he could look at her reflection and never at the Gorgon herself. This was how he was victorious. This was how he beheaded Medusa without getting turned to stone!"

Grant ignored the lecture. "For God's sake give that woman a gas mask, Kiefel!"

His voice muffled through the mask, Kiefel sighed. "When Perseus returned to Greece, he gave Athena Medusa's head, which she wore on her shield – her aegis – as a weapon, allowing her to turn her enemies to stone simply by showing them the head."

Grant shook his head in despair and banged his fist into the dirty floor. "You really are insane!"

"I am insane for liberating Medusa, but your government is not insane for storing it in secret for decades? How sane is it to withhold the real truth of our world from all the people?"

"I don't know what you're talking about."

"Of course not..." Kiefel offered a low, guttural belly laugh. "Of course you know nothing about Medusa being stored in Archive 7! I expect you also know nothing about why the severed head of Medusa – a Greek Gorgon – was in northern Norway? About who took it there and why?"

"As a matter of fact I do not!"

"Have you ever heard of Valhalla, Mr Grant?"

"Of course."

"Perhaps that will help you put the dots together, but in the meantime, I have business to attend to."

"I'm not playing your games, Kiefel. Whatever the hell that thing is, I know you can't possibly believe looking at some dead snakes can turn a man to stone!"

"I never said *that*, Mr Grant."

Kiefel slowly walked the head over to the female security guard. She kicked and struggled against the ropes binding her to the support post of the distillation unit.

"You see, when Poseidon turned her hair to snakes, this was the act of a spurned, enraged lover, and it became her curse – the true curse of Medusa was that she could never fall in love with anyone without turning them to stone. Now the curse of Medusa will fall on the entire world, starting with America which I intend to use as a testing ground. Jakob!"

Jakob padded across the room and gripped the security guard's head, forcing her to look at the severed, mummified head of Medusa. The young woman recoiled in terror.

"Now, Mr Grant, you will see the true power of Medusa – the world's most ancient doomsday weapon!"

Grant wanted to look away, but his inherent sense of leadership and responsibility forced him to behold the ancient evil that was unfolding before his very eyes. He couldn't turn his back on this poor woman, not now.

Kiefel held the skull up to the woman, whose head was now in the vice-like grip of Jakob's broad, gloved hands. He moved the skull closer until it was almost touching her terrified, sweat-streaked face, and her screams echoed in every room and corridor of the sprawling, abandoned processing plant.

CHAPTER EIGHTEEN

With Kiefel moving the skull ever closer, the young woman stared at it with wide, crazed eyes, and then began whispering an unintelligible Spanish prayer. She kicked more, and writhed like a trapped pig, but it was too late.

Grant watched with a sense of growing, desolate horror as the woman began to judder and shake uncontrollably, and then her skin slowly turned a strange putty color. A few seconds of agony later, the woman was silent and totally still.

Jakob staggered back, his trembling hands at his sides, and moved away from the dead, ossified guard as fast as he could.

"You've frozen her!" Grant muttered, incredulous.

"Wrong!" Kiefel said. "As I tried to explain to you before, this woman is not frozen – she is stone... behold!"

Grant watched as Kiefel took his pistol and tapped it against the young woman's head. It made a soul-draining *plink plink plink* sound. It sounded exactly like he was tapping the metal gun against a piece of granite.

Where a woman had once lived, there now stood a statue.

Kiefel ran a hand across the statue's face, lingering on its smooth marble-like cheek. "Don't you think she is so much more beautiful now? The ancient Greeks dismissed the love of statues as a psychological defect – agalmatophilia, they called it – but they were wrong, and so we are wrong today as well. Now, rendered in

119

perfectly smooth stone, this woman's beauty has increased tenfold!"

"What the hell have you done?" Grant said, mumbling his words in fear.

"I have reawakened an ancient force, Mr Grant. An ancient weapon – the original Doomsday weapon... and it's mine! Soon your whole country will be no more than a theme park full of statues for my personal amusement."

"God save us!" Grant said.

Kiefel spun around and stared at him through the mask. "And which god would that be, Mr Grant? Zeus? Apollo perhaps? Perseus?" As he said this last word his voice broke into laughter, and he walked the head back over to the box, gently lowering it inside and closing the lid tightly. He did the same to the steel lid and then removed his mask.

"Angelika, it is time for you to start your work with Medusa." He turned and pointed a gloved finger at some of his men. "Pick up this box and follow Angelika to the lab."

Grant shook his head in total disbelief at what his eyes and ears were telling him.

"What are you doing now?" he asked desperately.

"This is for me to know and you to find out, Mr Grant."

"You really are a madman, Klaus."

"Repeating the accusation over and over will not make it so, Charlie!" he snapped. "Could a madman orchestrate the decapitation of the entire United States Top Brass and put his own man in the Oval Office?"

Grant breathed harder as he took off his mask. He was starting to feel hot and sick. Partridge also removed his mask, following the President's lead.

"You mean..?"

"Ah – the penny drops! Yes, Teddy Kimble is in my pocket – is that the expression you Americans use?"

"I can't believe it!"

"A President and Vice President are too high up the tree to reach, and in fact so is your Speaker, but Kimble was easier to get to. That is why he is now in the Oval Office."

"My God, you killed two good men and kidnapped me just to put Kimble in the Oval Office?"

"Daring, aren't I?"

Grant struggled to understand why any of this was happening. There had to be something real at the bottom of it all. This had to be about more than just the lust for power.

"What is this insanity about, Kiefel – money? Power?"

Kiefel stared at him with ice cold eyes for a long moment without speaking. "You disappoint me, Mr Grant, but then Americans have a habit of doing that. Another habit of yours is reducing everything to those two things you just mentioned – money and power."

"Well if not that then what, damn it?!"

Kiefel paused again, he looked like he was mulling something over. Then, his facial expression turned darker than ever before. "Kiefel is my mother's maiden name, Mr Grant. Perhaps if I told you my real name – Kallweit – your memory will begin to work?"

A look of realization suddenly dawned on Charles Grant's face. "Wait a minute – your mother was Elfriede Kallweit?"

"Ah ha!" Kiefel exclaimed, his voice laced with bitterness. "Give this man a Cuban cigar – he has it!"

"That's what this is all about – your mother?"

"Your country executed my mother on trumped-up espionage charges in 1955. She was a good woman – a good East German, and loyal to the Soviet Union. You killed her. For this, Mr President, you and your nation will pay a terrible price."

"That's what this is all about – revenge? You murdered your way to me to avenge the death of your mother over sixty years ago?"

Kiefel glared at him. "You say death as if she had fallen over while picnicking, Mr President. My mother was shocked to death in Old Sparky – isn't that the quaint little expression you use to describe the electric chair? It took four shocks to kill her, Mr Grant. By the time they had finished, smoke poured from her head like a chimney."

"Elfriede Kallweit was notorious a Soviet spy! The scandal rocked the nation."

"My mother was innocent! The Americans needed a scapegoat and my mother was in the wrong place at the wrong time. For this, she was savagely killed by your so-called criminal justice system."

Grant stared at the man, unsure whether to feel pity or rage. "You can't seriously be suggesting the entire American people deserve to be punished because your traitor mother leaked defense secrets to the Soviets?"

Kiefel ignored the question. "After you murdered my dear Mutti, I was sent to live with my uncle and aunt in East Berlin. My father, as you may know, had died many years earlier in a farming accident. I was only a few months old. I grew up comforted by what was left of my family in the East, Mr Grant. There was nothing for me here after the murder."

"It was a legally-sanctioned execution after due-process! Elfriede Kallweit was found guilty of conspiracy to commit espionage and sending and receiving communications with Soviet double-agents, Kiefel. You're wrong, damn it!"

The German ignored Grant totally, and turned to the gum-chewing Angelika beside him. "You know where to take this, meine Liebling. Start work on it right away."

They kissed and he watched Angelika and the men take the box from the room.

"Fräulein Schwartz might look like a common punk to you, Mr Grant, but she is also a very accomplished chemist. Soon, I will have a weaponized version of this ancient doomsday machine, and then I really will be able to have some fun."

"Fun? What are you talking about?!"

Kiefel smiled and stroked his beard. "As I said, that is for me to know and you to find out."

CHAPTER NINETEEN

Devlin and Lea emerged from the Taxi on Tolka Quay and squinted in the Dublin rain as they walked the final fifty yards to their destination.

Lea looked at the junkyard through the rainy night and shivered. The sign above the gate read O'SULLIVAN'S SALVAGE. "Are you sure we can trust these guys?"

"Sure, what do you think I am – some kind of *eejit* or something?"

Lea smiled. "Sorry."

Devlin opened the heavy gate and swung it open to allow them both through. They dodged the puddles as they walked to the front office, lit low in the damp night.

Devlin knocked three times and took a step back.

A gravelly, low voice replied. "Come in, Danny. We don't want anyone hanging around out the front, do we now?"

Lea followed Devlin into the office, watching him carefully for any body language triggers. It was cold in here, and she could see her breath clouding out in front of her. Worse, the whole place stank of old engine oil and brake fluid and one of the overhead lights was faulty. It flickered on and off like a horrible yellow strobe and put her on edge.

An overweight man with a shaved head and thick moustache got up from his desk and padded over to them. Behind him, through a doorway that opened out onto a large workshop, a taller, thinner man with a long ponytail leaned against a car crusher with two muscular, tattooed arms folded high over his chest.

"Good to see you Danny Boy," said the first man. He smiled to reveal at least two missing teeth.

"Likewise, Mikey," Devlin said.

They shook hands and then the man looked at Lea. His eyes crawled from her face down to her boots and then all the way back up again. "And what have we here?"

Lea stood still and said nothing.

Devlin took a step forward and partially blocked the man's view of Lea. "This is an old friend of mine, Lea Donovan. Was in my unit. If you fuck with her you'll be sorry."

The man returned his gaze to Devlin. "Is that right?"

In a flash Lea elbowed Devlin out of the way, pulled a gun from her shoulder holster and pushed it into the folds of fat on the man's wide neck. "Sure it's right, ya great big lunchbox. Wanna try me out?"

A long moment of awkward silence followed and then the man burst into laughter. A second later Ponytail started laughing as well, and unfolded his arms.

"Oh... I like *her*, Mikey," Ponytail called through the door.

Lea holstered the weapon and took a step back, winking at the man.

"Lea Donovan, please meet Mikey O'Sullivan here with the barrel mark in his neck and Kyle Byrne hiding back there by the crusher. Pay no attention to either of them," Devlin said coolly. "Mikey's a real kingding at times and they can both be a couple of dry shites if they lose on the horses, like tonight, I'm guessing."

Mikey and Kyle exchanged a glance.

"Hey guys," Lea said casually.

"Good to meet you, Lea Donovan," Mikey said. "Now, Danny and Lea – would you like a drink to keep the cold out?"

They agreed to the drink and a moment later they were sitting around the desk. Mikey pulled a bottle of Irish whiskey from the drawer and poured out four doubles into old, chipped mugs.

Lea peered into hers with suspicion.

Mikey raised his mug. "Well, sláinte!"

Like it or not, Lea thought, she had to drink from the mug. She had done worse. She picked it up and they all chinked them together.

Devlin spoke first. "Not seen you around Dublin for a while, Mikey."

"I was over in Edinburgh visiting me brother. Old mate of his lives there – Graeme. We all hook up now and then in Kelly's – an Irish pub in Old Town that's always jammers. Had a few good times there I can tell you – the craic was ninety, Danny, I swear it. Great city – some of the best pubs I ever went to. You should go."

"I'll do that," Devlin said.

Lea sighed. "I think we're moving away from the point."

Danny looked at Lea and then to Mikey. "She has a point…"

Mikey smiled broadly. "Just sayin'…"

Kyle looked at Mikey and shook his head. "All right, so where are we at?"

"Where we're at," Lea said, "is that we need some help."

Kyle nodded. "Some muscle, you mean?"

"Call it what you like, but we need it."

"And you *do* owe me, Mikey," Devlin said. "You'll recall that little problem you had with those Roach muppets in Tyrone…"

Mikey looked embarrassed. "Sure, and I'm a man of my word, Danny. You shall have your help."

"We don't even know what they want yet!" Kyle said.

Mikey got serious. "It doesn't *matter* what they want, Kyle. I gave the man here my word. So Danny, what *is* it you want?"

"Lea can answer that better than I can."

Mikey poured more whiskey. "The floor is yours, Miss Donovan."

Lea took a breath. "It's like this… when I was a child my father was murdered right in front of my eyes. We were walking together out on the coast. He was going to teach me how to take a photograph. I had to go back to the car to get something for the camera, and when I got back he was gone. My father was there one minute, looking after me, and the next I was alone. They found his body at the bottom of the cliffs and ruled suicide."

"So how can we help?" Kyle said quietly.

"It was no suicide, Mr Byrne," she said. "I saw a man running from the cliffs. He was dressed in black from head to foot – he looked weird. I can't tell you how, but there was something about that man. He pushed my father off the cliff, I just know it in my heart."

"But you didn't see it happen?" Mikey said.

Lea shook her head. "My father never threw himself off a four hundred-foot cliff while he was looking after me, Mr O'Sullivan. He was a loving, kind man – a doctor who dedicated his life to healing people. If he was going to do anything like that – which he never would have even considered – he would hardly have taken me along with him to watch, now, would he?"

"So why did they rule it a suicide?"

"Simple. I was a young girl and they decided I was an unreliable witness. They said I had imagined the man in black in my grief, but I saw him running before I even knew my father was dead. The man in black murdered my father, Mr O'Sullivan, I know it."

"All right, I believe you. But I still don't know why you're talking to me."

"Very recently I received information from a reliable source that an old friend of my father's, a Sean McNamara, was brutally murdered in his home in Cork. Sean McNamara and my father had worked together on some kind of research relating to the medical industry a very long time ago."

"What research is that?" Kyle said.

Lea shrugged her shoulders. "I don't know. But I do know they were both killed for it, because before he died, McNamara sent a message saying he was killed by the same men who had killed Dad."

"And now you want revenge?" Mikey said.

"I want to know who killed my father and Sean McNamara, yes…and revenge wouldn't go amiss either, but what I want more than anything is my father's life's work – research files I never even knew existed until now, but now I know were the reason he was murdered by that bastard in black."

Mikey gave an understanding nod and took more of the whiskey. "So where do we start?"

"My parent's old holiday home on the west coast in Galway. It's still ours, but no one's been there for years. I think Dad's research is hidden there somewhere."

Mikey slammed his mug on the table and wiped his mouth. "Kyle, go and get some guns and any other treats you can think of. We're going on a picnic to Galway."

Kyle rose from the desk. "Sure thing, Mikey."

He returned a few moments later with a look of concern on his face. "One thing's already bothering me."

"Speak up, Kyle!" Mikey said.

"Well..." As he spoke, he casually pulled a sawn-off shotgun from a sports bag and began to load it. "Thing is, we know these pricks have already killed twice, sure. But what bothers me is the quarter of a century gap between the two murders."

Devlin nodded. "That's what I've thinking about. It's not your usual gangland hit or revenge murder. These guys are playing a long game, and are as cool as sea ice."

"Whoever they are, they've had it now Mikey O'Sullivan is on the case!"

"If you say so, Mikey," Kyle said sarcastically.

"I do, Kyle, I do." Mikey rubbed his stomach and yawned.

"So let's get going," Devlin said, pushing back from the desk and finishing his whiskey.

Lea paused for a moment. This wasn't just any old mission as far as she was concerned. This was something altogether different. This was about her father and she was already allowing her emotions to cloud her judgement. "Thanks, everyone, I really appreciate this."

"Not at all," Mikey said, patting her on the back and nearly knocking her over. "Come on Kyle! Get a move on!" He turned to Lea and lowered his voice. "Kyle's a lazy shite. If there was work in the bed, he'd sleep on the floor – you know what I mean?"

Lea smiled. "So you're both going to help then?"

"Sure," Mikey said. "But there's one condition."

Devlin eyed him up suspiciously. "I knew it! And what would that be?"

"We're taking Ciara," Mikey said. "I'm not making a journey like this without my Ciara."

Kyle rolled his eyes.

CHAPTER TWENTY

Hawke and Kim Taylor approached the heavily-armed PFPA men guarding the external doors at the entrance to the Pentagon. The Pentagon Force Protection Agency was a civilian law enforcement organization within the command structure of the Department of Defense. It was assigned to protect not only the world-famous Pentagon but also the Mark Center Building and other smaller DoD facilities in the city.

Kim showed her pass and Hawke followed her as she navigated her way deftly through the labyrinthine defense headquarters until they finally reached Brooke's sprawling suite of offices. They passed more yet guards at the door to the outer office of Brooke's private secretary and after a brief word with his personal assistant they entered a bustling, noisy room full of men and women talking into cell-phones and vying for their boss's attention.

Hawke took a look around the hectic office. "There are more guns around here than at your average firing range."

"He's the US Secretary of Defense and next in the presidential line of succession, plus we're in the middle of our worst terror attack, Hawke," Kim said, keeping her voice to a whisper. "What did you expect?"

Point taken, he thought. "We still need to speak to him."

He looked over at Brooke. Alex was beside him as an assistant was now directing the boss's attention to one of the many plasma screens neatly fitted into the far wall of the Secretary's office. Everyone in the room watched in silence as a second helicopter drone appeared on the capital's horizon and fired another Hellfire missile.

This time the target was the Lincoln Memorial, and a collective gasp of horror went around the room as the north side of the impressive monument exploded in a massive fireball. A few seconds later a grisly, black column of smoke billowed and plumed into the night sky, lit yellow by the memorial's powerful floodlights.

"It's another drone, sir!"

Brooke slammed his fist on his desk. "I can see that, damn it! Just blow the god-damn thing out of the sky like the last one."

Another flurry of phone calls was made, and Hawke watched as two F-15s flew over the city, one of them firing an AIM-9 Sidewinder missile at the drone. The enemy aircraft tried to take evasive action and dodged the missile, but the USAF fighter jets were too fast for it and after firing another heat-seeking Sidewinder they hit the target. Everyone in the room cheered as the drone exploded above the Potomac and crashed into the water in an orange fireball.

"Now's our chance," Kim said.

They stepped over to Brooke's desk.

"Mr Secretary," Kim said.

Brooke looked at them distractedly. "What is it? Oh..." His face warmed for a moment when he saw Hawke. "Joe, hi."

"We need to talk, Jack."

"Shoot – but make it fast. As you can see, those sons-of-bitches somehow just got another goddamned drone up."

"It's about the Smithsonian."

"What about it?"

"It's Frank Watkins, Jack."

Brooke smiled for a second and nodded his head. "How is the old bastard?"

"Dead, sir," Kim said.

Brooke's face dropped. "Dead?"

Hawke nodded. "Professional hit, and more than that – we found the President's order on his desk – the one sanctioning the release of an object from Archive 7."

"I can't believe Frank's dead... You think he was murdered by Kimble's men?"

"We can't be sure at this stage."

Brooke paused as he took the news on board. "So what did Kimble order from the archive?"

"We don't know what was released, or to whom, but whatever the hell it was, something very bad went on in that Archive, Jack. We found two men turned to stone."

Brooke's eyes widened with shock. "Turned to *stone*?"

Hawke nodded again. "But here's the thing – when we mentioned it to the President he just shut us down – told us point blank to leave it and get back to the White House." Hawke lowered his voice. "I think President Kimble is covering something up."

Brooke looked at the two of them, glancing over his shoulder as an admiral brushed past him with a cellphone in each hand.

"What is it, Dad?" Alex asked, suddenly concerned.

Brooke didn't reply.

Alex tried again. "Whatever the hell you know about this, Dad it's time to bring us in."

Brooke was silent for a long time before replying, his face tormented by indecision, his mind torn in two directions – his duty to protect national security interests on the one hand but his responsibility to help Hawke, Kim and Alex as much as possible to stop the threat on the other.

"Come with me."

He led them out of the main office into a smaller ante-room and closed the door.

"This is my private office. We can talk in here undisturbed."

"Sounds serious," Alex said.

Brooke ignored the comment. "What I'm about to tell you is highly classified. In fact, it's the second highest classification we have."

Hawke, Kim and Alex took their seats and watched the Defense Secretary as he thought about what to say next. This shit right here, Alex thought, is why my parents' marriage fell apart.

"Back in the late sixties, the international political landscape was very different to today. We were in the middle of the Cold War with the Soviet Union, and our foreign policy was, accordingly, slightly more..."

"Paranoid?" Alex said.

Brooke gave his daughter a withering glance. "I was going to say slightly more *interventionist* than today. You had to be there to understand how it was. Like today, covert intelligence gathering was a big part of that policy. We had listening stations all over the world in a bid to intercept communiqués passing back and forth between the Kremlin and various Soviet client states around the world. These proxy states – Cuba, North Vietnam, Mozambique – were very important to the USSR as part of their plan to expand communism around the world."

Hawke glanced at his watch. "Jack, we're short on time – I think we'd prefer the Bluffer's Guide if that's okay with you."

Alex winced, knowing that few people could talk to the Pentagon chief like that and get away with it, but when her father cracked a quick smile and leaned back

133

in his chair with his hands behind his head, she knew Hawke had worked his magic on yet another unsuspecting soul. Maybe it was the accent, she thought.

"Sure, I'm sorry. The bottom line is simple. The NSA commissioned the construction of a listening station in northern Norway – a strong NATO ally since 1949 – with a view to monitoring radio signals in the far north arctic region. You wouldn't believe what the Russians get up to up there... Anyway, so far so good, but here's where it gets its classification level. With the construction of the listening station going on up there it was decided to attach a science station alongside. Having the two side by side was a big saving in funding."

He paused again, and bit his lip in hesitation.

"Dad?"

"The men building the station found something in the ice core up there."

Alex and Hawke shared a glance. Both had the same question.

The obvious question.

"What did they find, Jack?"

Brooke rubbed his nose and jaw, still uncomfortable with the way the conversation was going. Alex recognized his body language easily enough. He had done the same moves the afternoon he told her he was moving out to live across town. She was just a teenager at the time, and she could recall every instant of that moment – what they were both wearing, the way the sun came through the window and lit the dust motes floating down to her carpet, the words her father had used – *it's like this honey, your mother and I have decided to...*

"Spit it out, Dad." Even after so many years, her words were tinged with the bitterness of that memory.

"They found the severed head of what we later learned was Medusa."

Alex looked at Hawke and knew he was thinking the same as her – an amazing revelation, but easier to accept given the events of the last few months. Kim Taylor on the other hand, was speechless with shock.

"Go on," Hawke said.

"It gets worse. You're aware of the mythological legend surrounding Medusa?"

Alex nodded gently.

"Sure," Hawke said. "Anyone who looked at Medusa got turned to stone."

Brooke sighed. "Turns out it's not just a legend."

"What do you mean?" Kim asked. "Is this even for real?"

"What happened at the Norwegian station came to light after the men working there stopped returning communications with a US air force base in Germany, which they used as a relay station. Obviously our guys got suspicious and a man named Colonel John Hill went up there to find out what was going on. At the time it was feared they'd been attacked by the Soviet Navy. What they found disabused them of that notion forever."

"What did they find, exactly?" Hawke asked.

"They found all the men at the station had been turned to stone, and worse than that, when they discovered Medusa, several members of the search and recovery team were also turned to stone, including Colonel Hill himself. After they discovered what was doing it, the surviving men took the necessary precautions and secured the head. It was brought to the US and secured in a facility here – the one you went to today – Archive 7."

"And it's been there ever since?" Alex asked.

135

Brooke nodded. "Until today. When you told me about those men being turned to stone I knew straight away what Kimble had ordered out of Archive 7, but why is anyone's guess."

"How many people know about this?" Hawke asked.

"Not many. Less than a dozen by my reckoning, and that may or may not include our new Commander-in-Chief," he said, referring to Kimble. "I don't want to go all Rumsfeld on you both, but I know not even I know everything. When you get as far up the greasy pole as I have, you start to learn things about the world... dark things."

"I can't believe this is happening," Kim said, rubbing her forehead.

A look of grim determination crossed Brooke's face. "Now I think we can all understand the importance of what's happening today. This isn't just about rescuing the President, or stopping these maniacs from killing millions of people. This is about the vital national security of the United Stated and some of our most highly classified secrets."

"So what's our next move?" Kim asked. "We still have no idea who's behind this."

Brooke sighed. "We have two problems – we need to know where these guys are operating out of – for that we wait to see where the Novak lead takes us. The other problem is we need to know just *how* this thing has the power to turn people to stone. That's why you're here, Alex. I know you can do that for me. Please remember this isn't something we can throw out to just anyone. No one can ever know about what we're talking of here, all right?"

Alex and Kim nodded, but Hawke wasn't so sure.

"And one more thing, while we're on this. You should all know that The Tomb of Eternity was quarantined by Eddie Kosinski's office."

"The Tomb of *what?*" Kim asked.

"On whose orders?" Hawke asked, ignoring Kim.

"An unknown official, and I can say no more than that... Now, we have to get back to these attacks."

Outside the office, Hawke, Kim and Alex walked back to the main office, still buzzing with people on phones, trawling through computer records and CCTV footage.

"You know what I'm thinking?" Alex said.

Kim was still speechless.

Hawke looked at Alex. "If that's the second highest classification, what the hell is the first?"

"Pretty much," Alex replied, and turned to Hawke and Kim. "Listen, I need to grab a coffee – I'll catch up with you in a second."

It was true that she needed a coffee, but it was also true that she needed time to herself to think about whether or not she should make another call to Ryan Bale. As she made her way along the corridor, she decided she needed to make that call.

CHAPTER TWENTY-ONE

Vincent Reno cracked his knuckles and walked toward Agent Kevin Novak. Not for the first time today he'd found himself thinking about his ex-wife Monique and their twin sons Léo and Louis. He hadn't seen his kids for weeks, but he worried about them all the time. The world was dangerous enough without scumbags like Kevin Novak adding a spark to the fuse. "Okay, mon ami, we need to talk."

Novak struggled against the ropes binding him to the kitchen table and blinked in the harsh strip-light shining in his eyes. "I don't know anything... I swear it."

Vincent powered a fist into his face, splitting his lip open for the second time tonight. "Not good enough. We know more than you think, but we need you to help us with some of the details, or... this is going to be a long night, n'est-ce pas?"

"Jesus, Doyle, who the hell is this guy?"

Vincent leaned forward and rolled up his sleeve to reveal a large tattoo of a burning grenade. "Légion Étrangère, mon ami." He gave a broad grin and nodded his head with pride. "You can call me *Reaper.*"

"Just tell us, Novak," Doyle said. "Right now you're going down for the rest of your life. If you help us out you could get some leniency."

"Look, I meant what I said..."

Vincent coiled his fist back.

"No!" Novak turned his head away in a vain attempt to dodge the punch. "Please – wait... let me finish. I'm just the little guy, all right? I shouldn't have helped them,

I know it now, but they offered me a lot of money, plus they said they'd kill Karen if I didn't go along with them."

Vincent turned to Doyle. "Who is Karen?"

"His kid sister."

"Ah, le chantage…"

Novak was now almost hyperventilating with fear. "I mean it, and now I'm in deep shit."

"I'll say you are," Doyle said. "You're part of a conspiracy to kidnap the President of the United States, Novak. They killed the Vice President and the Speaker."

"I had no idea they were going to do that. All they asked me to do was get them some information about the President's car, I swear it."

Vincent's eyes widened. "Ah – now we get somewhere, non?"

Doyle frowned. "Keep talking, Novak."

"This is a big operation, Doyle – bigger than you can imagine. The guy behind all this is one evil bastard and I'm not kidding. He owns people all over the world – and I'm not just talking about drug-dealers and small time cons, I mean he owns politicians and bankers. And the people who work for him – he has some kind of weird hold over them because they are scared shitless of him."

Vincent sighed. "Sounds like Monique…"

Doyle leaned over him. "Where can we find this son of a bitch?"

"I swear I don't know, and maybe you don't want to find him in case of where it leads…"

"What is that supposed to mean?"

"I got the feeling that maybe he wasn't at the top of the tree, if you catch my drift – like maybe he was following orders."

139

Vincent pulled the PAMAS from his belt and disengaged the safety. He ripped one of the cushions from a kitchen chair and held it down on Novak's chest.

"Woah!" Novak turned to Doyle for help. "What the fuck, man?"

"Where do we find this man?" the Frenchman repeated with steel-cold eyes.

"I already told you both – I never even met the guy…"

Vincent was losing patience, and glanced at his watch. "We're running out of time, Secret Service man. You give me what I want to know right now or I just kill you comme ça." He released the pressure on the cushion for a second to snap his fingers.

"I never even met him!"

"Okay," Doyle said with resignation. "Kill him."

Vincent nodded once and gripped the gun tight.

"All right – all right… listen. Maybe I can still help you guys out, just please, don't kill me. Karen needs me, you know?"

"We want names and addresses, not bullshit."

Novak sighed and stared at the ceiling. Blood poured down the sides of his face from his split lip and ran onto the table. He looked deflated and beaten. Vincent thought he was probably considering how a bullet would be preferable to life in a federal prison.

"I dealt with a couple of guys – one was an Australian – name was Pauling."

"And what was his part in all this?"

"I don't know exactly, but I think he was their technical guy. He asked me a lot of questions about computers and wanted the IP address of the President's car."

"And who did he work for?"

"An English guy. His name is Nick Collins, a real weasel of a guy."

"And how does the weasel fit into all this?"

"He's some kind of middleman with contacts in the arms industry."

Vincent pushed the gun harder. "That's all you've got, really?"

"All I know is he greases the wheels, you know? He's the link between the arms suppliers and the guy running this crazy show."

"You mean he supplied this loon with the weapons currently attacking this city?"

"He facilitated it, yeah."

"You have a real way with words, Novak," Doyle said in disgust. "I bet if you tried hard enough you could convince yourself you've got nothing to do with any of this."

"I'm not proud of what I did."

"Listen," Vincent said. "You believe this Collins guy can tell us where we might locate the people behind this attack?"

Novak nodded reluctantly.

"Where can we find him?"

"It's funny but you just missed him..."

Doyle moved closer. "You mean..?"

"He was the guy in the Viper?" Vincent asked.

"Sorry, but yeah."

"Where did he go?"

"I don't know much about him. I only met him a couple times. He just came tonight to give me my tickets out of here."

Doyle sighed. "We need more than that, Novak."

"I know that he was spending some time in Brown's on Capitol Hill."

Vincent looked at Doyle for clarification.

141

"It's an up-market cocktail lounge. A lot of the senators go there." He turned to Novak. "What was he doing there?"

"He sang cabaret in a cocktail dress, Doyle, what do you think?"

Vincent pushed the muzzle of the gun into the cushion, hard. "Don't get smart, mon ami. I move my finger a millimetre and your chest explodes."

"Sorry... he used the place to meet senators and that's all I know. That should get you started."

"I don't think so," Doyle said. "Brown's closed last week. Try harder."

Novak squinted with the effort of thinking with a gun pushed into his chest. He knew better than many what a nine mil round could do at point blank, and right now there was one with his name on it in a chamber ten inches from his heart. "All right, you could try Ivy City."

Vincent and Doyle shared an optimistic glance.

"What's in Ivy City?" Doyle said.

"A warehouse. I went there once to meet him. He was testing some chopper drones there because he used to be a helicopter pilot for the British Army or something. You need to hurry because he just told me he was moving out."

Vincent snarled. "Address, now."

Kevin Novak knew the game was up, and gave the men the address of the warehouse.

Vincent put the gun in his belt and made a call on his cell phone. A few seconds later Joe Hawke was on the line.

"You find anything?"

"Oh yeah," Vincent said. "Son of a bitch was packing his bags all ready to go on holiday. He has a ticket for Ecuador in his pocket."

"What did he say?"

"He's just the little guy, et cetera, et cetera…"

"Thought he might say that – but you charmed some information out of him, right?"

"Naturellement. There's an arms dealer named Collins, an English guy like you, Hawke."

"What are you trying to say, Frog?"

Vincent laughed. "Listen, this English guy has provided the fireworks for this party, and we have his address. He also told us about their tech guy, a man called Pauling who wanted to know all about the President's car."

"That explains how they pulled off the kidnapping."

"Right… but he also said this Collins guy mentioned something about moving out so we need to get going if we're going to catch him. According to Monsieur Novak this guy's a little weasel who knows where we can find the men behind this attack. He has a warehouse full of goodies."

"Where is this warehouse?"

"Ivy City."

"We can be with you in a few minutes," Hawke said and then paused. "Hang on just a second…"

"Joe, what is it?" Vincent said.

"A video just came up on YouTube – I think it might be our guy… whoever he is, he's about to play his first hand."

*

Mikey O'Sullivan walked them to the rear of the workshop and through a sliding door. In a small yard now, the big Dubliner pulled a key fob from his pocket and padded over to a car parked up beside a dark blue four-yard bin. The bin was covered in rust and so full of junk the lid couldn't shut, but the car was something special. It was a classic Audi, white with yellow stripes and a faded number '5' on the door panel.

"Meet my baby," Mikey said with pride. "A 1984 Quattro, redesigned instrument panel and new steering wheel design. This little baby right here won the Monte Carlo rally back in the early eighties." He stroked the hood as if it were a faithful pet, but snapped out of his daydream when Devlin coughed.

He turned to face them. "Of course, since then I've done a lot of work on her. I call her Ciara. If any one o' youse so much as scratches her, I'll blow your head off, okey dokey?"

He gave them a warm smile and opened the driver's door.

"Sure thing, Mikey," Devlin said.

Mikey cranked the seat forward to allow Devlin to climb into the back of the two-door rally car. Kyle strode out of the workshop with a shotgun over one shoulder and the gun-stuffed red leather sports bag in his hand. "Just some extra treats in case we get hungry on the way."

"Good job, Kyle, now hop in the back like a good lad so Miss Donovan can sit up front with me." Mikey winked at Lea as they all climbed in the car.

"All ready for a nice quiet drive to the coast?" Mikey said, turning the key in the ignition. The two liter engine roared to life with a retro rasping sound and the old instrument panel lit up. "There's my good girl," Mikey said, gently tapping the top of the vinyl steering wheel.

They drove through Dublin Port toward East Wall, turning left and driving down to the River Liffey before swinging right at a roundabout and moving west again. Ahead of them the outline of the Convention Center Dublin rose against the black Irish sky.

Mikey switched the radio off and sighed. "Terrible, this America business. I have a cousin in Boston – I hope she's all right."

Lea leaned forward in the passenger seat to check the mirror.

Devlin saw the look of concern on her face. "What do you see?"

"I think we have company," she said.

CHAPTER TWENTY-TWO

Klaus Kiefel looked into the camera and scowled at the world. Alan Pauling had made the final adjustments to the webcams a few moments ago and was now busy typing commands into a laptop.

"Are we ready to roll?" Kiefel said, straightening his roll-neck and adjusting his hair in the polished metal of the distillation unit.

"We're sure are, Klaus," Pauling said. "Just make sure you're ready to transfer my ten million dollars."

The German raised an eyebrow. "You'll get your money, Alan. Just make sure this works. I don't want it traced – understand?"

"There'll be no tracing this signal to anywhere," he said, and gave the boss the sign that the signal was live and broadcasting.

Kiefel stepped into the limelight. His fifteen minutes had arrived at last, and he held America in the palm of his hand.

"People of the United States… people of the world – you are about to witness the birth of a new nation right here in America… a new kind of revolution. You are about to witness a new kind of civilization run by a newer, different kind of law – a higher law!"

After a tense opening, Kiefel relaxed slightly and began to wander back and forth in front of the camera as if he were delivering a simple lecture on ancient Greek mythology.

"Your government has been lying to you all. You need to know this. What is casually dismissed as the insane ramblings of the conspiracy nut is in fact the truth. Area 51 is real, and so are all the things the conspiracy theorists say are inside it."

He paused for effect. "And so is the notorious Archive 7... This too is a real storage facility used by the United States Government to hide some of the most ancient secrets of this world from you, the common man and woman."

Kiefel paused a beat to let the words sink in, then he started to talk about his mother's execution. This was the moment he had been waiting for. This was his chance to get the ultimate revenge on a world he hated.

*

In Washington, Brooke looked at Kimble and his Chief-of-Staff Scott Anderson who were both in his office by way of a conference call, their faces lit large on a plasma screen to the left of the one where Kiefel's horror show was now unfolding.

"You getting this, Mr President?" Brooke asked, his raspy drawl dominating the room.

Kimble nodded grimly but said nothing. Anderson looked like he wanted to crawl into a hole.

Revelling in his new-found fame, Kiefel continued to strut up and down before the camera. "Your leaders have deceived you. They know ancient truths about your world that would shock you to your core, but they have kept them from you. Now, you will see a small part of the fabric of their lies and deceit come undone before your very eyes! You will see the light of reality and truth as it shines through from the ancient past and brightens the darkness you have been kept in."

Kiefel clicked his fingers and a tall, muscular man dragged a smaller, older man in a suit in front of the screen.

"My God!" Anderson said. "That's Dirk Partridge, one of the President's closest Secret Service agents!"

"Who's the ape hauling him across the room?" Kim asked.

"According to our facial recognition software, his name's Jakob Müller, a burned out gymnast from another age, now a small-time thug from Leipzig."

"I have a bad feeling about this," Hawke said.

"Me too," Alex whispered, moving closer to Hawke and putting a hand on his arm.

On the plasma screen, Kiefel smiled and continued. "This is United States Secret Service Agent Dirk Partridge. Shortly he will have the honor of dying for his country in the most ancient and wonderful of ways, and I would be honored if you join us for that."

Kiefel directed an insane grin at the camera and then the screen flicked to static.

"God damn it!" Brooke boomed. "Can't anyone shut this madman down?"

"We're working on it, sir," said one of his staffers. "But right now we can't even find his location."

"So shut down the internet!"

The staffer looked at him. "We can't do that, sir, not since the Cybersecurity Act of 2009."

Brooke said nothing for a moment, looking up at Kimble's face on the plasma screen across the room. Since Hawke had told him about the new President's reaction when he'd learned about Watkins's death back at the Smithsonian, Brooke had begun to harbor certain suspicions about his new Commander-in-Chief, but now wasn't the time to indulge in conspiracy theories or let his mind wander off-track.

Brooke looked from the President to the staffer. "That's just not true, son..."

Kimble looked at Anderson, equally shocked. Brooke considered that being in the Top Job for less than a few hours meant that Teddy Kimble probably knew a lot less about these things than your average conspiracy theorist.

"What are you talking about, Mr Secretary?" President Kimble said.

Anderson spoke up. "He's talking about the Kill Switch, sir."

"The *what*?"

"It's a cybercrime countermeasure, sir," Anderson said, his voice dropping to a whisper.

"Would someone tell me just what the hell we're talking about?" Kimble said.

Brooke sighed. "Everyone below codeword clearance please leave the room... except you three." He pointed at Alex, Hawke and Kim Taylor. "You ain't going anywhere. I need you."

When the room was clear, Brooke cleared his throat and walked out from behind his desk. "We're talking about the Kill Switch, Mr President. You won't have been briefed on it yet, of course. Its existence has been rumored a lot, I know... and there is even some kind of an accommodation for it in the Protecting Cyberspace as a National Asset Act of 2010, but..."

"Wait a minute," Kimble said, confused. "That Act expired years ago."

Anderson and Brooke exchanged a glance.

Anderson spoke first. "It *did*, sir, and it *didn't*."

Hawke listened with interest as Kimble reacted. "And just what the hell is that supposed to mean?"

"It means, Mr President," Brooke said, "that parts of the Act were taken on and... *initiated*."

"It means," Anderson continued, "that there is a Kill Switch in place, even though its use would be highly questionable in law, not to mention the outrage it would cause."

"But I strongly recommend you order its use right now, Mr President," Brooke said firmly. "We don't know what Kiefel is planning on doing, sir, but it might be in our interests to control the situation better than this, if you get my meaning... He can talk all he likes but something tells me things might start to get a little more graphic."

Kimble looked at Anderson and considered what he had been told.

"And how does this thing work?" he asked.

"You order me to kill the internet, and I'll make it happen."

"How fast?"

"Not long – an hour or so. It's a technical operation."

Kimble furrowed his brow with the stress of indecision. "I'm not sure about the Constitutional implications here, Jack. This is a civil liberties issue, you realize. The President can't be seen to be taking over the internet and policing freedom of expression like this."

"You can't be serious?" Brooke said. "We're not talking about freedom of expression, sir. This maniac could start killing people on live TV any moment!"

Kimble and Anderson shared a glance. "Leave it with me, Jack. I'll get back to you."

The screen went black and Brooke slammed his fist into the desk a second time. "Damn it!"

"Maybe he has a point, Dad," Alex said. "The Government shouldn't be controlling the internet."

Brooke looked at his daughter with his sharp, gray eyes. "Believe me, Teddy Kimble doesn't give a shit about civil liberties. He's stalling for some other reason.

150

Joe was right about Kimble – someone's pulling his strings... but who and where the hell is the puppet master?"

Hawke's cell phone rang and he snatched it from his pocket.

It was Vincent and he sounded unnerved. "Did you see that?"

"Sure did. We need to get to Ivy City in a hurry, Vincent." Hawke ran a hand through his hair. "...because things are really looking like shit from this end."

"Naturellement, mon ami. We can do this. When you hire Foreign Legion you get results."

Hawke smiled. It was good to hear the voice of an old friend once again.

"Okay – we'll coordinate on the way and team up when we get there."

"D'accord. This is the address."

Hawke wrote the address down. "We're out of here," he said.

A second later, he and Kim Taylor were running to her Government-issue Chevy Suburban in the parking lot of the Pentagon.

*

Ryan looked at the screen of his cell-phone and saw Alex Reeve was calling for the second time that night. It was well after midnight on Elysium, but he was awake, lying on the beach, counting stars and slapping at mosquitoes. Condensation from a can of Red Stripe lager was running over his hand. He thought of Maria back in the compound, lying in bed... Life was good, for some at least.

"Alex, hi. You can't seem to stay away from me."

"Get over yourself, nerd."

"To be called a nerd by you is a compliment."

"Listen, Ryan, I know you said Eden wasn't playing ball, but you need to hear this."

"Sounds like it!"

"Joe just got back from the Smithsonian and said the guards there were frozen – turned to stone. More than that, I just had a long conversation with Dad in which he proceeded to tell me some very interesting factoids about all of this."

"Sounds fascinating, not to mention highly classified."

"Sure, but I know you can handle it, right?"

"Right," he said confidently, noting the more serious tone in her voice.

"The short version is this is about Medusa, Ryan – as in ancient Greece, gods, and so on. If you'd seen the video you'd have no doubt, believe me."

"Medusa?" Ryan said excitedly. "She wasn't a god though. She was more of a... well, a *monster*, I suppose. Not sure how else you'd describe the Gorgon sisters, really."

"Right, and this is why I want you here, helping me with this. I can get you all the clearance you need."

"I don't know. Eden was pretty clear."

"But that was before we knew about Medusa. You have to tell him, Ryan. I don't know about you but I think this has ECHO written all over it. You have to convince Eden to give you guys the go ahead and the use of one of those jets he keeps locked up down there."

Ryan looked from the stars to his can of lager. "I'll speak with the old man, but no promises."

CHAPTER TWENTY-THREE

Mikey O'Sullivan glanced at Lea and then checked the rear-view. "You mean the Range Rover?" Behind them, the orange lights of the Dublin streets flashed on the shiny hood of a looming black Range Rover.

Lea nodded. "Been following us since the quay. Don't like the way it's keeping three or fours cars behind us all the time." The evening was getting on and the traffic, both pedestrian and road, was beginning to thin out for the night.

Mikey sighed heavily. "Could be Benny."

Lea looked at him. "Benny?"

"Sure, he's a bookie I might owe a few euros to, give or take."

In the back seat, Kyle tipped his head back and laughed. "Try fifteen thousand."

"You owe a bookie fifteen thousand euros?" Lea said.

Mikey shrugged his meaty shoulders. "Got a bad tip, you know? Bloody thing was off the bridle all the way around. It happens."

"Your luck with the horses is neither here nor there, Mikey," Devlin said. "Is it this mysterious bloody turf accountant on our arses or not?"

"Don't get narky with me, Danny Boy – I'm the one risking me arse for you at the drop of a hat!"

Kyle nodded his head appreciatively. "The man makes a good point, Danny."

Devlin rolled his eyes. "All right, then the flaming point's taken, but would you just answer me *please* – is it Benny Euro or not?"

Mikey smiled and squinted into his mirror once again, taking a longer look.

"No."

"No?" Lea said.

"I would say definitely not."

Kyle narrowed his eyes. "What makes you say that, Mikey?"

The Range Rover was closer now, and Mikey was able to get a much clearer view. "Because I know Benny Quinn can get nasty with his fists, but I'm pretty sure he doesn't know anyone with a submachine gun."

Lea, Devlin and Kyle all turned to Mikey in shock and spoke in perfect unison.

"What?!"

Mikey nodded. "Guy in the passenger seat seems to be holding a submachine gun."

Lea leaned forward again and checked her mirror. "Janey Bloody Mac, he ain't kidding!"

Before they had time to respond, the Range Rover accelerated and skidded around the remaining cars in between them.

"Time to get outta here!" Mikey said, and floored the accelerator.

The Quattro raced along the north bank of the Liffey, screeching past the Customs House, its heavy roar echoing off the stonework and drifting across the river.

"Are the bastards still behind us?" Devlin asked.

A gunshot blasted the mirror clean off the driver's door.

"Guess so," Kyle drawled.

"They shot Ciara!" Mikey exclaimed. "They bloody shot Ciara!"

In the back of the Quattro, out of Mikey's vision, Kyle face-palmed and lowered his voice. "Oh *God...*"

"What was that, Kyle?" Mikey said, trying to see him in the mirror.

"Nothing."

"I said they bloody shot Ciara!"

"Is she bleeding?" Kyle said.

Mikey narrowed his eyes. "You'll be bloody bleeding in a minute!"

Mikey swerved around a dawdling bus and accelerated along Eden Quay.

"Bloody hell, Mikey!" Lea shouted. "You're going against the traffic!"

"Thanks Miss Donovan – I hadn't noticed that."

Mikey changed down and powered the Audi the wrong way along a bus lane before swinging the wheel hard to the left and crossing the Liffey on O'Connell Bridge. The little skull-shaped air-freshener swung back and forth from the rear-view mirror as the big Irishman slammed on the brakes to avoid an old lady crossing the road. She looked up at the Quattro, startled.

"I won't have the elderly treated with disrespect," Mikey said, and waved at her cheerily. "You cross safely, my love." He turned to Lea, his voice lowering to a tone of confidential respect. "We all get vulnerable when we're old."

The lady stopped pulling her little tartan trolley bag and raised her finger at the car. "You shouldn't be on the road driving like dat, ya fuckin' eejit!"

Mikey changed into first and drove carefully around her. "She was just a little shocked, that's all."

As they crawled past her Mikey waved apologetically, but she was in full-flow now, and not to be pacified.

She waved her rubber-tipped walking stick in the air. "Ya tink Dublin's a fuckin' rally track now, do ya, ya stupid gombeen?"

"Sorry, Granny!" he said, and moved the car forward into D'Olier Street.

"Bloody Northsider..." Kyle mumbled.

"Now then, Kyle – don't be like that," Mikey said. "She's alright really, and... hang on a minute, I'm from Northside!"

"Who'd ya think I was talking about, you fool? Not that sweet little old lady you nearly drove over the top of, surely?"

Mikey laughed. "I was nowhere near driving over the top of her."

"Just as bloody well," Kyle said. "If you had you'd have made a right bloody mess."

"No, I don't think so," Mikey said, giving an evaluating shake of the head. "Maybe the front spoiler might have got smashed a bit though."

Kyle winked at Lea. "I was talking about the old lady, Mikey."

Seeing Mikey O'Sullivan's hard-exterior crumbled down by a little old lady made Lea smile briefly, but it was wiped from her face a second later when she instinctively glanced in her side mirror. "Bastards still behind us, Mikey."

Devlin twisted in the cramped rear seat and confirmed it. "They sure are – just hitting the bridge now."

Mikey didn't wait for a second, slamming down on the throttle and sending the Quattro lurching forward in a whine of squealing tires and blue rubber smoke. He weaved in and out of the light traffic along the north side of Trinity College and headed south through the city.

"We'll lose the bastards down here and then get out of town."

They took the corner fast, and Lea caught a sign outside a tourist shop. It was offering tours of the Cliffs of Moher. For a second she was back on the cliffs with her father, but the sound of bullets hitting the back of the Audi dragged her back from her past.

"They're still shooting at Ciara, Mikey!" Kyle shouted. "If you don't do something about it pretty soon, she'll think you love another."

Mikey said nothing, but focussed on dodging pedestrians crossing Grafton Street.

"Like maybe a Passat or something."

Mikey ignored Kyle once again, reserving his attention for more pedestrians, this time walking in and out of St. Stephen's Green. He turned the Audi toward the large monument on the northwest corner of the green and changed down.

"Oh, no!" Lea shouted. "You've got to be kidding!"

"Mikey never kids," she heard Kyle say from the back.

Devlin pulled his seatbelt forward so he could lean closer to the front seats. "What's the problem?"

"Sit back in your seat, Danny," Mikey said. "Ciara won't have been driven like this since Monte Carlo."

"What are you going to do?"

"We're going to drive them into the back-arse of nowhere and lose the bastards!"

Mikey blew the horn and sent a few pub-goers running out of the archway.

Lea shielded her eyes as Mikey powered the Quattro through Fusilier's Arch. On the other side of the archway, two metal bollards scraped either side of the car and tore off the remaining wing mirror on Lea's side.

"Bastards ain't getting a Range Rover through there, are they now?" Mikey said, swinging the wheel to the right and skidding onto the public walkway that stretched deep into the large park. He struck a trash can with the front left wing and sent it flying into the air behind them. It landed with a metallic smack in their wake as they powered forward into the park.

The Range Rover skidded violently to the right at the last minute to avoid the arch and roared south along St. Stephen's Green.

Lea checked her mirror and saw the gunmen swerve dangerously around a few drunken students meandering along the street. "That was close!" she said. "They don't care who they kill, it seems."

"I'll say," Mikey said with conviction. "They showed that when they shot at my Ciara."

A moment later they had no choice but to leave the park and rejoin the street.

Lea wound down the window and pulled a Glock from her holster. She clicked the seat-belt release and twisted around in her seat, a look of focussed determination on her face.

"What the hell are you doing, woman?" Mikey said, eyeing the Glock.

"Gonna take out those dirty little poxes, if that's okay with you."

"But we're in the middle of Dublin! Not even I would start a shooting war here. There's a Starbucks right there for God's sake!"

"So?"

Mikey shook his head and sighed. "It just doesn't feel right, that's all."

"Too bad – they have a bloody machine gun!"

She leaned out the window and fired at the pursuing Range Rover, striking the front left headlight and smashing the glass out of the housing. It swerved in response but powered up, not down. Drawing closer, the man in the passenger seat stood up until his upper body was outside the sunroof.

"Uh-oh," Lea said.

Devlin turned in his seat. "What does *uh-oh* mean?"

"Maybe we should get a move on, Mikey?" she said.

"What's up?"

"I think he's going to have another go with the MAT!"

Mikey sighed. "You hang out with some pretty crazy people, Danny – you know that?"

"Hey!" Lea said. "I am not crazy!"

"Tell that to the guys with the bloody machine gun aimed at my Ciara!"

Before she could respond, the man opened fire and peppered the back of the Quattro with the submachine gun. A line of bullets punctured the top of the boot and one hit the release mechanism, sending the boot-hatch into the air and blocking Mikey's rear-view. "That's just bloody fantastic – now I've not got any bloody mirrors to see what they're up to!"

Another burst of submachine gunfire tore through the open car and blasted the windshield into a thousand pieces. Lea screamed and covered her face to protect herself from the flying glass.

"Get these arseholes off our backs, Lea!" Mikey shouted.

"I'll handle it," Lea said, and leaned out the window once again.

"The woman's totally insane, Danny!"

Lea squinted through the sites. "Can't you go any steadier?"

She heard Mikey sigh and then the car slowed.

The sights lined up with the Range Rover and she opened fire – a rapid burst of six shots. They started at the grille and worked up the hood to the windshield, which exploded into shards. She fired again, merciless, and this time struck the driver in his chest and throat.

Inside the large vehicle, panic ensued, but nothing could be done as they left the road at speed and smashed head-on into the side of a department store, clipping a support pillar and spinning around ninety degrees. The Range Rover tipped on its side as it piled through the front display, smashing mannequins and sales bunting as it tore through the front of the store.

Lea climbed back in the Audi and holstered her gun. "Sorted."

"My poor Ciara…" Mikey said in a resigned tone.

"Sorry, Mikey!"

"You had to shoot at them, didn't you? We could have had a nice, simple car chase though the city, lost them in the estates somewhere, and then had our picnic on the coast, but no."

"They started it. Anyway, like I said…"

"I know, you're sorry – but I can't help feeling this is just the beginning."

Lea sunk into her seat as Mikey weaved the Quattro out of the city and headed west. She didn't say it, but she had the same feeling too.

CHAPTER TWENTY-FOUR

Kiefel watched Alan Pauling as he counted him down to the next live broadcast and gave him the silent signal to speak to the world once again. For Kiefel, holding the American population in thrall like this brought him joy beyond measure.

"People of America! The time has come for me to deliver on the promise I made to you in my previous statement. You will now behold the greatest weapon on earth, a power so mighty it will reduce a living man to solid stone right before your eyes. Never forget that it is I, Klaus Kiefel who controls this weapon."

On cue, Pauling increased the sound of the background music until Wagner's *Ride of the Valkyries* filled the room. Kiefel closed his eyes and smiled smugly for a moment before moving his hand in time with the string section as the French horns blared and boomed. "Ah, das ist viel besser, nicht wahr?"

Kiefel clicked his fingers and Jakob dragged Agent Dirk Partridge across the room. On his way to the hideous floor show, he knocked the camera and made the picture wobble for a few seconds. Out of frame, bound and gagged, Charles Grant was helpless and could only watch the insanity.

"Don't kick and squeal like..." he paused searching for the word before looking at Angelika and snapping his fingers. "Ein Ferkel?"

"Piglet," she said flatly

"Ah! Do not squeal like a piglet, Agent Partridge!" Kiefel said. "The whole world is watching... have some dignity, at least."

The senior Secret Service agent, only four years from his retirement, began to run out of energy as the German gymnast held him fast against a support post at the side of the distillation unit. Angelika tied him to the post with the same rope that had secured the security guard. She paused to kiss him on the cheek and mock him with a sadistic wink before gently tracing her finger down his sweating face.

As she tightened the final knot, Kiefel gave an order in German and everyone in the room put on their gas masks and gloves.

As Jakob fitted a mask to Grant, the President's heart sank as he realized he had no way of helping his loyal old friend.

Kiefel moved purposefully to the box and extracted the head for the second time, holding it aloft to the camera for the world to see.

"Behold, the Mighty Medusa!"

He carried the mummified skull over to Agent Partridge, who was now sweating profusely and unable to move his terrified eyes away from his fate.

"People of America!" Kiefel continued. "What you witness now is not merely a demonstration of my power, but the evidence about your world which you have long sought. This is the final proof that the history you learned in your schools was all lies! This is the final proof that the world is not what you think it is."

Kiefel raised the skull and held it in front of Partridge's face. Almost tenderly, Kiefel removed Partridge's glasses and handed them to Angelika. He lowered his voice. "This is your end time, Special Agent Partridge... *auf wiedersehen.*"

Partridge tried to speak but the terror coursing through his veins froze his words before they reached his lips. He stared at the hideous, twisted face of Medusa – its blue-black skin and pits for eyes – and began to hyperventilate.

Grant tried to scream through his mask but the gag muffled his desperate pleas.

"Silence!" Kiefel screamed.

Jakob padded over to Grant and powered a heavy fist into his stomach causing him to double over in agony. Winded and desperately trying to heave breath into his lungs, Grant knew there was nothing he could now do to save Partridge.

Concentrating once again on Partridge, Kiefel pushed the skull closer to the Secret Service agent, and he began to react the same way as the female security guard – juddering and more hyperventilation. Seconds later, the looked of crazed fear on the Secret Service agent's face was preserved in stone for eternity.

Grant looked away, horrified.

Angelika applauded and giggled insanely.

Kiefel beamed with pleasure and turned to the camera.

"People of America! If you enjoyed this performance, please tune in for the main show when I will turn your President to stone right before your eyes!"

He motioned at Pauling who cut the signal, and then he turned to Grant.

"I wonder what the viewing figures will be for our grand finale, Mr Grant, *hmm*?"

*

Hawke sat up front with Kim Taylor in the first of two Secret Service Cadillac Escalades as they made their way north-east along New York Avenue. Doyle and

Vincent followed behind with three SWAT men in the back.

They drove in silence. They had watched the terrible last few moments of Dirk Partridge's life on an iPad en route and no one had spoken since the signal was cut.

"We're there," Kim said at last. She braked and signalled to leave the highway.

They reached the Amtrak yard and pulled right to enter Ivy City, parking up a hundred yards down the road from the warehouse and surveying the industrial park for any signs of trouble. Hawke wondered how people like Kiefel always seemed to find places like this.

This was the industrial zone of the city, the part the rest of the world never saw.

The warehouse itself was a red-brick building that ran the full length of the block and was punctuated by three double roller-doors where trucks could make and take deliveries. A few yards behind a chain-link fence topped with razor-wire was a Ford F-150, jacked up on bricks in the parking area. The place didn't exactly look like it was overwhelmed with trade.

Doyle, Vincent and the SWAT guys joined them as they strapped on bullet-proof vests and loaded their guns.

"Nice place they have here," Vincent said.

Hawke smirked. "Just what I was thinking."

"All right everyone," Kim said. "We stick to the plan – and no heroics. This isn't just about rescuing President Grant. This is about the vital national security of the United States. We just don't know what these crackerjacks have got planned, but if it's got anything to do with what we all just saw on YouTube it's not going to be pretty so we can't risk any screw-ups, got it?"

They all nodded. No one would ever forget the look on Agent Partridge's face when Kiefel turned him to stone. The idea of that happening to millions of people across the country was unthinkable. As for his threat to do it to the President – they all understood the gravity of the situation and how that could never be allowed to happen, but time was running out.

"We got it," Doyle said. He cocked his SIG and scowled as he looked at the warehouse. "This is for Partridge. He taught me everything I know, and now that son of a bitch Kiefel is a dead man walking."

They jogged to a metal door a yard to the right of one of the roller-doors and Doyle kicked it in, almost tearing it from its hinges. After moving inside and seeing the office was clear, he flashed the others a pre-arranged hand signal and they fanned out into the warehouse space.

"Clear!" Kim shouted.

"Clear!" said Doyle. "Move on to the next warehouse."

They continued through the empty warehouse. Hawke rounded a corner, SIG raised in front of him, ready to fire, but found nothing except yet another expanse of concrete and bare metal shelving units. He moved forward with caution, his footfall quietly tapping on the polished concrete floor.

He rounded a second corner which revealed a short corridor lined with office doors, one of which was throwing a faint blue glow from its window onto the corridor carpet below.

He gave a signal and a moment later Kim Taylor was at his side.

They counted to three and then kicked the door in, immediately covering the entire room with their guns, ready to fire – but it was empty.

"Looks like they moved out in a hurry," Hawke said. He walked over to the desk and went through the drawers. In the third drawer down he found something.

"At last!"

Kim was covering the door as the Englishman made his search of the office, but when he spoke she glanced over and saw him pulling an Apple Mac laptop from the drawer.

Hawke smiled. "Bingo..."

"You think?" the American woman said.

"I bloody hope so, because whoever was here has moved everything else out!"

"Let me look at that," Kim said, and holstered her weapon. She walked to the desk and fired up the laptop.

"We need to get this back to Alex at the Pentagon," Hawke said. "It'll have a password on it."

"Never mind about that," she said dismissively, and pushed a flash-drive into one of the USB ports.

Hawke watched in amazement as the password screen faded to reveal the desktop. "How did you do that then?" he asked, already knowing the answer.

Kim smiled and sat down. "CIA classified."

Hawke smiled too. He knew he wasn't going to get any more than that out of Agent Taylor so he changed subject. "So what have we got on here?"

Kim was busy opening and checking files. "Not sure yet, but I'm copying everything to the flash-drive for analysis later anyway... ah – what's this?"

Hawke leaned in. "What have you found?"

"It's definitely the laptop of this Nick Collins guy, and I'm just going through the email history... looks like he's been spending a lot of time in the Bayou State."

Hawke looked at her, confused. "Eh?"

"Louisiana – there's talk here of a flight to New Orleans, and another email here booking a hotel in the French Quarter."

Hawke sighed. "That narrows it down, but not much..."

"I know, but… wait – did you hear that?"

"What?" Hawke looked up at the door and focussed on the silence of the warehouse. "Maybe it's the SWAT guys, or Doyle and Vincent?"

"No – I thought I heard a car outside the office."

Hawke moved to the window and squinted at the darkness of the car park. "You're right – someone's just pulled up in a Dodge Viper."

"And who would be driving to an empty warehouse at this time of night?"

They looked at each and spoke at the same time.

"Nick Collins!"

Hawke scowled. "Bastard must have come back for his computer before making like a swift and heading south for the winter no doubt."

Kim pulled her gun out again. "Not on my watch, he doesn't!"

They opened the outer office door quietly and went outside.

With his gun raised, Hawke ran forward through the car park in the shadows. Kim followed him until they were almost at the Viper.

They reached the car with their guns raised. "Freeze, Secret Service!"

Collins looked up, terrified, and re-started the engine.

Kim raised her weapon and fired at the Dodge Viper, but Collins reversed the powerful sports car at speed, its red striped roof flashing briefly in the pale glow of a streetlight on the perimeter of the car park. The bullet missed and struck a recycling unit, ricocheting off into the night.

"Damn it!" she screamed. "We need a car, Hawke!"

"On it!" Hawke called back, and sprinted to the front of the warehouse with the Suburban's keys in his hand.

CHAPTER TWENTY-FIVE

Alex Reeve was relieved to see Ryan's face when he walked through the door. It hadn't taken him long to make the short flight in the Gulfstream and she was impressed. She understood the agony he'd gone through after Sophie died in Japan, but now he looked different somehow – calmer, more at peace. Maybe the time he'd spent kicking back in the Caribbean had worked some magic on him.

"Hey," he said, and walked confidently over to her.

She looked at his clothes and shook her head. He was wearing a pair of black jeans and a black and red Spiderman t-shirt under a black denim jacket.

"What?" he said, smiling as he noticed her staring at him.

"Didn't you just spend the last few weeks on Elysium?"

"Yeah... so?"

"So I was expecting you to be dressed a little different than your usual funereal look, is all."

He shrugged his shoulders as he tossed his jacket over the back of a chair. "Why would I do that?"

"No reason, I guess. I just wondered what a Tropical Ryan would look like."

"He'd look like an even bigger wanker than miserable Emo Ryan," boomed a voice from the corridor.

Alex looked up and was more than a little surprised to see Scarlet Sloane enter the room.

"Oh yeah," Ryan said. "Eden insisted on my personal security tagging along."

"Your personal security, my *arse*," Scarlet said. "I'm here to save America. Where do I start?"

Alex rolled her eyes and returned her attention to Ryan. "You really should try the tropical look."

Ryan laughed. "Can you honestly see me in a pair of Bermuda shorts and a Hawaiian shirt?"

She looked at him for a few seconds, tipping her head to one side and pursing her lips, pretending to be in deep contemplation. "Sure..." She laughed.

He smiled. "Thanks for the call – I was getting cabin fever on that island."

"I'll say," Scarlet added.

"Just thought you might like to help," Alex said. "Surprised Eden didn't send you all up here."

Scarlet looked at her. "He said it 'wasn't in our remit'. Exact quotation."

"*Okay*... but where's Lea?"

Ryan sighed. "Chasing ghosts in Ireland."

"The silly cow," Scarlet added.

Alex looked confused for a second but let Ryan's enigmatic comment pass. "Anyway, listen up. I need you here right now but let's keep it between us. Hawke is pretty pissed about everyone keeping him in the dark about the ECHO thing."

Ryan looked indignant. "Hey! I never kept him in the dark! I found about it the same time he did."

"Eden had his reasons," Scarlet said. "We're not like the US military you know. ECHO is covert and highly specialist."

Alex gave her a look. "Well, whatever happened, I know he just wants to be away from it all for a while, so just keep your presence here between us, all right."

169

Ryan puffed out his chest. "When the President of the United States needs me to rescue him I can do whatever it takes, including keeping out of Joe's way."

Alex sighed and rolled her eyes. "I said *I* need you here, Ryan. The President did not ask for you to rescue him."

"Sure, but that's not what's going on my Facebook update."

She shook her head and whistled. "You put any of this on Facebook and you're the one who's going to need rescuing – from Gitmo Bay, probably."

Ryan laughed and sat beside her. "I take your point… now then – what have we got?"

Alex frowned and swivelled her laptop screen. "Thanks to facial recognition software, I can tell you that our man is one Klaus Kiefel, born in Dresden, in the Deutsche Demokratische Republik in 1951. He claims his mother was Elfriede Kallweit, the notorious spy who was executed in Los Angeles in 1955."

Scarlet sniffed. "Never heard of her."

"It was big here at the time, believe me. It was just after the whole McCarthyism thing was getting started. She worked for a defense contractor in San Diego and was busted passing blueprints to a Soviet agent. They were both members of a yacht club and used to meet off the coast of Catalina where no one knew what they were doing."

"Catalina?"

"It's an island off the coast of LA."

"Gotcha."

"Big, big scandal at the time."

Ryan snapped the ring-pull on a can of Pepsi Max and took a swig. "I'll take your word for it."

"Anyway, she was charged with conspiracy to commit espionage and passing classified

170

communications to the Soviets. She got the chair in fifty-five."

"I'm guessing by that last remark you don't mean she was awarded a professorship at UCLA?" asked Ryan.

Alex rolled her eyes. "I do *not* mean that, no. I mean she went to the electric chair."

"I know what you mean, Alex," Ryan said, smiling.

"So anyway, this guy Kiefel claims he is her son and that the time for America to pay for killing his mother has arrived."

"Ah that old spiel..."

"Right, but he's very serious, and claims he has... and I quote... 'some kind of ancient doomsday weapon that will shock the world to its foundations'... so this Medusa thing, in a word."

Scarlet spoke next. "What's Joe doing right now?"

"Following a lead in Ivy City."

Ryan cracked his knuckles and sat down beside Alex, firing up his laptop. "In that case, we better get to work."

"You can start by analysing the latest video."

Ryan and Scarlet shared a glance. "What video?"

"You mean you never saw it?"

"Saw what?"

Alex frowned and played them the film of Partridge's death. Like everyone else in the Pentagon, Alex was still struggling to make sense of the depraved horror show she had witnessed on the internet.

As the short film ended, Ryan ran a hand over his tangled hair and took a step back from the screen. "Holy crap."

"Seconded," added Scarlet, wincing.

Ryan immediately hit the keys and started looking into what might have happened, not believing for a second what his eyes had told him.

"Whatever the hell *did* happen," Alex said coolly, "that guy didn't just turn to stone because that's plain old-fashioned impossible, right?"

"Agreed, I think..." Ryan said. "And I say that even after the last few weeks have really made me question what 'impossible' means."

Scarlet drew up a chair. "You can say that again."

Alex looked at Ryan. "So where do we go from here?"

"We start with Medusa. That's the obvious starting point," Ryan said, pushing his glasses up the bridge of his nose.

"Medusa?" said a passing staffer. "What the hell are you talking about? That video was CGI... Medusa is a myth!" He leaned in closer to Ryan. "Ever heard of Greek *myth-o-logy*, son?"

"You could say that," Ryan muttered, and shared a smile with Alex and Scarlet.

The staffer narrowed his eyes. "What's that supposed to mean?"

"Listen, *Trent*," Alex said, peering at his name badge. "Ryan has forgotten more about Greek *myth-o-logy*, as you put it, than you will ever know, so just back off."

"That's pretty inappropriate behavior for an office like this," Trent said.

"Hardly," Scarlet said coolly. "I'd have told you to fuck off, so why don't you just do that instead?"

Trent looked at Scarlet for a moment, horrified. It looked like he was considering a range of responses, but in the end he went with the one based on the fact he was talking to his boss's daughter, his boss being the Defense Secretary of the United States. "Listen, whatever the hell that thing was, it sure as hell wasn't the mummified head of someone who never existed."

Scarlet grabbed his tie and pulled him toward her. "We know better, so go and fetch us some coffee, darling, yeah?"

Trent snatched his tie back and tried not to look embarrassed. They watched him walk away and shared a glance before erupting into laughter. "And pour some whisky in mine!" Scarlet shouted after him.

"I'm glad you came," Alex said. "Dad's under a lot of pressure and he needs all the help he can get. I know you're both very good at what you do."

"No problemo," Ryan said, beaming at the compliment. "There's only so many banana daiquiris you can drink on a tropical beach, although watching Scarlet fall off a windsurf board never gets old."

"Sounds like fun."

"If you think that's fun, you should have seen the time Ryan couldn't find the brake on his jet ski. I laughed for an hour."

Ryan turned to Alex, suddenly serious. "So why not come down when all this is over? Eden invited you both to join us, after all."

"I don't know... Like I said, Hawke was pretty pissed about not being included from the start."

Scarlet smiled. "That's just Joe. He'll get over it, believe me... anyway, since when did he make your decisions?"

"Since never, but it's not that simple. I only just started talking to my Dad again. We didn't talk for a long time – years, really..." she looked away, her eyes settling on some half-forgotten memory of childhood in the middle-distance. She wiped an incipient tear from her eye. "I can't just walk away now."

"I understand, but the offer's always there..." Ryan's voice returned to flippant mode. "It's not just pissing about on jet skis, you know. We're always busy down at

173

ECHO HQ. As we speak, Eden has people in Mexico monitoring unusual activity at an archaeological site in the jungle. We might be needed to spring into action at a second's notice."

She laughed.

"What?"

"Just thinking about you springing into action, that's all."

"What's funny about that?"

"Ryan... *Hawke* springs into action, you kind of slide into it."

Ryan feigned offense, putting his hand on his heart and pretending to cry. "I can't say that didn't hurt me, Alex."

"She shouldn't have said you slide into action," Scarlet said, placing a comforting hand on Ryan's shoulder.

"Thanks, Scarlet."

"You have to be dragged into action kicking and screaming."

Ryan gave a fake laugh, and Alex let a few seconds pass before changing the subject. "So how's things with Agent Snowcat? Last time I saw her she was using you as a sun bed."

"That is *so* funny, Alex," Ryan replied, trying to look nonchalant but clearly pleased she had brought the subject up.

"Well?"

"She's fine, thanks."

"Back in Mother Russia?"

"Hardly... after James Matheson made his little phone call when she and Hawke were on the run in Cairo that's the last place she'd be. As far as the Government of the Russian Federation is concerned Maria Kurikova is *persona non grata*."

"So she's with you on Elysium?"

"Sure is," Scarlet said, raising her eyebrows. "Now we get borscht on Tuesdays. Yummy." She pretended to vomit.

Ryan nodded, ignoring the former SAS woman. "She sure is, and we're getting along just fine. She has excellent offensive techniques in the Sambo and Systema schools of Russian martial arts."

"And you would know that *how*?"

He looked at her and winked.

"Oh... that's *gross*, Ryan," she said, but half-returning his smile. "Keep your disgusting little bedroom habits to yourself in future."

"Sorry... it's just a joke."

"Which is exactly what Maria said when she saw inside Ryan's underpants for the first time."

"Hey!"

Alex suppressed a laugh. "So why isn't she here keeping an eye on you?"

"Eden only wanted to send a couple of us up here, so..." Ryan glanced at Scarlet who had now grown tired of the conversation and crossed the room to harass Trent. "So you got the short straw..."

She smiled, and was happy that he had found someone to help him get over the terrible loss of Sophie Durand. She wondered if she would ever find someone who would make her happy. She knew who that man was, but she knew he was in love with someone else. She kept the thought to herself and decided to change the subject. "Okay, Mr Bale... let's get to work. That crazy son-of-a-bitch is somehow using the severed head of an ancient monster to turn people to stone, and we're going to find out just how the hell to stop it!"

"I bet you never thought you'd say that sentence in your whole life."

"Never!" She held out her hand to shake. "Deal?"
Ryan smiled and shook her hand firmly. "Deal!"

CHAPTER TWENTY-SIX

Hawke floored the accelerator down hard and they shot off in pursuit of the English arms dealer currently racing a Dodge Viper down New York Avenue and toward the center of Washington DC. He hadn't even had time to tell Vincent and the others what he was doing.

"Where the hell is he going?" Kim said.

"Search me, but we're going there too."

She pulled her cell-phone from her jacket and made a call to her boss at the CIA requesting back-up. Then she called Vincent and told him what had happened over on their side of the warehouse complex.

Now, in the distance they saw a puff of smoke as Collins hit the brakes to take a corner. They heard the tires squeal from a block behind his speeding Viper.

"We can't lose him now!" Kim said. "We only have New Orleans as a destination – it's just not enough."

"Yeah, I worked that out all by myself... hold on!"

Hawke braked for the same corner but it was still too fast. Kim gripped hold of the door handle and screamed as the Suburban tipped over onto two wheels. Hawke struggled to control the heavy car at such a speed, but swung the wheel around and brought it crashing back to the ground. With all four wheels on the asphalt, he slammed the throttle down and the Chevy leaped forward once more in pursuit of the fleeing Englishman.

Hawke checked his mirror instinctively for cops, but the curfew had thinned their numbers and the coast was clear.

"Where the hell is the little bastard going?" he asked.

Kim frowned. "Looks like he's heading to Georgetown for some reason."

"Can you think why? There must be something... why would a man on the run go there? I'm betting it isn't the coffee shops."

"Well, he sure ain't going to the university either... wait a minute!"

Hawke shot her a glance. "What is it, Kim?"

"It's a long shot but there *is* something. There's a helipad at the Georgetown University Hospital."

"That's got to be it!" Hawke said. "Remember what Novak said about how Collins had tested the drones because he was a helicopter pilot?   "

They took another corner, then Hawke slammed the throttle down to power out of the bend and close the gap with Collins's Viper.

"Well this is Georgetown all right," Kim said. "And sure enough – he's going to the hospital."

"Look!" Hawke said, pointing out the windshield. "There's a chopper on the roof, rotors already whirring."

"Let's shut this little bastard's escape route down!" Kim said, pulling out her gun as Hawke skidded to a halt behind the Dodge.

They ran up an external fire escape and hit the roof just in time to see Collins climbing into the chopper beside the pilot. Hawke wasted no time and fired, shattering the side window glass and striking the pilot in the neck. He slumped forward, but Collins took to the controls.

Hawke sprinted to the chopper and swung open the door before Collins had raised enough power to get airborne.

Collins cursed as he raised the collective, but the lack of sufficient power meant there was no response.

As Kim stood back covering Hawke with her pistol, the English SBS man opened the door of the chopper, punched Nick Collins in the face and unclipped his seatbelt.

"I'm afraid your flight is over," he said, and dragged him from the helicopter into the warm Washington night. "Make a move for it and you die."

Collins looked up at him from his place leaning up against the chopper's starboard skid. "You're English?"

"Never mind about me, mate. We're the ones asking the questions, not you."

Collins accepted the rebuke and realized he wasn't going to get anywhere with the man currently holding a chunky black pistol twelve inches from his forehead. "What do want with me?" he said, nervously.

Kim strode forward. "So you like Cajun food, is that right?"

Collins looked up confused. "I'm sorry?"

She leaned in closer and lowered her voice. "Don't screw around with me, asshole. What's your interest in Louisiana?"

Collins looked up and smirked. "I love Dixieland music."

Hawke punched him in the face, and by the sound of it fractured his cheekbone. Collins screamed out in pain, and Kim Taylor looked on with horror. Hawke took hold of Collins's hand and put him in a thumb lock.

Collins screamed out in pain again, blood pouring down his face.

Hawke was unmoved. "Answer our questions or I'll break your thumb, got it?"

"Get off me!"

"After that I'll break your wrist and then your shoulder before moving to your other side, understand? By the time I've finished with you you'll look you've

179

been on a hot wash cycle in a high speed washing machine."

Kim stepped forward and lowered her voice. "Can I see you a second, Hawke?"

Hawke wiped the blood from his hand and glanced from Collins to Kim. "What, *now*?"

"Yes, *now*!"

"Sure." He turned back to Collins. "I'm a just few yards away. If you move I'll shoot you dead before you take three steps – got it?"

Collins nodded glumly and rubbed his thumb.

Hawke followed Kim a few yards away from the chopper.

"What the hell was that?" Kim said.

"What?"

"You broke his cheekbone and you nearly broke his thumb, damn it!"

"You mean you want me to stop going easy on him?"

"Are you trying to be funny?"

"Only ever so slightly."

"Well, you're not making me laugh, got it?"

"Come on, Kim. He's our only chance."

"He's in federal custody, Hawke. You can't beat information out of prisoners."

Hawke shook his head in disbelief. "And this from the people who brought us water-boarding!"

"I'm sorry?"

"Forget it... listen – I hate to burst your bubble but that guy isn't going to dump on the sort of man who kidnaps the American President without a certain amount of incentive, if you catch my drift."

"You're not hitting him again, Hawke – if you do I'll have you arrested."

Hawke was silent for a few moments. "Fine – but let me handle it, all right?"

180

"No more broken bones, okay?"

"Spoilsport."

Hawke padded back over to Collins.

"We know you're involved in the plot to kidnap the President," he said. "Right now you're in so much shit you'd probably be better off if I just shot you."

Nick Collins tried to laugh, but Hawke brought a rapid end to his amusement with a hefty kick in the ribs.

Kim Taylor sighed and rubbed her forehead. "What did I just say?"

Hawke ignored her. "You're going to tell us all we need to know about the plot – not only where the President is, but what Kiefel's interest in ancient Greek archaeology is." He waved his gun in Collins's face. "I want to know what was stored at the warehouse as well, where it is now and what the hell Dixieland has got to do with anything."

Collins was now beginning to look nervous. Hawke didn't think he looked like the kind of guy to be involved with an operation like this and thought maybe he was beginning to have serious regrets. He was probably thinking he'd got away with it, but now this.

Collins breathed out a long sigh of relief. Maybe he was glad it was over. "I don't know much, but I'll tell you everything I know, I swear."

"Start talking."

"I was approached a few weeks ago about hiring out some space in the warehouse. We're not exactly over-run with business and maybe I didn't ask as many questions as I should have."

"We need more than that," Kim said, holstering her gun and moving closer to the man.

"What's going down is big. Bigger than anything you could imagine."

"Yeah, yeah," Hawke said. "Heard it all before, mate."

"It's true, I swear it!"

"Save you're swearing for the courthouse," Kim said.

"What was in the warehouse?"

"We stored drones at the warehouse. Helicopter drones."

"The ones in the attack?" Kim asked.

Collins nodded.

"How many drones?" Hawke asked.

"Four."

"But we only destroyed two over DC," Kim said.

Hawke pushed his gun into Collins's neck. "Where are the other two?"

"Kiefel's heavies took them down to New Orleans ages ago. They have a location there they're using as some kind of laboratory."

"And where is this mysterious location?"

"All I know is the guy who delivered the flatbed to the warehouse mentioned something about driving down to an abandoned processing plant in an industrial part of the city somewhere... St. Tammany Parish, I think."

Kim spun around and started to speak into her earpiece.

"You've been most helpful," Hawke said.

"Does this mean I get immunity?" Collins said nervously.

"From the US authorities, maybe, but from me, sadly no."

Without saying another word, Hawke powered his fist into Collins's face and knocked him out cold. "We have to get to New Orleans in a hurry," he said.

Kim turned to face him, her hair blowing in the helicopter's downdraft. "On it."

CHAPTER TWENTY-SEVEN

Joe Hawke ignored the high-performance takeoff of the Learjet 31. His mind was still processing the totally unexpected sight of Scarlet Sloane as she drove across the airport asphalt on a stolen motorbike and skidded to a halt a yard from his legs.

"Only you could lose a President," she had said as the rubber smoke drifted into the air.

Now, as Vincent, Doyle and a team of SWAT men slept in the small cabin, the two of them and Kim Taylor studied maps of the processing plant. He knew the flight from Washington DC to New Orleans would take less than two hours in the Lear, and that didn't leave much time to organize a strategy to save Charles Grant and bring Kiefel's plans to a halt.

After discussing their strategy for the tenth time, he shut his eyes for some important rest before the assault, but struggled to sleep. Instead, he recalled his earlier conversation with Alex Reeve and realized somewhere over Alabama that she had been right, as usual. Thankfully, Scarlet had stayed out of it, but he knew it was time to speak to Lea Donovan.

He had thought about calling her before, but the events of the last few hours had overtaken him. Now he had a few moments he knew what he had to do. He switched on his phone and gave her the call he should have made a long time ago.

Her voice was clipped and distant. "So you remembered my number then?"

Not a good start. She sounded as angry as he'd imagined she might, but he had a right to be angry too.

"Where are you?" he said, trying to chill things down.

"I'm in Ireland."

"Visiting family?"

"If you call chasing my father's ghost off a cliff visiting family, then yeah... I'm visiting family." She sounded as unhappy as he'd ever known her and he regretted more than ever walking out on her back in Luxor.

"I don't understand," he said.

"You don't need to understand." Her voice grew weaker as the reception faltered. She sounded so far away. She *was* so far away.

"Don't be like that, Lea. Do you need any help?"

"I have help, Joe. You're not the only action-figure in the toy store you know."

Touché, he thought. Presuming a woman with Lea's contacts and experience was sitting around waiting for his help was stupid and presumptuous.

"So what's going on?" he said after another awkward silence.

"An old friend of Dad's and Rich's was murdered, so I'm looking into it."

"You think the murder is connected to your father's death?"

Her reply was succinct, to say the least. "Yes."

Another long silence stretched out between them.

"What about you?" she asked at last. The phone line crackled and accentuated the distance between them.

"I'm in America."

"America?" she sounded shocked. "I thought maybe you went back to London."

He knew there was no point in delaying the inevitable. "I've been staying with Alex at her father's cabin in Idaho for a few weeks."

A longer silence.

"Is there something you want to tell me Joe Hawke?"

Uh-oh, both names. "If you mean is there anything going on between me and Alex, then no, there isn't. She's just a very old friend of mine. I don't think of her like that, and she doesn't think of me like that."

She changed the subject. "You're up to your arse in this terror attack, aren't you?"

"You could say that. I'm calling from a jet. We're flying to New Orleans to rescue President Grant. I'm surprised ECHO isn't all over it as a matter of fact."

"Rich has his reasons."

"Enigmatic."

"I could tell you more, but as an outsider you don't have clearance."

"Funny, but that's what Scarlet Sloane just said to me."

"Scarlet's there?"

"Yeah – she landed in the US a few moments ago. Eden sent her and Ryan up here as soon as he found out Medusa was involved in all this. He can't help himself."

"Listen, Joe… I have to go."

He nodded, even though she couldn't see him. It was an instinctive reaction. "Sure."

"I'll call."

Sure, he thought as the line went dead.

*

Lea switched her phone off with a scowl, folded her arms and stared out of the windshield without blinking. Outside the car, the Irish countryside flashed by in a rain-streaked blur and she caught her reflection in the window. She looked like she was about ready to murder someone.

"They'll hypnotize you, you realize that."

Lea thought about ignoring him, but she had the crazy idea Mikey O'Sullivan wasn't the type to be ignored. "What will?"

"The windscreen wipers," he said, pointing a meaty finger at them as they swished back and forth in the heavy rain. "If you stare at them like that you're sure to be mesmerized."

"Is that true, Danny?" Lea said, turning her head slightly to the back.

"You can forget about asking him for back-up – they're both dead to the world."

She turned to see the Guinness and whiskey had finally caught up with Danny Devlin, and Kyle too had succumbed to the gentle purr of the Audi Quattro's classic inline five cylinder engine.

"So I take it that was your boyfriend – is that what they're called these days? I don't know anymore."

"Oh, there's lots of words to describe Joe Hawke. I'm not sure if *boyfriend* is at the top of my list right now, Mikey."

He smiled. "You know, my daughter isn't much younger than you. Maeve's her name. She says I'm not allowed to talk about stuff like this because it's so embarrassing."

For some reason she was surprised that Mikey had a daughter. She couldn't imagine him living anywhere other than among the oil stains and old carburettors of the salvage yard. He seemed to fit in there just right. Imagining him in a house, with a carpet and wallpaper, and a wife and kids was almost impossible. For a while she let his words hang in the air, but then she spoke. It seemed rude not to. "She sounds like a smart girl."

He was ready with his reply, and said it with the weary pride that constant repetition brings. "That she certainly is – a lot smarter than her old man and that's for sure."

The engine rumbled away under the hood as the car ate up the miles and made its way across the country toward the west coast. Mikey's reference to 'her old man' made her think of her father as she closed her eyes. A heartbeat later she was asleep.

CHAPTER TWENTY-EIGHT

"This report is freaking me out," Ryan said, passing it to Alex. "Read the bottom of page two." She took the report, delivered a few moments ago by one of her father's senior personal assistants. On the front page of the dossier the words TOP SECRET CODEWORD were stamped in bright red letters.

Alex scanned the page. "Oh my God... this is what Dad was telling me about and it's just... terrible. It says here that the three men were discovered at a US listening base in northern Norway and that they resembled statues."

"Your dad knew about this?"

"No, not my dad... the US Secretary of Defense knew about it." She sighed. "There's a big difference – just ask my mom."

"Alex, I have a funny feeling that all this stuff links together. I wonder just how much your Dad knows..."

"I don't know. Even if I were closer to him I'd never ask. He'd only ever tell me what he wants."

Ryan shook his head in disbelief and whistled. "It says there that in the attempt to work out what happened five other men were turned to stone. It says that they had it assayed but that despite numerous tests on the statues, they could never prove exactly what kind of stone it was, but it resembled a type of granite with flecks of gold in it."

They both stared at a series of black and white six-by-fours, taken when the men were discovered back in 1968. The twisted, agonized faces of the men looked just like the one they had seen on the face of Dirk Partridge in Kiefel's horror show – but here there were three blocks of human-shaped stone standing in the Arctic snow, dead and still.

"I think we're putting the dots together. We know we're dealing with the Medusa myth…"

"But it's not just a myth now."

"Right. We know it was found in the Arctic ice nearly fifty years ago, brought back to the US and placed in top secret storage in Archive 7. Somehow, our man Kiefel found out about it and wanted to use it against America, but…"

"But he knew it required no less than an Executive Order to have it released and that without that he could never get it out of a place like Archive 7."

"So there was only one option – put his puppet in the Oval Office and have him release the weapon by Executive Order."

"Which means we can't trust Kimble."

"Right."

"Right… but where the hell do we go now? I'm struggling to believe this is really happening…. it's like black magic or something."

Ryan frowned. "No, it's not that, there's no such thing."

"I'm not so sure anymore, Ryan, and if we can't work out how this thing is turning people to stone we don't have a chance of stopping it. You heard him – he's going to kill President Grant with it – and what if he weaponizes it and disperses it all over the US?"

"We're not going to let that happen, Alex."

"That's easy to say, but what if this thing really is some kind of curse? We can't fight that with bullets and laptops."

Ryan sighed and tapped his fingers on the desk for a moment. She saw he was going into one of his daydreams.

"Ryan, please tell me you're on this and not thinking about blasting some giggle weed or something."

He turned sharply and fixed his eyes on her. "Is that what you think I'm thinking about?"

"Sorry… all this talk of curses is just freaking me out."

"Luckily for you, and the people of America I might add, Ryan Bale is thinking about neither giggle weed *nor* curses."

"And what *is* Ryan the Great thinking about?"

He smiled broadly and put his hands behind his head. "Aside from the elephant in the room, you mean?"

"The elephant being why the severed head of a Greek Gorgon was found in ice tens of thousands of years old well north of the Arctic Circle?"

Ryan nodded. "Yes, aside from *that* elephant… I'm thinking nanoparticles."

Alex smiled as she pushed her hair back behind her ears. "I knew you were going to say that!"

"How?"

"Because that's what I was thinking and you're always five seconds behind me."

"You're almost as amusing as Scarlet," Ryan said with a sarcastic smile. "Last I heard you thought it was a curse."

"All right, I give in. You win." As she spoke, Ryan was busy tapping away on his laptop.

"I usually do…"

"You are so *arrogant*. I had no idea."

Ryan ignored her. "While you were prattling on just then, I just found this – it's a fascinating peer-reviewed article regarding the biodiversity of gold nanoparticles and ions..."

"Biodiversity?"

Ryan scanned the document. "Sure. They use silver nanoparticles all the time in manufacturing all kinds of things from cosmetics to socks because when they're oxidized they become toxic to bacteria and it helps to stop germs from spreading."

"I did *not* know that."

"You surprise me..."

"Hey – when it comes to hacking I could kick your ass down one side of the street and back up the other."

"You know, I can't see that happening... but I *can* begin to see what all this is about."

Alex suppressed a scream of frustration. "Please explain to me just what the hell all this means!"

"No problemo. I remember reading a few years back about how some scientists had discovered that a certain type of bacteria can actually change ions into solid gold."

"You mean like alchemy or something?"

Ryan smiled. "That's how they would have described it five hundred years ago, but today we know better. This has nothing to do with the prima materia, if that's what you're thinking."

"Say Philosopher's Stone if you mean Philosopher's Stone."

He smiled at her. "Sure... but the principle is similar though – we're talking about the transition of matter from one state to another."

A roll of the eyes. "Explain."

"This is all about bacteria."

"Explain better than that."

"The scientists discovered a bacteria called *delftia acidovorans* which have a self-defense mechanism when they come into contact with gold."

"Why?"

"Because they form on gold deposits but exposure to gold ions kills them, so it does its thing and releases a chemical which basically turns the gold ions into gold nanoparticles when the gold ions are dissolved in H2O..."

"Say water if you mean water."

"Sure... because when gold ions are dissolved in water they become toxic, and their toxicity poses a danger to the bacteria which is already in the water. For this reason the bacteria releases a protein which protects them, but it also has the side-effect of turning soluble gold ions into actual solid gold."

"I don't understand the difference."

"The difference is that ionic gold is soluble in water but metallic gold – the stuff your rings are made from – is not. This bacteria transforms gold ions into regular gold."

"And a gold ion is..?"

"A gold ion is a single atom of gold that is lacking three electrons. There are other experiments going on in this field – one used a different bacteria called *cupriavidus metallidurans* to create pure 24-carat gold from gold chloride, a toxic chemical."

"Sounds like something King Midas would have loved."

"Funny you should mention that because on my researches I was reading all about how..." he paused. "Forget it – I digress. The fact is this just has to be about some kind of airborne bacteria that is getting transferred from the severed head into the victims and transforming their very molecular structure to a different state."

"I'm starting to get a headache."

"Look, we don't need a chemistry lesson to stop Kiefel, at least not yet. All we need to know right now is this must have something to do with the bacteria, or something very like it. If that bacteria can release a protein to defend itself from toxic attack, it's not out of the question that something similar is going on now."

"So you definitely think something similar might be going on with Medusa?"

Ryan nodded vehemently. "Definitely. If there is some kind of ancient bacteria on there, it could be capable of triggering some kind of reaction at the molecular level and somehow transforming the ions in the human body into a solid state."

"So it would look like someone was turned to stone?"

"Got it in one – and take a look at this."

"What is it?"

"While you were talking I tracked this down."

"You flatter me."

Ryan looked at her, confused for a second. "I was *listening* at the same time..."

"Sure – show me what you have."

"It's a paper on a laboratory experiment in England a few years back all about how bacteria can turn flesh to stone."

"I think I preferred it when we talking about gold and Midas."

"Yes, but these people are turning to stone not gold. I said the process was *similar*."

"I was at high school a while back now, Ryan, but isn't that what fossils are?"

"Sort of, yeah. The process of mineralization you're describing takes millions and millions of years, but the experiment at the English lab took place over just a few weeks."

He directed her attention to the paper and she scanned through it. "This is fascinating – I had no idea. So they kept shrimps in isolation under special conditions in seawater and they turned to stone?"

"Yeah – thanks to the way the bacteria interacted with the process. The shrimps' soft tissue was turned into calcium phosphate. If Kiefel really does have the head of Medusa – severed by Perseus all those millennia ago – then it's possible it contains some kind of unknown bacteria."

"Capable of something similar to the shrimp experiment?"

"Indeed, only whatever the hell it is, its capacity to ossify is obviously considerably more powerful."

"So you think this is what the entire Medusa myth might have been based on?"

Ryan shrugged and cracked open another Pepsi. "Sure, why not? You didn't think it was hocus pocus or anything did you?"

Now Alex shrugged. "Ryan, since Poseidon I've learned anything is possible."

He smiled and gave a short laugh. "I hear you."

"And Ryan?"

"Yeah?"

"Please never refer to yourself in the third person in my presence ever again. It's weird."

Ryan smiled and gave a casual one-finger salute. "Gotcha."

"Thanks – we have to tell Hawke straight away."

"Agreed – I'm on it."

"And another thing…" Suddenly Alex winced in pain and doubled over in her chair, holding her thighs.

"What's the matter?" Ryan asked, rushing forward and holding her shoulders.

"Nothing..." She sounded in pain. "It's nothing at all..."

"It doesn't sound like nothing, Alex. What's going on?"

"I said it's nothing, really. Just a pain in my legs, is all."

"It's a pain in your legs and you say it's nothing... This could be something to do with the elixir, Alex! You can't just ignore this."

"Sure, I know that, but there's no time for that now. We have to stop Kiefel from destroying America!"

CHAPTER TWENTY-NINE

Vincent Reno watched out of the window as the Learjet 31 touched down at Naval Air Station Joint Reserve Base New Orleans on the outskirts of the city around midnight. The tires of its main undercarriage squealed on the asphalt and sent up a puff of white smoke into the dark Louisiana night.

The Frenchman was last to leave the aircraft, with Hawke, Scarlet, Agents Doyle and Taylor and the SWAT men walking ahead. As he stepped outside onto the apron he immediately noticed the much higher humidity down here in the Deep South.

Hawke wiped sweat from his brow. "Reminds me of my jungle training in the rainforests of Belize. That was a long time ago... when I was a much younger bloke."

"Another era then," Scarlet said with a smirk. "Didn't you train against velociraptors back in those days?"

"By the way," Hawke said, deadpan. "Your sense of humor called and asked when you're going to find it again."

Vincent moved between them and put his heavy arms over their shoulders. "You crazy English guys love each other really, oui?"

Agent Doyle spoke a series of commands into his headset and gave the signal to move out. They wasted no time in climbing into the Jeeps and speeding out of the airbase on their way to the processing plant.

Their journey took them through the French Quarter of the city which was usually buzzing with jazz and people drinking and partying on Bourbon Street but tonight the nationwide curfew had brought a blanket of grim silence over the Big Easy.

Somewhere, in the far distance, Vincent heard the sound of an unknown man singing Amazing Grace from a rooftop. The words carried in the silence, and left a surreal end-of-the-world feeling in Vincent's mind as they moved through the deserted streets and drove along the impressive causeway north across Lake Pontchartrain.

They reached St. Tammany Parish on the north side of the estuary and closed in on the target. Here, the land was still mostly below sea level, and the night was even hotter and more humid than back at the air base.

Vincent watched the flat, featureless landscape flash past as they continued to race north. It was a hot night, and the drab olive-colored trees reminded him vaguely of Provence. His mind drifted once again to his sons. It was all he needed to get the focus and determination required to terminate Kiefel and his underlings.

He pulled his phone out of his pocket and made a call to Marseille. He hadn't spoken to Monique for longer than he could remember, but now seemed like as good a time as ever. Like millions of other people in the world, wherever she was she had probably seen the YouTube film of Dirk Partridge and would be scared. He needed to reassure her and the boys that they were doing all they could to end the threat.

It rang for a long time, but there was no reply. He nodded his head sadly. Caller ID had struck again. Monique probably thought he was drunk and calling from a bar in Algiers like the last time. He switched the phone off, put it back in his pocket and glanced outside.

He stroked his handlebar moustache and after a moment to clear his head he loaded his trusty PAMAS G-1. The idea of his children being exposed to this nightmare and turned to stone filled him with a barely controllable fear, but he fought it back. It was what the Legion had trained him to do. There was always time to drown your sorrows, but now was never that time. Now was always about fighting.

"No one home?"

He turned to see Hawke beside him. "Not this time, mon ami. I expect they have gone to her mother's."

Reaper wiped the sweat from his brow and readied his weapon as they pulled up as near to the perimeter of the processing plant as they could get without giving themselves away. It was a thick mangrove forest. They shut the engines off and climbed out the Jeeps with their weapons.

Doyle was technically in charge of the operation, but had been briefed by Hawke on the best ingress strategy. Now, he led the team around the far edge of the mangrove forest and over the scrubby dead grass which formed a boundary between the processing plant and the rest of the world. Here, on a raised bank, they were able to establish a good overwatch position from which to survey the plant.

Hawke took a night-vision monocular and scanned the plant. "I see the Presidential limo down there. Its rear door is still open and it looks like it's been abandoned."

"Anything else?" Doyle asked.

"No, which is what worries me. Where is Kiefel's transport?"

"Only one way to find out," Scarlet said.

They reached the perimeter fence and with the aid of a pair of bolt-cutters they were through and crossed the outer zone in seconds. Vincent now saw why Kiefel would choose such a place to weaponize the bacteria – not only was it miles from anywhere but the place itself was labyrinthine in its construction.

As they got closer the true scale of the place dawned on them. The plant was a vast compound of various buildings, storage units and chimneys, all reflecting the bright Louisiana moonlight on their rusted metal exteriors. The wild jumble of buildings stretching all over the expansive compound was not exactly conducive to an easy search and rescue mission.

"Let's get in there!" Vincent said. "You think I want to be in this country any longer than I absolutely have to, Doyle?"

Hawke suppressed a laugh.

Doyle smiled. "Oh yeah, and I wish I lived in France *so* much."

The American Secret Service agent gave the order to move forward, and they headed straight across the enormous car park. Once it would have been full, but now the factory's disused status had turned it into real tumbleweed territory. Moments later they were pushing into the plant itself, where they fanned out and each took their own section to search.

After searching part of the isomerisation plant, Vincent heard Doyle's voice over the radio – he and Hawke had found what they were looking for.

By the time Vincent arrived, Doyle was in already in a rage.

"Damn it!" Doyle screamed. "They've moved out."

Vincent felt his anguish as he watched the American agent walk across the room and behold his old boss and mentor for the first time. Now, frozen in stone forever, Dirk Partridge stared into eternity, lifeless. Someone had slid Partridge's bifocals back onto his stone face. A form of casual mockery which they all knew was the ultimate act of disrespect.

"I swear I'll kill them all for this!" Doyle said.

Then they heard a creaking sound above them. They spun around and aimed their weapons on the air-conditioning duct grille.

"Don't shoot! Please, don't shoot, man!"

"Get down now!" Doyle screamed.

A man in a security guard uniform lowered himself out of the duct and landed with a gentle thump on the desk. He clambered down to the ground, his terrified face drained of color.

"Who are you?" Doyle asked.

"Name's Logan. I was working tonight's shift with Jenny Sanchez…" The man looked at his former colleague, now no more than a granite statue. "We got separated and when I ran out of bullets I hid up in the aircon ducts. I did *nothing* to save her!"

"What happened here, Logan?"

"They used the equipment in the distillation unit to weaponize the bacteria. That *thing*… I'll never forget what it looked like as long as I live…"

"We need more details than that."

"Whatever the hell they extracted from the head they installed into a couple of canisters. They said they were going to spray LA and New York with them."

"Where, exactly?"

"The place in LA belongs to the big boss – Kiefel, his name was. God *damn* it, that guy was crazy!"

"And what about New York?"

"I swear I don't know – they never said no more about it."

Hawke frowned. "Great – New York – that narrows it down."

Vincent sighed. "So what now?"

Hawke took a second. "You take Kim Taylor here and some SWAT and get over to LA. Me, Cairo and Doyle will go to New York in the meantime. We'll get

Alex and Ryan to work on the specific locations while we're in the air."

Vincent shrugged his shoulders. "It's as good a plan as any."

"So let's get on it."

*

The Learjet cruised thirty-five thousand feet above Virginia on a bearing of forty degrees. It would be landing in New York in a little over an hour and Hawke tried to clear his head. Now, he knew a man like Klaus Kiefel was capable of anything, and taking him out before he could execute the President or release the bacteria over Manhattan would be the greatest challenge he had faced.

Behind him, he heard Scarlet Sloane talking to Agent Doyle. A thin smile appeared on his lips when the next image in his mind was that of a cougar stalking a bunny rabbit. He had no doubts about Doyle's ability to fight a man like Kiefel, but defending himself against Cairo Sloane was a different matter altogether. On that score, the smart money either stayed in his pocket or backed Scarlet.

His mind turned to his other friends – those who were elsewhere in their own corners of the world, fighting other battles. He wondered how Vincent and Kim were holding up flying over to California to take out Kiefel's underlings and stop the annihilation of LA... then he thought about Lea, hunting down her past on the Irish coast – was she alone? He wished he could help her, but he guessed she didn't need it. Then, at some undefined moment, exhaustion finally overtook Joe Hawke and he started to fall asleep.

CHAPTER THIRTY

Charles Grant had faced many challenges in his life, from his time commanding a unit of special operations men in Vietnam's Khánh Hòa province all the way through his acting career, his time in the Senate and then the ultimate fight to the Oval Office itself. Tonight, however, he knew he faced the toughest test of his entire life – and perhaps the final test. Knowing the whole nation was watching, he steeled himself, determined to die with dignity. He knew this moment would be carved in history for eternity.

Now he watched, helpless, as the terrorists moved around him on the rear deck of the Perseus, Kiefel's super yacht. They had landed a few moments ago, having flown up from New Orleans out of a private airfield, taking full advantage of Kiefel's capacity to persuade Kimble to let their plane pass. Now, they were preparing for the final broadcast – Charles Grant's death. He knew it was no coincidence that Klaus Kiefel had moved the show to the Perseus – while the Americans were dealing with Manhattan and Los Angeles being turned into a statue park, he could slip into international waters.

He watched the German with disgust as he launched into another lecture on the many failings of America, but the final horror was only now revealed as Kiefel commanded Jakob to tie the President into his chair and position him on the deck so there was no way to tell they

THE CURSE OF MEDUSA

were in Midtown Manhattan. This meant it was time to die.

Kiefel raised his hands and used them to frame Grant as if he were checking the ergonomics of a piece of furniture. "Ja... das ist *perfekt*, nicht wahr?"

Jakob nodded, humorless, while Angelika smiled and made a comment in German too fast for Grant to catch.

Kiefel turned to Grant and grinned.

"I hope you're ready for your close-up, Charlie – it's Showtime!"

*

The atmosphere in the Situation Room was grim when the appointed hour arrived and everyone gathered around the plasma TV. President Kimble in particular looked very nervous, and had to lean against the desk for support as the image they had all been dreading flicked to life on the screen.

"Greetings America!" Kiefel said. He was standing beside Charles Grant who was now tied to what looked like a deck chair. He was gagged and blinking wildly in terror.

"He looks furious," Anderson said.

The President's executive secretary, Margot, dried her eyes with a gentle dab of her pocket handkerchief before turning away from the screen. "He looks scared, to me."

"He looks confused," added General McAlister, clenching his jaw.

Kiefel smiled grotesquely into the camera. "You know by now that I have the power to turn man to stone, and you also know I am prepared to use that power. Here, you see before you your former Commander-in-Chief, Charles Grant."

Kiefel made a big show of looking at his watch. "It is incumbent upon me to tell you Mr Grant has less than an hour to live. How sad."

Grant struggled against the ropes but they were too tight.

"After Mr Grant has been turned into a garden ornament for my estate, I will turn this awesome power on the American people. Only in this way will my mother be avenged."

The image was cut and the screen went black.

In the Situation Room, all eyes turned to the President, but it was Brooke, still irritated at being summoned back to the White House by Kimble, who spoke next.

"Someone get me Joe Hawke!"

*

President Edward D. Kimble couldn't seem to stop his fingers from drumming on the edge of the Resolute Desk. After the video of Grant on the yacht, he had returned from the Situation Room alone, more than a little shaken by what he had seen.

Now, he glanced at the imposing grandfather clock by the door – the same one Charles Grant had installed on his first day as Commander-in-Chief. He felt an uncomfortable wave of nausea rise in his stomach. If everything was going according to plan, his German puppet-master would be televising the execution of his predecessor very soon. All that remained then would be Kiefel's pièce de résistance – his long-held desire to turn large swathes of the global population into a theme park full of human statues, starting with America.

Maybe, just maybe, Kimble thought... *I could use my new power as the President to liberate Klaus Kiefel from his madness – permanently...*

The thought was an intriguing one. Perhaps, he thought, he was settling into the Big Chair at last.

It was time to give Klaus Kiefel a call and put an end to the insanity.

CHAPTER THIRTY-ONE

Racing north, thirty-five thousand feet above America, Hawke and his team watched the latest film with equal revulsion. Scarlet had woken Hawke to see the live YouTube broadcast, and he'd watched it in a state of genuine disbelief. Before anyone could voice a reaction, the pilot communicated to them that the US Secretary of Defense was on an incoming call from the Oval Office. Seconds later they were gathered around the screen on the cabin partition wall.

Hawke watched as the Oval Office appeared on the screen. The atmosphere looked bleak.

"Joe, this is Jack Brooke. I take it you just saw the broadcast?"

"Us and the rest of the planet," Hawke said.

"We need to work faster on this, Joe…"

"I know, Jack… I know."

Hawke watched Anderson pacing up and down the room behind Brooke. He ran a hand through his graying hair. "We need to find out where the hell they are and in a hurry."

"We have the location of the target in LA," Brooke said. "Kiefel owns a luxury beach house in Santa Monica. He sent two of his people out there – his lover Angelika Schwartz and the Australian Alan Pauling, his tech guy. We already told Agent Taylor and Vincent Reno and they're on their way."

"But we're still in the dark about the location in New York…"

Kimble was silent.

"Did you hear me, sir?" Anderson said.

"Mr President!" McAlister's bassy voice filled the room. Kimble looked up, shocked, as if shaken from a reverie.

"Sorry, what?"

"It is critical we locate this place. We cannot let this maniac execute a former President live on the internet, not to mention whatever the hell he has planned next."

"Right, yes," Kimble said. "What do you suggest, General?"

"Get this latest video analysed. I know the last ones gave us nothing, but if there's anything on there at all – a certain type of unique sound, anything – then we might get something to go on, and then we can..."

"Wait a minute," Hawke said.

Silence fell over the room and everyone turned to face the Englishman on the screen.

"What is it, Hawke?" McAlister said.

"Play back the video once again."

"Which one?"

"The last one – the one we just watched a second ago. Play it back there and I'll do the same up here."

A staffer re-played the YouTube video and the same grim silence fell over the room.

"We're wasting time!" Anderson boomed. "You heard him – he's going to kill Grant any minute now!"

"No – look carefully," Hawke said. "Do you see?"

"What is it, Hawke?" Kimble said, leaving his desk for the first time and walking over to the TV. '"What do you see?"

"Look at Grant – the way he's blinking."

"He's terrified, God damn it!" Anderson said. "What the hell does that have to do with anything? Turn this off!"

McAlister stepped forward and raised his hand. "No – wait. I think I know what's going on here."

"And just what the hell is that?" Anderson said.

"Remember Jeremiah Denton?"

"Who?" Anderson said.

"You're obviously too young to remember," McAlister said. "Or too ignorant to know."

"Wait just a God damn minute, General!" Anderson snapped. "I'm the Chief-of-Staff to the President of the United States and you will address me with..."

McAlister cut him off. "Ah, shut up!"

Anderson looked to Kimble for back-up, but the President shook his head and spoke. His voice sounded anxious. "Admiral Denton was a US Navy man, wasn't he, General?"

"That's right, sir."

"Continue."

"Yes, Mr President. Jeremiah Denton was a naval aviator in the Vietnam War who was shot down over Thanh Hoa in the north. He was held as a prisoner of war for eight years, half of which was spent in solitary confinement."

"What has this got to do with our current situation, General?" Anderson said.

Hawke passed a hand over his eyes and tried to get more focus. "Admiral Denton was paraded on TV by the Vietnamese as a war trophy. His presence was supposed to show the world that American POWs were being treated with respect, but Denton managed to tell the entire world otherwise. Right under the noses of the enemy, while being filmed for their disgusting little propaganda exercise, he told the entire world that he, and the other men being held as POWs, were all being tortured."

"And how did he do that?" Anderson said

"Haven't you worked it out yet?" Hawke said, sighing. "Bloody career politicians!"

"Don't wast our time, Hawke!"

"He blinked the word *torture* in Morse code while he was on TV, right in front of his torturers. He was a true hero."

Anderson looked at him like he was crazy. "And you think President Grant was doing the same?"

"I bloody know he was, because when you were shitting your pants about how I was wasting your precious time I translated the Morse and worked out what he was saying."

For the first time, Anderson was speechless.

McAlister smiled and looked at the Englishman, expectant. "What did he say, Hawke?"

"Unfortunately I couldn't get the entire message because Kiefel's elbow moves in front of the President's eyes at the start and blocks some of it. But the fragment remaining clearly says something about Perseus."

Anderson scoffed. "What good is that?"

"Thanks to Logan back at the processing plant, we already know he was moved to New York City, so now we have this Perseus clue to go on as well. I don't know about you but I'd rather have that information than nothing. Get Ryan and Alex on it right away."

"Agreed," Brooke said firmly. "If anyone can get to the bottom of this shit, then it's my Alex."

*

As the jet screeched down on the asphalt in New York, Hawke readied himself for a fight. He looked outside and saw a military helicopter already on stand-by on the apron, fuelled up, blades whirring and waiting for them. Doyle and Scarlet were already kitted up with their gear and waiting to go. It hadn't taken Alex and Ryan more than a few minutes to discover that a super yacht named the Perseus was sailed into New York Harbor several weeks ago and was still there, moored to a pier on the west side of Midtown Manhattan.

A few short minutes after touch-down they were climbing above the airport in the same chopper Hawke had spied from the jet and banking in the direction of the Hudson River.

He watched almost dreamily as the world's most famous skyline approached from the west. They rose higher into the air over the East River and Roosevelt Island, and moments later they were crossing the southern tip of Central Park. It was full-dark and lit by countless thousands of sparkling street lights, but Hawke recalled with a faint smile the last time he had seen it when he, Lea and Ryan were in pursuit of Kaspar Vetsch. They had torn half the park up in the chase and eventually wound up in the custody of the CIA. All of that seemed like another age to him now.

Tonight, the curfew had turned Manhattan into a ghost town, and everyone was locked in their apartments waiting for the danger to pass. Everyone except Hawke and his friends.

The chopper began to descend as they approached Hell's Kitchen and after a few words were squawked through their earpieces, the pilot deftly lowered the collective and brought the helicopter down into the middle of DeWitt Clinton Park. Before the skids had touched down on the grass, Hawke, Scarlet and Doyle were prepping their weapons.

They sprinted across the park and over 12th Avenue until they reached the east bank of the Hudson and saw the Perseus moored up on Pier 84.

Hawke checked his gun one last time and briefed the others. "All right, we know we can't storm the yacht fast enough to save the President and stop Kiefel from releasing the weapon. That's why we're going underwater."

"Once a bloody frogman, always a bloody frogman," Scarlet said.

"Don't start all this SAS-SBS bullshit," Hawke said smiling. "The only reason you joined the SAS is because you can't smoke cigarettes underwater." He turned and looked at her straight in the eyes, deadpan. "Be honest."

"I could slap you sometimes, Joe."

"Will these things still work?" Doyle asked, pointing at his gun. "We don't do a whole lot of underwater espionage training in the Secret Service."

"They'll fire underwater, sure," Hawke said, "but obviously the range will be reduced. We don't have to worry about that because we're not going to do any underwater firing. This mission is about a covert insertion on that bloody yacht and then when we're on board we find the President. You will then swim with him back to the shore while Cairo and I take-out Kiefel and his cronies and secure the weapon."

"Got it."

"I'm sure I don't have to tell anyone here that when we're on board hold the bolts on your weapons back and drain the water from the chambers before you fire."

They crouched low as they made their way along the pier on the east bank of the Hudson River. Then they used a line of rowan trees as cover as they drew nearer to the Perseus and reached the water-line.

Hawke slipped into the river first. He immediately felt the dark, cold water of the Hudson as it surrounded him. His years in the Special Boat Service meant if anywhere was home, then this was it, but he knew a US

Secret Service agent like Doyle, and even to a certain extent Scarlet with her SAS background, wouldn't be as comfortable underwater as he was. Diving was an unsettling experience for some even at the best of times, never mind in dark, cold, moving water at night, with explosives strapped to your back and the possibility of people shooting at you.

He held his breath and dived silently into the black water.

CHAPTER THIRTY-TWO

Vincent Reno paused at the entrance to the luxury Santa Monica beachfront estate and took a few seconds to take it all in. It was in the Spanish Colonial revival style, stretching right down to the beach. It didn't seem the sort of place that would suit a militant German terrorist with a revenge obsession, but despite the ornate statues and carefully manicured gardens, he knew Angelika Schwartz and Alan Pauling were here. They had to stop them before they launched the drone and released the weaponized bacteria into the skies above America's second largest city.

Kim Taylor finished briefing the SWAT team and joined Vincent at the hacienda's outer gates. She whistled through her front teeth as she cast her eye over what she could see of the property through the black wrought-iron gates.

"Place like this must cost twenty million dollars," she said, shaking her head.

Vincent nodded and smiled. "Amazing what a few arms deals can purchase…"

"Must have a hell of an ocean view out the back."

Vincent gave a Gallic shrug and tipped his head. "I prefer the mountains."

"You can have your mountains," the American agent said. "I want to see that ocean view."

"But this place is like Fort Knox," Vincent said. "Are we going over the walls?"

Kim shook her head and grinned. "No, we're doing it the fun way."

"You give up the element of surprise?" asked the Frenchman with surprise.

"This *is* the surprise," she said, as she ordered an explosive breaching of the gate. "They already know we're here thanks to Pauling's extensive surveillance," she said, pointing to the cameras all over the property. "Plus the perimeter's covered by our guys. This assault is about going in hard, fast and nasty."

Vincent nodded his head in appreciation and flicked his cigarette into the impressive bank of blue agapanthus flowers swaying in the breeze along the outer wall. "I can do hard, fast and nasty." He took a deep breath and looked up at the moon, now setting over the ocean. "Ce soir, la lune rêve avec une plus de paresse, ainsi qu'une beauté, sur de nombreux coussins... "

Kim Taylor stared at him, confused. "What hell is that?"

"Just some words for the moon, mon ami. Maybe one day I tell you what they mean." Vincent checked his PAMAS before holstering it and then readied a Heckler & Koch submachine gun for combat.

"If we get through this alive then that's a deal. I always wanted to impress someone with French poetry."

Vincent smiled, recalling the time he met Monique in Montpelier. "With these words, Agent Taylor, you cannot fail."

The SWAT man advanced with some Cordtex and deftly wrapped the pentaerythritol tetranitrate detcord around the central gate-bars either side of the substantial lock before withdrawing to cover. Seconds later the high-explosive detonated and blasted the entire central section of the gates to oblivion. Vincent, Kim and the SWAT team were through and into the property before the smoke had cleared.

The SWAT men sprinted to their designated areas at the sides and rear of the hacienda while Vincent and Kim headed for the main entrance. The hacienda was built around an opulent central courtyard with an expansive swimming pool at its center, and they knew from the satellite surveillance that the helicopter drone was parked on the west lawn in between the pool and the property's beach-front perimeter wall.

Now, Vincent and Kim blasted their way toward the hacienda's thick oak-panelled double doors at the main entrance before the Frenchman threw a SWAT-issue flash-bang grenade into the hall. The explosion rocked the stone Tuscan-order columns either side of the entrance and then a second later belched a thin cloud of white smoke out of the hole where the door used to be.

They entered the hall, guns raised and ready for booby-traps, but there was nothing there.

"Clear!" Kim shouted, adhering to protocol in a way that put the briefest of smiles on Vincent Reno's face.

Glancing up at the top of a long-winding staircase of white marble to ensure there was no one above waiting to pour fire on them, they moved forward into the main section of the hacienda, passing through the largest kitchen Vincent had ever seen.

A vision of his twin boys waiting patiently for breakfast while their mother ground the coffee and warmed the milk flashed in and out of his mind in less than a second. He had to concentrate – those boys needed a father to guide them, not a grave to visit. In his line of work he had seen that happen too many times.

Now, exiting the kitchen and making their way into a games room the fighting began. They dived for cover behind a pool table, and while Kim radioed the attack to the other SWAT men, Vincent peered around the table to see a woman with spiky hair he instantly recognized.

"Angelika Schwartz!" he called to Kim. "Ten meters, behind the bar."

Kim nodded to show she understood and radioed the information back to HQ.

As bullets raced over their heads and drilled into the wall behind them, Vincent struggled to get an angle with the submachine gun so shouldered it and switched to the PAMAS, firing a ferocious succession of nine mils at the enormous Jägermeister bar mirror on the wall above where Angelika was taking cover. It shattered into thousands of lethal shards which rained down on the German hired-gun. He heard her scream and then the sound of her boots crunching on the glass as she tried to extricate herself from the situation.

Vincent was merciless. Thinking again of his boys, he fired another series of bullets at the woman as she sprinted across the room and dived through the open window into the courtyard. As she ran, she fired her Heckler & Koch USP blindly at them, blasting chunks out of the pool table and sending a shower of tulipwood and maple splinters into the air. One of her bullets hit a No. 8 ball and it exploded into a cloud of phenolic resin which impressed the Frenchman more than it should have.

More submachine-gun fire was coming now from their right, and they darted their eyes outside the games room to see Angelika had rallied two more men with weapons to defend the property. Behind them, on the far side of the pool, Vincent saw Alan Pauling in the dim glow of an exterior louvred wall-light as he fitted the canister of weaponized bacteria to the helicopter drone and crouch-walked across the lawn to the pool house.

"Bastard must be controlling it from there!" Kim shouted, pinned down by the submachine-gun fire. "We have to get to him before he takes that thing off and flies it over L.A!"

Vincent nodded grimly, visualizing all the thousands of innocent men, woman and children sleeping in their beds as they breathed in the bacteria and were instantly turned to stone forever. "That's the name of the game, mon ami!"

*

On board the Perseus, Kiefel stared at the muscle-bound Jakob with undisguised hatred for a few moments, scowling at the interruption.

"*Was*?!" he barked at him in German.

"Telefon!" Jakob said, and took a cautious step toward the boss.

Kiefel snatched the phone from him and spoke. "Who is this?"

"It's the President," Kimble said.

Kiefel immediately noticed a change in his tone. He sounded... less frightened.

"What do you want, Teddy? I'm busy."

"I've been thinking over the terms and conditions of our agreement and I think it's time to modify the details."

"What are you talking about? If you cross me I'll release your files to the world."

"Is that worth your life, Klaus? That is the question you must ask yourself."

Kiefel scowled. "You're calling my bluff, Teddy? I never thought you had it in you."

"Don't push me, Klaus. I know we had a deal but I can't let you murder Grant."

"Perhaps you give me some time to think it over."

"Well..."

Kiefel cut the phone call and turned to Jakob. "Contact the girl in Washington. See to it that President Kimble has an accident."

"Jawohl," said Jakob.

"And ready the helicopter. It's time to start Operation Medusa."

Jakob nodded and left the cabin.

CHAPTER THIRTY-THREE

Hawke was the first to reach the hull of the Perseus, and gently made his way around to the portside boarding ladder, remaining submerged the entire time. They knew from their CIA briefing while on the flight from New Orleans that the yacht had two stainless steel retractable gangways, controlled by a simple hydraulic system, but the control pads were on deck. They also knew that on the portside near the bow there was a non-retractable ladder, so this was their entry point.

Hawke emerged from the water in silence and drew his SIG. He pulled himself from the water as quietly as he could and climbed up the ladder. On the deck now, he slipped into the shadows and waited for the others. Not for the first time in his life he wondered why he wasn't in bed, waiting for the dawn of another day in a normal life. That was what most people did, he thought. Who the hell chose to spend their time in freezing cold water under enemy boats?

He did, he guessed, and that was something he just had to live with. For one thing, he had too much trouble imagining himself doing anything else, and that's what had frightened him about leaving the SBS and starting up his security company. Colliding with Lea Donovan and Sir Richard Eden back at the British Museum that day had in many ways saved his life.

As he waited in the silence of the night, he thought he heard one of Kiefel's goons on the deck above him moving toward the steps leading down to him, but it was nothing, and then out of nowhere his mind turned to his family. Maybe it was because Alex had been asking him about it all so recently, he wasn't sure. Alex, and especially Lea, had a right to know about his family and his background, but for some reason he was reluctant to share that part of his life with them.

Talking about himself wasn't something he was used to, and neither was he very good at it. Sharing private information with others wasn't exactly high on the list in the Royal Marines Commandos, and it certainly wasn't something that the men in his unit of the SBS liked to spend their free time doing either. He had lived like that for so long that now it was normal to compartmentalize his life into subunits like this and keep them apart from one another. When someone asked him to start talking about his family, his first thought was always the same – why?

Now the same noise – a muffled footfall on the deck directly above his head. He held his breath and readied his pistol as he waited, frozen like a statue in the shadow of the steps, but again no one came. Instead, he heard some tuneless whistling and then someone spat into the river.

Doyle emerged over the side of the yacht, slightly breathless with the effort of the underwater swim but otherwise in good shape, and as he moved silently into the shadows to join Hawke, they both watched with relief as Scarlet appeared, the top of her wet hair and shoulders reflecting some moonlight as the clouds shifted above the city.

Besides, he thought, his mind returning to family – it wasn't just him who liked to keep things to himself. What was Lea doing right now? She was chasing ghosts across Ireland – ghosts he knew nothing about… and she was fighting a battle he knew nothing about, against an enemy he knew nothing about. She had kept it from him in the way he had never told her, or anyone else, about his life growing up in London. Maybe, he thought as he watched Scarlet extract her SIG and cock it, it was time for everyone to start being more honest with each other.

But now it was time to focus. They shared a look which they all knew meant it was time to move out, and began the mission to save the President and secure the weapon.

Halfway up one of the external staircases they noticed a guard who was asleep, lulled by the moonlight and the motion of the yacht on the river. Scarlet won paper, scissors, rock and stalked up to him, grabbing him roughly around the neck with one hand and jamming the muzzle of her SIG into his face.

"Call out and you're dead before you hit the water, yes?"

The man nodded, his eyes wide open with fear and surprise. "Ja – Ich verstehe."

"Good. Where is Kiefel?" To help things along, Scarlet pushed the gun harder into the man's cheek.

"Oberstleutnant Kiefel is on the rear deck with the President."

"Excellent – and where is the weapon?"

"The weapon is being fitted to a helicopter drone on the helipad as we speak – directly above us here on the top deck."

Scarlet moved the weapon and pushed the rim of the suppressor into the man's chest.

"Nicht schießen! Ich habe Kinder... *I have children!*"

"Wrong," Scarlet said. "Sie *hatten* Kinder – you *had* children."

The man opened his mouth to scream, but Scarlet discharged the weapon before he could make a sound. His dead body slumped onto the deck, and Hawke and Doyle lowered him into the water to get him out of sight.

"I had no idea you spoke German," Hawke said, impressed.

"Picked it up in Bielefeld."

"That's right – I forgot the army spends so much time in Germany. Maybe that's where you got your sense of humor?"

Scarlet smiled. "Maybe you should start collecting better jokes?"

"Like your collection of medieval bollock daggers you mean?" Hawke said.

"How do you know about that?" Scarlet said, raising an eyebrow.

Doyle stepped out of the shadows. "I hate to break up the obvious sexual tension, but I want everyone to remember that we are not to move against the President until we have secured the weapon. If Kiefel gets wind of this operation before we can disable the drone and secure the canister, all he has to do is push a button and that thing's airborne over Manhattan and we're all dead, clear?"

"Clear as daylight," Scarlet said.

"Good. Let's move out."

They divided into two units, as planned. Hawke and Scarlet made their way up the steps to the top deck and the helipad while Doyle moved toward the stern where Kiefel was holding President Grant.

It was time to end Kiefel's assault on America.

CHAPTER THIRTY-FOUR

Seeing Taobh na Gréine for the first time in so many years brought back some serious memories for Lea Donovan. It didn't take her long to work out the last time she had set foot on the property. It was the day she and her mother had locked the place up after her father's death. Her mother had vowed never to return and she had kept to her vow. She was good at sticking to a vow.

Lea didn't have to try so hard. She was only a young girl, and did as her mother told her. Then when she was older she joined the army and left the county. She needed no vow to stay away from Taobh na Gréine.

"So, are we going in or are we going to stand here all damned night?" She turned to see Danny Devlin at her side. The sea breeze was ruffling his greying hair and part of his face was obscured behind his trademark up-turned coat collars.

She nodded. "Of course we're going in. We've got to go in. I want to know why someone murdered my father, and the answer's in this cottage."

Now it was Devlin's turn to nod in understanding. "So, you have a key?"

"Dad always kept one under that pot over there by the garage – where he used to keep his motorbike."

Lea walked across the drive, her boots crunching on the loose gravel chips. She shivered and pulled her coat up around her as she knelt to tip up the pot. Spending so much time in the Caribbean she always forgot how cold Ireland could get sometimes, even in the summer.

"Sod it."

"Not there?"

She shook her head. "Stupid to think it would be here after so long. Mum probably took it somewhere. She hated the place after Dad died."

"So how are we going to get in?"

Before Lea could reply, they all heard the sound of breaking glass. Lea stood and turned to see Mikey grinning at them. "By the way, I just put a brick through the kitchen window."

"A genius solution," Devlin said.

Lea reached inside the shattered window and flicked open the lock. "And so stealthy, too."

Inside now, they began the search. Mikey and Kyle took downstairs while Lea and Devlin searched the bedrooms upstairs. Luckily, her mother had removed most of their belongings over the years, so the ghost-count was lower than Lea had feared, but there were still occasional items that transported her back in time – the rocking chair by the window, the smell of some leftover linen in the airing cupboard... the pencil marks on the back of the door where her father had measured her height when she was growing up.

She felt a flood of relief that whoever had killed McNamara hadn't known about the cottage or they would have destroyed this place as well. She thanked God her mother had bought it in her maiden name before the marriage.

After clambering down from the loft hatch, Devlin announced the whole place had been searched from top to bottom, and when Mikey and Kyle emerged through the bedroom door, they concurred.

"Wait a minute!" Lea said. "There's somewhere we haven't tried yet – when I was a kid, me and my brothers used to play hide and seek here. I used to hide in a secret place I thought only I knew about. They never found me when I hid there, but Dad must have known about it."

"Where is it?"

"Downstairs in the kitchen – there's a hatch in the larder floor leading to a small cellar where they used to store meat in the old days when it got too hot."

They hurried downstairs and Lea opened the hatch with bated breath… this was the moment that her entire journey hinged on. If it wasn't in here then it was lost forever.

"Is it there, Lea?" Devlin asked, trying to look over her shoulder.

Lea smiled, then her eyes filled with tears. "I think so, Danny… I hope so."

She picked it up and blew a heavy layer of dust from the box-file. "Oh my God… this must be it."

She stared at the file for what seemed like forever, her eyes wide with anxiety. She pulled it from the small compartment and walked it out into the candle light of the main kitchen.

Devlin moved closer. "What's the problem?"

"I… I'm scared of what I might find in here, that's all."

"Do you want Uncle Mikey to look first?"

She looked up, startled by O'Sullivan's booming voice so close. He too was standing almost beside her, and Kyle a foot to his right. It seemed everyone was more than a little curious about the contents of Dr Harry Donovan's enigmatic box-file.

Lea tried to smile, but it wouldn't come. "No… this is something I have to do. Maybe this is where my whole life has been pointing."

Lea walked to the table and took another moment simply to stare at the old, dusty box-file before her. She knew the last person to have touched it would have been her father, and that alone made her sad before she even opened it to see what he had been researching - what he had looked into that had cost him his life – what had caused some bastard to take her father away from her when she was so young.

"Jeez, would ya just open the thing already!"

"Can it, Mikey," Devlin said, his voice suddenly all business. "She'll open it when she's ready. In the meantime, now we've found the fucking thing maybe you and Lurch over there could go outside and keep an eye out. It's not like we had an easy time getting here. Whoever tried to take us out back in Dublin might not give up as easily as you two jokers."

Mikey took the hint and he and Kyle picked up the shotguns and went outside the cottage where they stood either side of the door.

Devlin put a hand on her shoulder. "In your own time, Lea. They can wait. We can all wait."

"I hope that's a fatherly hand, Danny, and nothing else."

He smiled, and removed the hand. "It's a reassuring hand, Lea. That's all."

Lea managed an insincere smile and opened the box-file.

Then she gasped so loudly she almost made Kyle Byrne jump out of his skin.

Mikey looked at Kyle and suppressed a chuckle. He leaned his head into the kitchen and lowered his voice. "What the hell is it, woman?"

Lea was silent for a few moments. When she spoke, her voice was trembling.

"It's worse than I could have imagined."

CHAPTER THIRTY-FIVE

Vincent Reno watched with admiration as Kim Taylor fought her way closer to the luxury pool house. It was a hard slog through half a dozen men paid handsomely by Kiefel to defend the drone.

In response, the French mercenary fired a non-stop barrage of rounds into the defensive positions held by Kiefel's men and kept them pinned down, but he was also being kept busy by Angelika Schwartz and her impressive determination to blow his head off.

Vincent saw a chance to hit the drone and he started to fire. Pauling saw what was happening and ran for cover, leaving the canister behind. A second later Vincent hit the drone and it exploded all over the rear yard, sending a fireball into the night sky.

Then, using the cover of a row of California palms, he sprinted in the shadows until he was across the south lawn and finally joined Kim at the pool house. It didn't take too long for a very dangerous and angry Angelika Schwartz to snatch the canister and join Pauling. A second later she had picked off another two of Kim's men with startling ease and accuracy before ordering Pauling in broken English to retreat to the back room of the pool house.

She shoved the Australian through the door and walked backwards, firing lethal shots as she went, pausing only to tear some cloth off her shirt and stuff it into Pauling's vodka bottle. She lit the end of the cloth with the burning cigarette in her mouth and tossed the bottle at the entrance of the pool house. It struck the arched doorway and smashed, spreading vodka all over the walls and pool chairs. Instantly the burning cloth ignited the spirit and moments later the front of the pool house was ablaze.

"Move forward!" Kim shouted, unperturbed by the flames. "They're on the back foot."

Vincent was the first inside, covering his face from the heat of the fire with the back of his arm. He moved forward, gun raised while Kim and her remaining men were just a pace behind. Somewhere in here, he thought, Klaus Kiefel's West Coast operation was about to come to an abrupt end.

They reached the changing room – a large, expansive affair of polished teak floorboards and fluffy white towels hanging over the backs of wooden pool chairs. Vincent caught a fast movement in the corner of his eye and turned his head to see Angelika blasting the lock out of an external door at the rear of the pool house. She fired two or three shots at them blindly before the two of them exited the pool house and slammed the door.

Then they heard another isolated shot.

Vincent and Kim were there a second later, and while the Frenchman tried to open the door, the American agent used her palm mic to order more of her men to the rear of the building to cut them off.

"Is anyone reading this?"

"What's the problem?" Vincent asked.

"No response. I think all my men are down. What's the problem with you?"

"Damned door is stuck," the Frenchman said. He tried to shoulder it open but it didn't move an inch.

"They must have pushed something up against it," Kim said.

Vincent frowned. "Step aside."

THE CURSE OF MEDUSA

When Kim was safely out of the way the former Foreign Legion man fired a long burst of bullets into the top panel of the door until it was reduced to matchwood. He then smashed out what was left with the butt of the gun and peered through the hole to see the problem.

Alan Pauling was dead and wedged up against the door.

"She must have shot him and used him as a kind of door wedge," Kim said.

Vincent nodded his head thoughtfully. "Why can't I find a woman like that?"

*

In the tense silence of the Oval Office, President Kimble waited anxiously for the telephone to ring. He was almost totally sure that Kiefel would call off the murder of Grant if it meant saving his own life.

Almost.

Now, he watched as the young woman brought the coffee into the room. Her name was Veronika Fischer, but it had become Veronica Fisher when Kiefel had arranged for her to apply for the job six months ago.

"Just put it down there," Kimble said without a smile. A lot was riding on the next few minutes. If Kiefel didn't comply he knew he would have to give the order to kill him.

Veronika gently placed the coffee on the small table either side of the couches in the center of the room. "Would you like me to pour the cream and sugar?" she asked in a faultless Maine accent. Her beautiful smile sealed the deal.

"Yes… thanks – one sugar only please."

The former spy and mercenary gently poured the cream into one of the cups and filled the rest of the cup with hot, fresh coffee until it was almost at the brim. Then, with equally placid movements she spooned one rounded teaspoon of sugar into the warm drink and smoothly stirred until the grains had all dissolved and the coffee was ready for the President.

He watched her as she picked up the cup by the rim of the fine china saucer and stepped slowly over to him. She gave him another one of those smiles. He could get used to those, he thought.

Kimble continued to stare at the phone as she gently placed the cup and saucer on his desk. He barely noticed when she broke protocol and moved around behind him to return to the tray in the corner of the room.

He was about to ask what she was doing when she made things a little clearer by drawing her leather belt off her waist and slipping it around his neck, pulling it as tight as she could.

"Mit freundlicher Empfehlung von Herr Kiefel," she said with cold hatred.

Kimble spoke not a word of German, but he knew from the last word what was happening and he knew why – his attempt to blackmail Kiefel had gone badly wrong.

He kicked out against the heavy desk and reached up with his hands, but she was pulling the belt so tight he couldn't even get his fingers beneath it to pull it away from his neck. It bit into the flesh on his throat and pushed down hard on his windpipe.

He tried to call out, but the constriction just wouldn't allow it, and now he felt the blood pooling in his head, making him dizzy.

"Margot!" he croaked as the belt crushed down on his windpipe. "Margot, get help!"

With a final burst of energy he managed to stagger up from the chair and drag the woman halfway across the room, where he spun around and fell backwards. They both fell down, the woman first. Her back smashed into the coffee tray and the shattered crockery pushed into her back. She cried out, but never let go off the belt.

Kimble turned again, driven by the base instinct to survive and using his heavier weight to gain some superiority against the woman, but it was too little too late. They tripped back over and this time went forward with Kimble's face smashing into the small coffee table. It collapsed under the weight of the two of them, its daintily carved mahogany legs buckling outwards and snapping into splinters.

"Margot! Call the Secret Service..!"

They rolled twice more, and Kimble was able to look under the couch through the open door leading to Margot's office. He strained as he stared out into his executive secretary's room and realized all hope was gone when he saw Margot's dead body on the floor. A look of abject terror was frozen on her face by the nascent rigor mortis, and a telephone cord was still digging deep into the soft skin of her throat.

Now, he could feel the weight of the woman as she tightened the slim leather belt around his neck, her knees pushing into the small of his back and stopping him from moving. The blood rushed into his head as he strained for the final breath he would ever take, and then his world began to fade.

His last sounds were that of the woman whispering something in German... *"Sie werden als Verräter sterben..."*

Her words were drowned out by the sound of his own tortured breathing, and then the room began to go dark. At first, his cortisol-flooded brain told him the lights were fading, but then he realized with a last gasp of horror that he was losing consciousness.

His last sight was that of the Presidential Seal on the rug, now seen up-close with his face pushed into the carpet weave.

An ignominious way to die, he thought, and then it was over.

CHAPTER THIRTY-SIX

Hawke and Scarlet used the cover of night and the shadows caused by the beams supporting the radar arch above the helipad to move unnoticed toward Jakob. He was fitting the canister to a manned helicopter drone, and the Englishman moved silently forward and raised his silenced weapon, ready to shoot him.

Then a car backfired on the West Side Highway. Hawke cursed – another curfew breaker, or looters maybe.

Jakob spun around instinctively and saw Hawke and Scarlet in the shadows just a few yards from him. In a second the German bodybuilder leaped into the helicopter and raised the collective, slowly lifting it into the air.

Hawke and Scarlet fired at the chopper drone but realized with horror that there was a chain gun fitted to the front of it. They dived for cover behind a lifeboat when Jakob opened fire on them, holding the manned drone in a steady hover about fifty feet above the yacht. The downdraft from the blades lifted water from the pool and sprayed it all over them as the heavy duty rounds from the chain gun drilled into the deck, tearing up the polished teak and shredding the fiber-glass sides of the pool.

Inside the drone, Jakob was laughing hysterically.

"We have to stop him!" Hawke yelled. "The canister is attached to the bottom of the chopper. They're obviously planning on flying through Manhattan and releasing it into the atmosphere there."

"What do you propose?" Scarlet shouted over the sound of the rotors and chain gun. "Using your martial arts skills to karate chop the bullets away?"

"No... Actually I want to use you as bait..."

"You're so romantic, Joe – I almost wish I never had to set eyes on you again."

"But I know you'd miss me," he said.

"Only if I sneezed when I pull the trigger."

Hawke gave her a look, and then without another word, Scarlet leaped up from their cover behind the lifeboat and sprinted toward the front of the yacht. Jakob immediately turned to fire on her, giving Hawke the chance he was looking for. He ran forward and gripped the starboard skid of the drone with both hands, as if he were about to do a chin-up exercise, and then pulled himself up until his body was hanging over it.

Scarlet disappeared inside the yacht, and Jakob gave up the chase. He turned the drone toward the Manhattan skyline and began to gain altitude rapidly. Hawke clung on for his life. He knew he had seconds to make the decision of whether or not to let go – either he let go now while he was still low enough to survive the fall or he would be forced to hold on for the whole ride – whatever that meant.

In his mind there was no decision – if he let go now Jakob would be on his way over Manhattan in seconds and Kiefel would have won. Wherever this thing was going, Hawke knew he was going along for the ride, and his eyes desperately stared with more than a small degree of terror at the canister he had seen Jakob fitting to the base. If that thing opened its deadly cargo while he was hanging onto the drone, there was going to be a perfect life-size statue of Joe Hawke on the bottom of the Hudson River.

It was then he noticed that it was on a timer – counting down from five minutes. That didn't give him a lot of time to get things sorted out as far as he was concerned, but it was all he had to work with. Unfortunately, the canister was fitted to a specially constructed bracket and bolted into place. It was impossible to get it loose without shooting at it and that went against his long-standing policy of not shooting at any aircraft that he was hanging off the bottom of – so he had to think again.

It was time to persuade Jakob Müller to turn the helicopter around.

*

Scarlet felt a maternal *awww* moment when she watched Agent Doyle taking cover behind Kiefel's upper deck bar. She peered around the door of the room and saw the German laughing deeply as he took casual pot-shots at the American, one hand on his hip in a display of nonchalant mockery.

"Would you like a vodka, my friend?" Kiefel asked. He shot the vodka bottle and sprayed the drink all over Doyle's head. "Or perhaps a bourbon is more your thing?" Another shot blasted through a bottle of Jim Beam and the spirit showered down over him mixing with the vodka.

"Mock this, you bastard," she said, and spun around the door frame with her Heckler & Koch submachine gun.

Kiefel turned in horror as the Englishwoman gripped the powerful weapon and unleashed a merciless volley of automatic fire at him. He dived for cover amidst the deathly *dunk dunk dunk* sound as the bullets exploded from the gun's muzzle and traced all around him.

Doyle looked up and nodded. "Am I glad to see you! Ran out of bullets about two minutes ago…"

"Here, take this," she said. Without so much as glancing at Doyle, she pulled the SIG from her belt and tossed it at him. She also tossed him a gas mask from her pack. "Wear it, now."

Kiefel fled the room, and Doyle took the weapon, checked it was loaded and moved forward in pursuit of the German. Scarlet paused to toss her lighter into the pool of spirits behind the bar, igniting them in a rush of flames which started to burn their way up the sides of Kiefel's luxury bar. "One good turn deserves another."

Outside, she saw Doyle chasing Kiefel down to the front deck. She watched in horror as the German dragged a man out of a chair and held a gun to his head. It was President Grant. Kiefel fumbled with the camera, desperate now, but determined to get his revenge.

"Get back or I kill him! It's all being broadcast live on the internet!"

Doyle froze where he was, but Scarlet saw her chance. She made her way down the side steps, out of sight.

"Where are you, English lady?" Kiefel called out. "Come out or I kill Mr Grant. I count to ten."

"Ten…" Scarlet thought. "That should just about give me enough time."

*

Hawke clambered over the skid and wrenched open the door on the passenger's side of the drone. Hundreds of feet above the ground, the night air whistled around him and the downdraft buffeted him as he tried to climb inside.

Jakob saw him immediately and turned in the pilot's seat, lashing out with his left leg and smashing his boot into Hawke's chest. The SBS man flew back out the open door and fell backwards toward the ground, his arms flailing out in front of him helplessly. In a heartbeat he wrapped his legs around the skid and clung on for his life as the German began to violently swerve the chopper from side to side to shake him off.

Now hanging upside down, Hawke heaved himself up in the airborne sit-up from hell until he could grasp hold of the metal skid with his hands again. Jakob leaned over to see what was happening and pulled a gun from his pocket. At the same time, he leaned forward on the cyclic and plunged the drone down into a shallow nosedive. Hawke slid forward on the skid until he was now hanging off the front.

Jakob then levelled the drone and aimed it north along Fifth Avenue before activating the Drone Automatic Flight Control System and shifting over to the passenger's seat.

He casually aimed the gun at Hawke and took a pot shot. It missed, ricocheting off the skid with a metallic ping. Hawke flinched, unable to protect himself while both hands were gripping the skid.

"You really are very irritating!" Jakob shouted. His voice was barely audible over the sound of the helicopter's massive turbine engine.

With all his might, Hawke leaped to the other skid and clambered up inside the drone from the other side. It took Jakob half a second to move across again and try the same trick with his boot, but this time Hawke grabbed his ankle twisted it around hard.

Jakob screamed and fired his pistol wildly at Hawke, missing each time because of his rage. Hawke twisted it again the other way until he heard something pretty chunky crack and give way inside the ankle, and now Jakob was howling in agony.

Hawke took advantage of his pain to get inside the drone and push the German out the other side. Jakob tumbled out but hooked his good ankle inside Hawke's jacket on the way, pulling him forward with the same momentum. Jakob fell backwards, grabbing the skids and Hawke fell past him, now suspended five hundred feet above Manhattan and held in place by Jakob's boot inside his jacket.

Jakob looked down at him and despite the pain in his ankle, grinned. "Now we must say *auf wiedersehen*, Englishman!"

He started to twist his boot out of the jacket, and for a second Hawke thought it was over, but then he looped his legs around the drone's skids and gave Jakob's good ankle a hard twist and pulled down at the same time.

The German screamed in agony and leaned forward instinctively to grab his ankle, allowing Hawke to grasp his belt and yank him down over his head.

Jakob tumbled forward now, helpless to fight against the momentum produced by his full bodyweight as it fell forward out of the drone. His face filled with fear as he realized what had happened, and he reached out pathetically for help as he went, but Hawke declined the invitation, pausing only to snatch the German's parachute as he fell forward and rip it from his back.

Jakob Müller tumbled away from the drone, screaming as he dropped down through the air like a rock. Hawke watched without emotion as the German fell toward the top of the Chrysler Building. "Surely not..." he said to himself, but he was wrong.

A second later Jakob smashed into the vertex on top of the deco skyscraper – the 186 foot-long spike on its roof, and was instantly impaled. His body, now skewered like a kebab, ground to a halt as the friction of the gleaming vertex against the insides of his broken body slowly increased until the German came to a terrible, horrendous stop.

*

Vincent and Kim clambered over Alan Pauling's corpse and continued their pursuit of Angelika Schwartz. The German chemist hadn't hesitated to shoot Pauling through the middle of his forehead simply to use his body to block the door, which told the former French Foreign Legion man more about his quarry than endless interrogations ever would. She was as cold as steel and twice as hard.

Kim now looked at Pauling with disgust as she reloaded her gun. "Where did she go?"

Vincent squinted into the darkness as he scanned the horizon. "There! She's running south along the beach toward the pier."

They wasted no time in sprinting after the German woman. Vincent knew Kim was now motivated not only by the hideous murder of her colleague Dirk Partridge, back in the New Orleans processing plant, but also by the slaughter of all her men in the siege of Kiefel's beachfront estate.

As for him, he still needed nothing else to drive his pursuit and neutralization of Schwartz other than the thought of his children being exposed to the bacteria. He knew he had only one duty to them, and that was to kill her and secure the canister. He speeded up as fast as he could, pounding along the sand of Santa Monica State Beach toward the pier.

Angelika vaulted over the car park fence and sprinted to the pier, slipping under the pedestrian walkway. Vincent aimed and took a shot, but missed and smashed a chunk of concrete from one of the walkway's support beams. He cursed and powered forward, once again straining in the dark to see where she had gone.

"I can't see her!" Kim screamed. "The bitch has got away... Damn it all!"

Then the German woman gave her position away by shooting at them and striking Kim in the shoulder. Vincent spun around just in time to see his partner fly backwards with the force of the round and collapse in a heap against one of the car park's toll booths.

"Go on without me!" she screamed.

The Frenchman had no time to think and instantly dived for cover in the shadows beneath the pier to escape the same fate as Agent Taylor. At least in wounding Kim, Angelika had given her position up, he thought grimly, and climbed up the steps to the boardwalk.

Now, silence fell as he moved forward along the pier. The only sound was the gentle hum of occasional curfew-breaking traffic on Ocean Avenue somewhere behind him. He felt the eerie atmosphere of the pier – bustling with laughter and joy in the day, but now deserted by everyone and everything except a psychopath and a night wind. And somewhere close-by that psychopath was hiding in the shadows.

He moved cautiously forward, gun-raised and ready to fire in a heartbeat. He weaved his way forward to the end of the pier – he knew she was here somewhere. As he went, he checked the stalls and restaurants – now locked up and empty – for any signs of break-ins, but there was no sign of her.

He checked behind a Coke vending machine as he made his way forward but it was clear just like everywhere else. He peered inside the Ice Cream and Treats bar, but still nothing. Angelika Schwartz would be getting a treat very soon, he thought.

Then he saw her at the base of the Ferris wheel. She was moving slowly in the shadows, trying to get around behind him so she could escape back to the beach. He fired a shot and it struck her in the shoulder. She spun around one-eighty and he thought he'd done the job, but then she scampered to her feet and disappeared once again into the night.

He vaulted over the fence where people queued for tickets and saw her at once – she was trying to climb over the rail at the end of the pier. As she clambered over the rail she dropped the canister. Pausing for half a second to retrieve it, Vincent saw his chance and seized it.

He fired and the bullet hit her in the center of her head, just as she had done to Pauling. She dropped like a bag of concrete over the end of the pier landing with a splash in the Pacific below. Vincent ran forward as the canister rolled slowly to the edge and snatched it up in his hands.

He sighed with relief. His boys, wherever they were sleeping, were safe.

CHAPTER THIRTY-SEVEN

Scarlet appeared on the deck wearing a gas mask and holding the Medusa box. At once she saw Kiefel register what had happened while at the same time half a dozen military helicopters flew over the water and surrounded them.

Kiefel, now trapped like a wounded wolf, was more dangerous than ever. Scarlet watched in horror as he dragged the injured President at gunpoint to the edge of the yacht. The German's desperate swivel-eyed stare told her he knew what would happen if he could no longer use Grant as a human shield.

"It's over, Kiefel!" Doyle screamed. "Just let the President walk away and you can live."

"Get away from me!" The German's head craned wildly as he strained to monitor the latest military chopper arriving on the scene, shining its powerful Xenon short-arc lamp down on him and tracking him as he moved closer to the edge.

"Give it up, Klaus!" Scarlet shouted, keeping her gun aimed squarely at Kiefel's throat. She knew from her training that putting a nine mil through his throat was the quickest way to cut the nerve signals from his brain to his trigger finger. "You're lit up like Christmas – you can't get away!"

"I said get away from me, you animals… and put that gun down at once or I shoot the President."

"Fine with me," Scarlet said. "In fact, why should you have all the fun?"

Without wasting a second she moved her gun to the right and shot President Grant in the shoulder. He spun out of Kiefel's grip and fell overboard.

Doyle gasped in horror. "What the hell?"

"Save your President, Doyle. He hasn't got long with that wound."

Still stunned, Doyle immediately dived in after him while Kiefel turned and fired several shots at him as he disappeared into the black water. Scarlet was sure Grant would be fine. It was a clear through and through shot as they said in the trade, and her aim was good enough to know the bullet had gone on its way without hitting anything important.

Kiefel now held his gun in his outstretched arm. It trembled in his hand.

"That's a Heckler & Koch USP Compact 45 ACP, Klaus, which means it carries twelve rounds. If I'm not mistaken you fired nine at me and Doyle back there after you reloaded, and three right then at the water. You're out of bullets, and out of luck."

"So you're going to shoot me, is that it?"

"You'd like that, wouldn't you?" she said. As she spoke, she dragged the metal box out from behind the forward lifeboat. Above their heads several men were shouting orders through megaphones attached to the circling choppers.

Kiefel recognized the box at once. "Was machen sie? What are you doing with that?"

"Irony can be beautiful, Klaus, and it can be ugly."

Scarlet opened the outer box, calmly and quietly. "For you, it's going to be ugly."

She opened the inner box and had to work hard not to recoil in horror at what she saw looking back up at her.

The severed head of Medusa.

She lifted it from the box and walked toward Kiefel.

Covered in sweat, he stumbled back, pointing his empty gun at the Englishwoman's heart and clicking uselessly on the trigger. He started to climb over the forward rail with a view to jumping in the water, but it was too late. Now he knew why she was wearing the gas mask and gloves.

She held the head up to him and the breeze did the rest.

Scarlet watched in silence as he gripped at his throat, choking. His eyes bulged like boiled eggs as he strained for more air, and then his body began juddering violently. Right before her eyes, almost as smooth as some kind of CGI, she saw him transition to stone and turn into a statue. He reached out to her, his arms extended in a desperate entreaty for mercy, but none was forthcoming.

In the final second before he was solid stone, she stepped up to him and whispered in his ear. "I'm going to take you home and use you as a towel rack."

As Kiefel finalized the transition to solid granite, he tipped back and crashed into the river with a tremendous splash. Scarlet was disappointed – she'd been serious about the towel rack idea – but, as they said in the movies, que sera, sera.

*

Devlin knelt beside Lea and looked her in the face. She was still in shock and hadn't spoken for several minutes.

"What is it, Lea? Jesus woman, you've gone as white as a ghost!"

"It's... I don't know. It's freaking me out is what it's doing, Danny."

"I don't understand."

Devlin peered over her shoulder and gently flicked through the paperwork that had stunned Lea. "What are these words, Lea – Mengloth, Frigg, Eir…?"

"I don't know – something to do with Norse mythology if I can read Dad's handwriting properly."

"Well, he *was* a doctor."

She looked at him. "Really, *now* you make jokes about my Dad?"

"Sorry."

"Forget it. His handwriting *was* atrocious, but this here definitely says Norse, and something about runic inscriptions and here is something about the power of healing."

"So what's freaking you out?"

"This word here, Danny. This word here is what's freaking me out."

She put her finger gently to the page, underlining a single, simple word written in her father's hand, but legible as it was in large capital letters and underlined three times. She couldn't bear to look at it, and turned her head away. She stared at the clouds outside the window as Danny followed her hand and read the word.

"Athanatoi."

A long pause. "I hate that word, Danny."

"What does it mean?"

"It means trouble, Danny. Real, big trouble." She wiped a tear away from her eye and took a deep breath. "What the hell was Dad doing?"

Before anyone could answer, a strange voice emanated from the shadows.

"Tu veux une clope, Miss Donovan?"

They scrambled for their guns but it was too late. Before they could defend themselves the man stepped into the light and shouted an order at them to stay where they were. To back up his point, he pointed the barrel of a MAT-49 submachine gun at them. "And if you think you can rush me, then you should know I have a colleague standing just there."

They turned to see where the first man was pointing, and another man with a MAT-49 stepped through the door.

"We made use of your side door – allow me to introduce myself. You can call me Lefevre, and this is Devos."

"I don't give a rat's arse who you are!" Mikey lunged for the shotgun on the table, grabbing the stock with the tips of his fat fingers but not quite getting hold of it. It slipped from his hand but he never knew it. Lea watched in horror as the two men opened fire on him and filled him full of lead. The bullets tore through his jacket and exploded in his chest and throat, propelling the large Irishman back through the open door and blasting him down on the gravel drive where he landed with a sickening crunch.

"No!" Kyle screamed, reaching for the same shotgun. He was closer and more agile, and managed to grab hold of the barrel and pull it toward him before the two men turned their weapons on him too. They drilled dozens of needless rounds through his body until he resembled a human pin-cushion, collapsing to the floor in a cloud of gun-smoke when the men had finally finished.

"Same happens to you two if you try anything, oui?"

Lea was too stunned to reply, and despite his extensive experience in the military, even Devlin could barely believe his eyes.

"Give me the file, Miss Donovan."

"How do you know who I am?" Lea said. "Who are you?"

"I know exactly who you are, Irishwoman. You think I do a job tracking down Henry Donovan's research files and not find out about his daughter? Bringing the notes to my employer will make me a very rich man, but there is a great bonus. I know a man in the Far East named Luk who is going to pay me a small fortune to deliver you to him... Now – get up slowly."

"Mr Luk?" Lea's stomach turned with nausea as she recalled his torture chamber back on Dragon Island.

The man pointed the gun at the door and Lea rose slowly from the table.

"We're going outside," the man said. He pointed the gun at Devlin. "You, sadly, are staying in here." Without saying another word he shot Devlin in the darkness. Lea screamed as she watched her former CO collapse to the floor wordlessly.

The other gunman, the one who had not yet spoken, began to pour petrol around the inside of the kitchen and up the outside walls of the cottage. He took a final drag on his cigarette and casually flicked it at the small cottage.

Lea jumped back as the flames raced up the side of her childhood holiday home and began to eat their way inside like a pack of hungry wolves. "You *bastards*..." she tried to say, but it came out weaker than a whisper and sounded not angry, but pathetic. She tried to run inside to save Danny but the men held her back.

She turned to the man, her heart full of hate and rage. It was then she saw they both had tattoos on their arms – tattoos of a specific kind of burning grenade she had seen somewhere before.

"Bonne nuit, Miss Donovan," he said.

She felt the butt of a submachine gun smash into the side of her head and then everything went black.

CHAPTER THIRTY-EIGHT

The streets of New York, now unsettlingly far below, flashed by as Hawke strained to keep a grip of the drone's skid, but it was getting harder with every passing second. He glanced behind him to see the Perseus was now ablaze, with most of the top deck and bow on fire and black smoke rising into the air over the Hudson River. It was surrounded by military and coast guard choppers.

Slowly he clawed his way back up over the skid and then scrambled inside the drone, strapping himself inside the pilot's seat. He deactivated the auto-pilot but nothing happened.

"Scarlet, are you receiving this?"

"Sure."

"I take it from the bonfire you caught up with Kiefel?"

"Let's just say he's enjoying his hobby from a new perspective."

"What the hell does that mean?"

"It means he's decided to go into marine biology."

Hawke looked confused. "Forget it – you can tell me later. Listen – we have a problem. The weapon is on a timer and the drone's autopilot can't be disconnected. I think the only way to disarm it is to hack it. I need you to patch me through to Ryan, in a hurry."

"You mean you can't disable it yourself?"

"You could say that, yes."

He heard her sigh. "If you want a job doing then call the SAS," she mumbled to herself. "I'll be with you in a second, *Josiah*."

"Not unless you can fly five hundred feet into the air, you won't."

"Oh, *please* don't tell me you were stupid enough to hang on to the skids when that maniac took off?"

"Something like that."

"You total prat."

"Well, thanks for your unwavering support and respect, but right now I'm in a slightly precarious position, so please just get me Ryan."

Seconds later, Ryan was patched through.

"Joe, what's up?"

"Mate, need some help."

"Yes, I heard. Scarlet just told me something about you being trapped in a helicopter drone loaded with a deadly weaponized bacteria?"

"That just about sums it up, yes."

Then he heard Alex's voice. "You don't have to do this to impress me, Joe."

"Yes, as amusing as your jokes may be, can I remind you all that I'm currently in a drone five hundred feet above Manhattan with the world's deadliest cargo underneath my arse!"

He heard Scarlet sigh again, and then speak. "I have an idea!"

"Let's hear it," Hawke said.

"Why don't we just get the USAF to shoot it down like the one in DC?"

A pregnant pause.

"Oh yes," she continued. "That's right - we can't do that because there's a numbnuts called Joe Hawke trapped inside it."

"Thanks for your input, Cairo, but we're running out of time. It's obviously on a pre-programmed route. Is there any way you can hack it, Ryan, and bring it under our control before the timer releases the bacteria?"

"Yeah, I think so – how long have we got?"

"According to a readout here in the cockpit, we only have a minute left before the canister is programmed to disperse the agent. I tried to deactivate the autopilot as I just said but Kiefel must have had Jakob fix it so it couldn't be switched off after he jumped out the drone."

"Smashing," Ryan said.

"So you can hack the thing, yeah?"

"I think so."

"Me too," Alex said. "It's been done before, at least."

"That's right," Ryan said. "The Iranians recently hacked a USAF drone flying over their border by hacking into its GPS system and uploading a maldrone."

"A what?" Hawke shouted.

"Drone malware, basically. I can use it to hack the drone and connect it to my laptop. That would bring it under my control, theoretically, at least."

"Theoretically, Ryan, I'm about to get covered in Medusa's lethal bacteria and turned to stone, and if that's not enough motivation there's a strong southerly right now and when Kiefel's little timer releases this shit it's blowing all over one of the most densely populated places on earth... so can we just get a move on, please?"

"Already on it," Alex said. "We already know the drone's IP address because it's one of ours, and I just hacked it and disconnected it from its internal GPS guidance system. Anything Kiefel programmed in there is now old news."

Hawke breathed a sigh of relief. "What now?"

"Now I'm turning it around..."

"Woah!" Hawke yelled as the drone banked hard to the right and steered sharply away from midtown Manhattan.

"How long have we got on that timer, Joe?" Ryan asked.

"Sixty seconds."

"The SWAT guys have got a sealed unit for us to land it in but it's on a US Navy ship just off the coast," Alex said, and then added grimly, "We don't have time to lower the drone so you can get out, Joe."

"Don't worry about that," Hawke said as he strapped Jakob's backpack on. "Our German friend left me a get out of jail free card. Just fly the drone over to the yacht and then take her out to the ship!"

Hawke moved to the drone's door and waited as Ryan flew the drone back to the Hudson then he leaped out and immediately pulled the cord on the BASE jump parachute. He glided safely to earth and landed with a gentle thump beside Cairo at the base of the Statue of Liberty. She was standing a few yards from the container holding Medusa.

"What the hell happened to Jakob, anyway?" Alex asked over the headset.

"He dropped out of city life," Hawke said.

"You mean the Big Apple didn't work its magic on him?"

"No – he didn't see the point of it."

Scarlet rolled her eyes and they watched the drone, guided by Ryan and Alex, as it landed inside the sealed unit on board the ship in the distance.

"Can you believe we don't even get a pension for this work?" Scarlet said.

"You're still talking about money, Cairo, and... wait – I don't believe it!"

"What is it?"

Hawke pointed at a small Coast Guard tender as it moved toward them. "Look who's on the bow."

"Who am I looking at, Joe?"

"The smug bastard waving at us."

"Who is it?"

Hawke couldn't help but grin. "It's Eddie Bloody Kosinski, and he's coming to get Medusa."

Hawke and Scarlet shared a glance, and then burst into laughter.

*

Moments later their humor was subdued by the sight of Agent Doyle pulling President Grant from the Hudson River. The Commander-in-Chief had the wound Scarlet had aimed for, and was fine, but still needed medical attention. As the team of doctors swarmed around him on his way to Marine One, he called Hawke and Scarlet over.

"Mr Hawke, I can only thank you from the bottom of my heart…"

"Don't mention it," Hawke said.

"You saved a nation tonight, Mr Hawke, and maybe the world. We all owe you a debt of gratitude."

Hawke gave a nod but made no further reply, aware that he was suddenly the center of attention.

As they loaded his stretcher into the back of the giant helicopter, Grant turned to Scarlet.

"As for you – you saved the life of the Commander-in-Chief tonight, and more than that, a husband and a father. I'll never forget what you did, even if it was slightly unorthodox."

"No problem, Mr President," Scarlet said.

"If you ever need anything…"

Now he was inside the chopper and the blades began to speed up. Slowly, the large machine lifted off the ground.

"I'll bear that in mind!" Scarlet shouted, but her words were drowned out by the turbine and then the President was gone into the night.

CHAPTER THIRTY-NINE

Lea winced as the pulsing agony of the deep laceration on her head coursed through her temple and into her jaw. She felt the blood from the wound welling in her eye socket and for a moment she thought she was going to pass out again.

Only now did she feel the duct tape over her mouth and the cable-ties on her wrists behind her back. A weird stench of motor oil hung around her nostrils and a wave of nausea rippled over her as she struggled to see in the darkness, her arms now numb as the weight of her own body crushed down on them.

She didn't know where she was. The last thing she remembered was trying to go back inside to pull Danny Devlin from the flames as they burned down her parent's old holiday home. She never even got the chance to drag him from the fire and toxic smoke before one of the men had hit her in the head with his gun and then everything had gone black as night.

Wherever she was now, it was a small, closely confined space. For a dreadful second, she thought she was in a coffin, but then she realized her cheek was pushed against some kind of hard carpet, and as far as she knew, the interior of coffins weren't usually carpeted.

She breathed a short sigh of relief before another wave of panic rose in her when she heard an engine fire up and then a familiar rumbling vibration – she was in the boot of car, and it didn't take her long to work out which one.

The gunmen's Audi A7.

Now it was all coming back.

She remembered what Lefevre had said about Mr Luk – was he really going to take her back to Hong Kong and hand her over so that psychopath could subject her to death by a thousand cuts? She felt sick at the thought, but she was given no time to think. The engine revved and she felt the car lurch violently forward, forcing her to the back of the boot and striking her head on the internal boot release. She cried out as the metal release catch dug into the fresh wound on her head, but her cry was muffled by the duct tape on her mouth into a pitiful moan.

She knew the roads around here better than anyone, and by following the turns of the car she knew where they were heading – south-east toward the coast, and that could mean only one thing. The men were taking her to Connemara Airport where they no doubt had some kind of aircraft fuelled up and ready to take her – and her father's research files – to god knows where, but Luk rose in her terrified mind once again.

She heard an indistinct mumbling from the front of the car and then the leader of the two men started shouting. This was followed by a drastic swing to the left and the squealing of tires. Then the car went straight again and there was a rapid acceleration.

Her mind drifted to Joe Hawke, whom she had last seen in Egypt so many weeks ago. The former SBS man had saved her before, but not this time. This time he didn't even know which continent she was on. Her only hope was the one man who knew where she was, but the last time she had seen Danny Devlin he had been half-dead from a bullet wound and smoke inhalation and was now unconscious and surrounded by flames.

255

Danny Devlin coughed the burning smoke from his lungs and staggered from the flames with his hand over his mouth. His face was smeared with soot and he stopped on the patio and violently threw up. He rushed his hands to his side and breathed a sigh of relief when he saw the bullet had only produced a flesh wound – searing half an inch of his torso away and leaving what would be an impressive scar – but he would live.

He searched around him for any sign of Lea and the two men, but saw only the corpses of Mikey O'Sullivan and Kyle Byrne. He snatched up one of their shotguns, and prepared to fight. It was then he heard the sound of a car and looked up to the cliff road to see a pair of red brake lights rapidly receding into the stormy Irish night.

Lefevre must have taken Lea and the research files!

He searched Mikey for the keys to the Quattro and sprinted to the front of the property, but when he turned the corner he saw the classic Audi was on fire just like everything else. The gas tank had already exploded and now all that was left was a char-grilled shell of black, twisted metal with flames all over the remains of the bent chassis.

He cursed as his eyes crawled desperately over the property for another means of giving chase and rescuing Lea when he suddenly remembered what Lea had said about her father's old motorbike in the garage, which had somehow escaped the attention of these maniacs and was thankfully untouched by fire.

The heavy wooden doors scraped against the gravel as he swung them open. There, in the corner was what could only be a motorcycle, concealed beneath an old brown dustsheet.

He wrenched the cloth away to reveal what he had been praying for – a motorbike, and not only a bike but a stunning black 1967 Norton Commando, just as Lea had described to him on their journey to the cottage.

He offered another prayer that the keys were still in it, as was her father's habit, and they were. The holy trinity of prayers was completed when he climbed on top and switched it on. It roared to life and he sighed with relief when he saw there was at least a quarter of a tank of fuel in her.

Without wasting a second he slung the shotgun over his shoulder and raced out of the garage, spraying gravel chips up in the air behind him in a great sweeping arc as he skidded out of the drive and joined the coast road on his way to catch up with the fleeing Audi A7.

As he sped along the narrow, winding lane which followed the coast, his headlight illuminated the rainfall which the Atlantic westerly was driving into his face with terrific velocity. *This, Danny*, he told himself, *is a real bloody stupid night to be chasing after a gimp like this Lefevre bloke.*

He hit a straight and accelerated to sixty, confident that on a road like this he could easily catch up with a car on something like the Commando, but then the tiny red rear lights disappeared from view. Had they turned a corner or had Lefevre killed the lights?

Devlin knew you'd have to be insane to drive blind on roads like this on a stormy night with no moon, but then was that enough to rule out Lefevre? He wasn't sure. All he knew was that he wasn't going to turn *his* light off because that was a four hundred foot drop to a raging ocean just a few yards to his right. He scowled in frustration but all he could do was speed up and continue the pursuit.

257

He turned a shallow bend on the road and suddenly saw the red lights once again. He was gaining now, and the Audi was less than two or three hundred yards ahead of him.

*

"You see *what*?" Lefevre drawled in Belgian French.

"A headlight," Devos replied. He nodded his head at the Audi's rear-view mirror. "Maybe two hundred meters behind us. Must be Devlin."

"Impossible. We killed Devlin."

Lefevre leaned forward and peered into his own wing mirror. He cursed loudly and smashed his hand down on the dashboard. He narrowed his eyes as he stared once again at the approaching headlight of the pursuing motorcycle and pulled a Heckler & Koch USP from inside his jacket. He checked the semi-automatic pistol's magazine and pushed down the electric window. A burst of rain blasted into the car but Lefevre didn't notice. He simply released his seatbelt and turned to Devos. "Keep driving."

Devos nodded as Lefevre swivelled in the seat and climbed halfway out the speeding car. To stop himself flying out, he anchored himself with his left hand on the grab handle while he calmly raised the USP and aimed it at the headlight of the pursuing bike.

He fired, and missed.

He cursed and wiped the rain from his face with his forearm.

He aimed again and fired a second time, but the bike was still behind them, and now it was swerving from side to side in an attempt to evade the bullets.

258

Romain Lefevre wiped the rain from his eyes again and aimed his pistol at Danny Devlin a third time. He wasn't the kind who believed in giving up.

*

And now the bastards are shooting at you, Danny! he screamed into the howling wind.

Devlin blinked and rubbed the rainwater from his eyes as the Commando powered forward closer to the Audi. As if things weren't dangerous enough he now had to swerve the bike violently to the left and right to avoid getting hit by their bullets. The risk was skidding on a patch of smooth asphalt and going for a short flight to an early death over the cliff-edge to his right, but he had no choice. It was that or take a bullet in the chest at sixty miles an hour.

Either side of him, the hedgerows raced by in a blur as he pursued his quarry. He wanted to return fire on the bastards with the shotgun – that would sort the wheat from the chaff – but he knew Lea was in the car and couldn't risk hitting her with such an inaccurate weapon. His only play was to give pursuit until they got wherever they were going and then wing it. The Danny Devlin Masterplan.

The fact Lefevre hadn't simply stopped the car and had it out with him right here meant that he was more interested in getting away with his prize than killing him, and that meant he'd decided not to take any risks tonight.

Whatever was in Harry Donovan's research files was obviously of enormous importance to Lefevre – or more likely – to the person Lefevre was working for. In Devlin's estimation, Lefevre didn't seem the type to have either the inclination or funding to raid Irish cottages in the dead of night in search of decades-old medical research papers. No, he was definitely working for someone else, and that was why the killer was in such a rush to get to Connemara Airport.

Devlin revved the 750cc engine and increased to seventy miles per hour, storm, wind, rain and bullets be damned.

Lea Donovan was in that car.

CHAPTER FORTY

Devos changed down to third to get more torque as he powered the Audi into a sharp bend on the coast road. The engine growled deeply and the Belgian contract killer slammed his foot down on the throttle to gain speed as they hit the next straight.

To his right he saw a brief flash of moonlight on the surface of Galway Bay before it was smothered but yet more storm clouds. The wipers, set on maximum speed to clear the heavy deluge from the windshield, flashed back and forth in a mesmerizing blur. He flicked his eyes to the rear-view and saw the damned headlight was still behind them.

"You want me to slow down?" he called out to Lefevre.

"Non!" The other man shouted. He was still outside the car and firing shots at the motorcycle. He climbed back inside and pushed the window up. "We are being paid to deliver the files, not take unnecessary risks with Irish fools. We'll kill him at the airport."

Devos nodded in agreement but his grin was sort-lived.

"What is it?" Lefevre asked.

"He's right behind us!" Devos said.

*

When Danny Devlin saw Lefevre climb back inside the car, he knew he had only once chance left. He increased the speed to over eighty and raced the bike until it was

261

almost on the rear fender of the Audi. He knew he'd only have seconds to act before they took evasive action, so he killed the light and offered another prayer. He was about to do the most insane thing of his life. Almost...

With no light, and under cover of the storm, he was invisible for a few seconds. He put his head down low and accelerated alongside the fleeing car. The bike had stable and powerful acceleration, and a second later he was almost past the Audi.

Then they saw him, as he knew they would, and immediately swerved their car into his path.

He knew what he had to do, and he knew he had to act fast. As the car's front wing struck the Commando he leaped into the air and slammed down on the Audi's hood. The Norton spun off out of control and careered to a stop at the side of the road.

Devlin clung to the air vent ridge at the top of the hood. The Audi began to swerve in an attempt to fling him off and share the same fate as the Norton Commando, but he held on for his life – a task made easier by the strength in his fingers he had built up over so many years of free-climbing.

He knew what had to happen next – and it did. A few seconds after he landed on the car the side window came down and Lefevre climbed halfway out with his USP, grinning at him.

He gave the Irishman a *c'est la vie* shrug and aimed the pistol at his face.

Devlin had anticipated the move, and using the forward momentum of the speeding car to keep him in place, he snatched the shotgun from his shoulder and fired twice at Lefevre.

The shot shredded through the Belgian's chest and throat. The top of his dead body now slumped out of the car, his hands scraping along the road.

Devlin watched Devos through the windshield as he saw what had happened, his panicky face lit a ghostly blue by the A7's dash. In desperation to get rid of the Irish devil now clinging to his car, he swerved more violently than ever.

As the car skidded over to the left, Lefevre's body was rammed into a hedge and got snagged in the twisted branches, pulling him from the car. The corpse landed with a wet smack on the asphalt as the others raced forward.

Devlin had no time left. He knew Devos had only one play left and was about to do it. If he hit the brakes he would go flying like an Iceland Gull and hit the road at speed where he would stay for a few seconds with every bone in his body broken before Devos ran him down with the Audi.

Devlin raised the shotgun and fired it at the glass, shattering it totally. He then fired a second shot through the smashed glass at Devos, filling his chest full of lead and killing the man instantly. The Belgian killer convulsed for a few seconds and the car began to swerve uncontrollably.

Devlin crawled on to the roof and slipped down inside the vehicle through Lefevre's open window. He immediately grabbed the wheel and kept the speeding Audi on the road while at the same time forcing his right leg down in between Devos's legs and hitting the brakes.

The Audi came to a juddering halt in the middle of the lane.

The race was over.

Devlin breathed a sigh of relief and closed his eyes for a second. So this is what happens if you take a phone call from Lea Donovan, he thought.

Talking of whom, he looked around the car for her but saw nothing.

Then he heard a deep thumping from the trunk.

He flicked the release catch and it sprung gently open as he ran around to the rear and cut the cable-ties from her wrists and ankles. Finally he pulled the duct tape and oily rag from her mouth.

Lea looked at him and frowned. "Well, *you* took your fucking time, Danny Devlin – don't tell me... we drove past a pub on the way and you nipped in for a swift half of the bloody black stuff!"

"You wouldn't begrudge me that though – not a pint o' plain, would ya?"

She rolled her eyes, pulled herself out of the boot and dusted herself down before giving the man a hug. "Thanks Danny, I owe you more than a pint of plain."

"Don't mention it."

Lea leaned against the car and put her hands on her head in shock as she watched her childhood holiday home burning in the low light of the Irish summer morning. Around her, life continued as normal – a marsh harrier's piercing shriek filled the air and she looked up to see it banking hard to the right and flying over the ocean, and the eternal sound of the Atlantic as it folded over in waves of surf all along the coast.

Her stretch of coast, where she had played as a child...

And now part of that childhood was ablaze and burning to cinders and ash right before her eyes. She wiped away a tear and opened the Audi's rear door. She took back the box-file of research papers that Lefevre had taken from her and they began to walk slowly back along the road to the Norton Commando.

She picked it up with tremendous effort and sat on it.

"What's going on here then?" Devlin said.

Lea gave him an innocent look. "What?"

"I'm driving the bike, not you!"

"Like hell you are Danny Devlin. This is my Dad's bike and I'm getting it somewhere safe. You can come if you want, ya silly horse."

Devlin pulled up the collars of his jacket and shivered. He looked out at sea for a long time and said nothing.

"You look very serious, Danny. You're not going to start quoting Yeats or anything, are ya?"

"Me? Nah. I was just thinking - is it too early to get properly langered, young Lea?"

She looked at him expressionless for a few seconds and then smiled. "Get on the bike, Danny... pub's this way."

Devlin rubbed his hands together and climbed aboard, putting his arms around her waist to hang on as she turned the key in the ignition. "You know I could quote Yeats If you'd like me to."

"Yeah... not so much," she said. "And put this in your jacket." She handed him the precious box-file. "I don't know what it means, but I know it's coming with me."

"Sure thing."

Devlin took the file and slid it inside his jacket before zipping it up.

Lea turned the accelerator and the old engine revved to life. She smiled when she heard it – the sound reminded her of her father and all the hours he spent working on it in the garage. The old man only ever rode the thing when he was here on the coast, and if she closed her eyes she could still hear him telling her all about how it worked...

"The left side of a bike is about the gears, Lea, look..." he showed her the clutch on the left side of the handlebars, and the gear pedal operated by the left foot. *"The right side is all about speed and brakes..."* She watched as he tapped the right handlebar to show her the

accelerator and then moved his hand down to the brake pedal operated by the right foot. She smiled at the memory – memories were the only place her father lived now. At least there she could keep him safe.

"So are we getting a drink or not?" Devlin said. "I haven't had a night like that since me honeymoon…"

"It's sunrise, Danny," she said. "Of course we bloody are!"

She'd ridden the bike enough times, with and without her father's blessing, to know well enough where the clutch engaged so she let it out with confidence and the bike began to roll forward.

The Norton Commando shot away into the rising sun with a beautiful, old-fashioned roar.

EPILOGUE

The Isle of Elysium nestles in the bright, turquoise waters of the Caribbean Sea, an isolated utopia far from the rest of the world. It offers the perfect balance of white sandy beaches, dramatic waterfalls and gentle rolling hills of untouched rainforest. Previously owned by the French Government and used as a tropical naval training facility, the island was bought by a consortium led by Sir Richard Eden. Not long after that it all but dropped off the map.

Now, a lone woman stood on its northern shore and shaded her eyes as she watched a Gulfstream IV in its silent approach to the island. The strong sun glinted off the bright, white paint of the jet as it turned and lined up with the runway for its final approach. Behind her, cicadas chirped loudly in the palm trees which ran along the beach, and less than a hundred yards out to sea she saw a pod of dolphins breach the blue surface of the ocean on their way west.

And she was nervous.

She had made a similar flight to the island less than a week ago, saying goodbye to Danny Devlin at Dublin Airport and flying away from home for the thousandth time. She too had been on one of the three ECHO Gulfstreams as she brought her late father's mysterious research notes back to her new home, and her new family. Maybe she would show them to Ryan to see what he could make of them, or maybe not. She knew in her heart everyone had a right to know her father had known something about the Athanatoi, but she was frightened to dig any further.

In the deep blue sky, she watched the jet slow down as the pilot extended the flaps to full and lowered the main gear. Now, almost close enough to touch, her sense of anxiety seemed to subside.

The jet landed with the sharp squeal of rubber on asphalt as the wheels touched down, and moments later it was trundling toward the tiny airport. As it passed her, she tried to look inside and see him, but it went by too fast, and she was distracted by the mechanical whine of hydraulics as the flaps and airbrakes retracted in readiness for parking and the engine shutdown sequence.

Then, the door opened and there he was, standing tall with his bag over his shoulder. An old army-surplus boonie hat on his head obscured his face and a pair of aviator shades covered his eyes. He looked like he'd been sleeping, but he was here at last.

Lea met Hawke on the landing strip and for a moment they were unsure what to do – unsure if they were still together or not. It ended when Hawke took her in his arms and kissed her, and the ice was broken.

Before she could say anything, Alex Brooke stepped off the plane and walked over to join them. For a second, Lea thought she looked like she was in pain, but then the moment passed.

Lea tried to conceal her disappointment. She didn't know Alex well enough to hate her, and she knew she'd been a good friend to Hawke after the hell back in Egypt, but she was suspicious that the former CIA agent had tried to make a move on Hawke while he was staying with her in America.

The three of them barely spoke as they crossed the asphalt and headed toward the low, modern glass-and-steel entrance of the Elysium HQ. Each of them had their own problems. She knew what they had been through in America in their attempt to hunt down Klaus Kiefel.

As for Lea, her mind was still buzzing with everything that had happened in Ireland. She was pleased she had rescued her father's life's work, even if she had no idea what any of it meant. It was enough to know she had saved it from falling into the hands of Lefevre and Devos. Even if she didn't know who they were working for, she had won, and all thanks to Danny Devlin. She looked at her watch and saw it was well into opening time back at Flynn's. She smiled when she pictured her old CO propping up the bar once again, gripping a pint of Guinness among the wreckage of the fire-fight.

"I'll leave you two to it, I think," Alex said, and walked ahead.

Hawke turned to Lea and took off his shades. He scanned the area, looking beyond the heat shimmer on the airfield. He was looking at a tropical island maybe ten square miles in size, with elevated ground to the west and east and a lower sea-level dip in the middle which seemed to house some kind of metallic compound. It was partially obscured behind a low line of macaúba palms and the sun flashed brightly on its roof.

Behind the airfield, to the north, a strip of white sandy beach cut between two different shades of blue – the deep azure of the tropical sky, and a bright cerulean strip of ocean, warm and inviting. He watched someone – Scarlet maybe? – windsurfing a few hundred yards out, the bright red sail cutting into the calmer colors. The ubiquitous sun flashed on the boom of the windsurf board and he looked away. He could see the attraction of the place, it had to be said.

"So this is the mysterious mission control?" he said quietly.

"Sure is…" Lea's words drifted into the heat shimmer. "Joe, listen… about the island and ECHO – I really wanted to tell you about it but…"

"Forget about it," he said, a tone of finality in his voice.

She pulled her head back and gave him a look. "Forget about what?"

"About your apology – there's no need."

"About *my* apology?" She felt the fury rising in her as she looked at him. "I was *going* to say I really wanted to tell you about it… *but*… you shouldn't have been such a *bastard* when you finally heard about it from Eden!"

"An apology's not on the cards then?"

Lea screamed. "No, you're not getting a sodding apology because I never did anything to apologize for!"

Hawke turned to her. "So we're going to have a row about this, are we?"

Lea looked defiant. "You bet your arse, Joe Hawke!"

Hawke smiled. It felt like he was home at last.

THE END

AUTHOR'S NOTE

This novel put both Hawke and me a little out of our comfort zones, as we both prefer a good old-fashioned international hunt for ancient relics and treasures. While I felt that thanks to the presence of Medusa this was still in that ball park, the murky world of Washington politics put a different slant on things. As regular readers will know by now, I like a good helping of humor in my adventure novels and I hope I managed to achieve that in this story.

As it happens, Joe will return in VALHALLA GOLD (Joe Hawke #5), which is a return to his regular world of hunting down ancient lost treasures and taking out super-villains in the process... and he also gets a chance to visit some exciting international locations as well as build some bridges with old friends and play in the Caribbean on jet skis for a while... I just thought he deserved a holiday. I hope you can join us for that. It should be released in the Spring of 2016 (or the Autumn of 2016 if you're reading this Down Under).

Finally, I want to thank everyone who has left me a review on Amazon. It really means a lot to a writer when a reader takes time out to leave a review, even if it is just a line or two. Reviews are an essential part of the writing process and will really help the Joe Hawke series, so, sincerely, my thanks to you. Also, don't forget you can keep up-to-date with the series on my Facebook page here: http://bit.ly/RobJonesNovels, and my website here: www.robjonesnovels.com

Anyway, I have to go – Joe Hawke just called and asked if I want a beer. Frankly, I think I could drink him under the table. What do you reckon?

With best wishes, dear Mystery Reader,

Rob

The Joe Hawke Series

The Vault of Poseidon (Joe Hawke #1)
Thunder God (Joe Hawke #2)
The Tomb of Eternity (Joe Hawke #3)
The Curse of Medusa (Joe Hawke #4)
Valhalla Gold (Joe Hawke #5)
The Aztec Prophecy (Joe Hawke #6)
The Secret of Atlantis (Joe Hawke #7)
The Lost City (Joe Hawke #8)

The Sword of Fire (Joe Hawke #9) is scheduled for release in the spring of 2017

For free stories, regular news and updates, please join my Facebook page

https://www.facebook.com/RobJonesNovels/

Or Twitter

@AuthorRobJones

Made in the USA
Monee, IL
27 November 2020

49817229R00166